IN LOVE WITH THE KING OF HOUSTON

Carmen Lashay

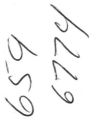

Text **Treasured** to **444999**

To subscribe to our Mailing List.

Interested in becoming a part of the Treasured Publications family?

Submit manuscripts to

Info@Treasuredpub.com

PROLOGUE

"Ok, class, time to sing the goodbye song like we always do before we end the school day," Ms. Martha said to her pre-kindergarten class.

All sixteen of the budding, four year olds eagerly jumped up to join hands and stand in a circle, Ms. Martha included.

"Are we ready?" she asked, looking around at all the happy faces smiling back at her. Noticing Yemani, her loner student, off in the playroom corner, she dropped hands with the students, and walked over to Yemani, bending down until she was eye level with her.

"Yemani, it's time to sing the goodbye song, care to join the class?"

"No, thank you," Yemani said in her usual stubborn manner. She was always known to do the complete opposite of the other students. Being that she was four and not five, making her the youngest in the class, she still was the most daring of the bunch.

"Didn't you tell me your Big Momma and Pappa were coming home today? Don't you want to hurry up and get home to them?" Ms. Martha asked, knowing she would be quick to jump at the mention of their name. Although she had a pair of loving parents who adored her, it was her grandparents whom she insisted on living with, and I guess her parents didn't seem to have a problem with that. All week, since we learned numbers, she had been counting down the day until they returned. A huge smile graced her face as she quickly jumped up and practically flew to the circle with the other students.

"You can stand by me, Yemani," Desiree, one of the other students, said, dropping hands with a student to grab onto Yemani's hand.

Getting up and walking back to rejoin the students, Ms. Martha said," Ok class, now is everyone ready?"

"Yesss!" they screamed.

"Ok, one, two." By the time she got to three, they had already all started singing off key and very loudly.

"It's time to go home; it's time to go home, it's time to say goodbye. I had some much fun, and you have so much fun, we all had so much fun, and now we say goodbye. Goodbye, goodbye, see you again." As they finished the song, as tradition, everyone turned to the person closest to them and hugged them. Usually, they all ended up in a threeway hug or hugging each other more than once. As the bell rung and the announcer came over the intercom to call everyone to their busses and car pick up, the kids grabbed their book bags and rushed to their respective destinations. Yemeni and Desiree, who were both car pick up, walked to the car pick up line and waited for the group of kids from other classes to join so they could all walk to the front with Ms. Simmons, the after-school worker.

"Do you want to be my friend?" Desiree asked Yemani.

"Why?"

"Because you always play by yourself. You can play with me."

"You play with Shelly, and I don't like Shelly; she had cooties," Yemeni said.

"Well, if Shelly has cooties then we can just play without her," Desiree said as if this was the perfect solution.

"Ok."

As the girls walked outside with the group, each went their separate ways, running to their parents.

"Mommy, mommy, is Big Ma and Pappa home yet?" Yemani asked as she ran into her mother's arms.

"We actually have to drive to Monroe and pick them up, baby. Did you remember what momma said?" Her mother asked.

"Yes, you said they left on a airplane. Can we go on an airplane momma?"

"One day, pudding. Now let's go pick daddy up so we can get Big Ma and Pappa."

"Yahhh!!" She yelled, hopping in the car as her mom got her situated in her booster seat and closed the door.

After they picked up her father, they were off to Monroe.

"We almost an hour late because you had to have that burrito for lunch," Caroline, Yemani's mom, said to her husband.

"How was I supposed to know that shit would tear my stomach up?" he said, rubbing his belly. Pulling into the airport, they parked at the pickup area and looked around for Caroline's parents. Giving it another 20 minutes, the family decided to go park and look for them.

"Just call your mom again, you know they could have gotten lost," Dave said to his wife, who he knew would likely to start panicking soon.

"My mom is always so punctual; it's not like her to be late."

"Come on," he said, picking Yemani up as they crossed the parking lot together into the busy airport. Walking inside, they found out exactly what terminal they were to exit from. Getting closer to the terminal, they noticed uniformed policemen and a crowd of people gathered around, some crying, some trying to listen.

"I wonder what's going on?" Dave asked.

"Yeah, good question," Caroline said. "Excuse me, sir, do you know what's going on?" she asked a nearby worker.

"Flight 815 caught some bad weather, and lightening struck it, causing the plane to go down. That's all we know at the moment, and we are doing the best we can to give you guys up to date information," he said.

"Oh my God!" she screamed.

"Calm down, baby, I'm sure they are fine," Dave said unsurely as he looked up and for the first time realizing what everyone else was looking at, the news was on the scene covering the story. Walking closer with his family, he saw it said survivors had been found and they would keep everyone updated on the progress as they were trying to get through the debris. The plane had broken apart three ways, and so everyone was scattered everywhere.

"Daddy, I don't see Big Mamma," Yemeni said, looking around for her grandparents.

"They coming, baby, they just got held up," Dave said, trying to console his wife and keep his daughter in a state of bliss as she excitedly awaited the arrival of her grandparents, whom he wasn't sure if she would ever see again. After a few hours of waiting at the airport, they decided to head home but still keep up with the news just in case they started releasing names. There were 532 passengers aboard, and so far, they had rescued 200 and counting, all of whom were alive.

"Daddy, why Big Momma and Papa didn't come home today? I thought we were going to get them?" Yemani asked her father once they were home and situated.

"Something happened, baby, but they will be home tomorrow. I promise, princess."

"Ok," she sadly said as she put her head down and walked to her room. Dave only hoped he could keep that promise.

Open the floodgates of heaven

Let it rain, let it rain.

As the choir sang *Let It Rain by Michael Smith*, Yemeni sat in the front row of the pew between her distraught mother, and her stone-faced father, staring unblinkingly ahead at the two white caskets in front of her. Her parents had done the best they could at explaining to her that Big Momma and Pappa were in heaven now, but she still doesn't fully understand what that meant. Flight 815 recovered 250 passengers from a flight list of 532. Charles Skinner, known to

Yemani as Pappa, was in the restroom when the plane descended from the sky. He was dead on impact. However, Janice Skinner had survived the crash but later died the same day of a heart attack after they informed that her husband of 59 years was dead. They married young and never had the chance of going on a honeymoon, so their kids sent them to the Bahamas. They were on their way back when the crash happened. As the viewing of the body started, Desiree walked up to Yemani and handed her, her Miss America dolly. It was her favorite one, but she wanted her new best friend to have it.

"I hope this makes you feel better," Desiree said, hugging her and walking off with her parents. When it was time for the family to view the body, Yemani walked up and immediately tried to climb in the casket with her Big Momma, whom she always climbed in bed with.

"Momma, you said Big Momma was in heaven, but she is right there. Mommy, how is she in heaven when I can see her? I won't be bad anymore if you give Big Momma some medicine to make her feel better," she cried, which only made her mother cry harder. Not understanding why her Big Momma and Pappa were not waking up, Yemani held onto her dad and cried her little eyes out. This was the first time tragedy had struck her in twos, but it definitely wasn't done with her yet.

PRESENT DAY: 15 years later.

CHAPTER 1

Life is like a box of chocolates, you never know what you're going to get...

YEMANI

"Yemani, are you listening to me?" My mom said as I tried to tune her out and focus on the tv.

"Yes, mom, I heard you."

"You promised me you would revisit this scholarship in a year. It's been past a year, Yemani. You are so smart and talented, baby; I don't want you to throw that away because of fears you have," she said. She always insisted I leave this small town and live my life. I can't see myself doing that. Yeah, sometimes I complained and stayed in trouble, but the truth is I never wanted to leave. Before I continue, my name is Yemani Jacobs and I'm two months shy of my 19th birthday. I live in a very small town called Sicily Island, Louisiana, where the population barely reaches 500 people. We are such a close-knit town that everybody, except for about a handful of people, are related. We are so small that we literally barely have one of anything. If you want to go to a grocery store, you have to go over to the nearest town because Barron's will charge you damn near $5 for a simple canned good. I guess they figured since they were the only grocery store and some people didn't have a car, they could capitalize off of that.

"Are you listening to me?" My mom said, slicing through my thoughts as she pushed a paper towards me.

"What is this?"

"I took the liberty of calling the scholarship office, requesting to accept the scholarship because your deadline was nearing before the offer was removed from the table. This is the letter they sent detailing what they are paying you for room and board down to books. It's a full ride scholarship. I even pulled some strings to get you to room with Desiree. School starts two weeks before your birthday, so consider this an early birthday gift."

“How about I get a trip to Vegas for my birthday?”

“How about you register for school first, and we'll see?”

Rolling my eyes, very frustrated at this point, I said, “Mom, did you even talk to me before you did this?" I said, getting annoyed.

"No, because I would only keep getting excuses after excuses. I love you, baby and you have so much potential. You have to let this fear go and go off and live your life. Do this for me, and I'll throw in a Brahmin bag with that Vegas trip. Don't you want to be with your partner in crime in the big city, anyway?”

Desiree, my best friend since kindergarten, and I had both gotten academic scholarships to the University of Houston, but I decided to postpone accepting mines while Desiree broke her neck trying to get away. I just didn't want to leave my parents. I had detachment issues that I never fully dealt with ever since my grandparents died.

"Aren't you supposed to be getting dressed for your anniversary dinner?" I asked her, changing the subject.

"Your father is still at the store, so I have a little while before I need to get up," she said, walking into the living room. After my grandparents died, my parents got a small settlement, which they used to open a store in Ferriday. They also paid off bills and purchased new cars. Since I received a full ride scholarship, they didn't need to put any up for my schooling. I started to wonder would my Big Momma be disappointed that I wasn't living out my dream of being a dental hygienist. Even at four, I knew exactly what I wanted to be when I grew up. I worked hard all throughout school to graduate top of my class, but when the time came to go away, practically everyone else left for their desired college but me. I couldn't even bring myself to pack. My, so-called boyfriend, Tyron left and didn't bother to call me.

The last time I seen him was when we had a failed attempt at having sex. It hurt so bad, I immediately pushed him away, causing him to get mad and storm off. He probably went to the town slut, Tangie's house, who he didn't know that I knew they were fucking.

RING! RING!

Looking down, I noticed my best friend calling me. I must have talked her up.

"Hey, boo thang," I said to her as I got up and walked outside.

"Hey, heifer. What you up to in that death trap?"

"It's not that bad; this was home for you up until a year ago."

"And the best thing I did was leave, and if you were smart, you would get out as well," she said, matter of factly.

"Come on, not you too, Dezzy. I just had to get a lecture from my mom, and she even took it a step further as to call the scholarship office and accept the shit for me. Why can't y'all see that I am content with my decisions? Besides, I was thinking of signing up for online classes."

"Your mom loves you and just wants the best for you, that's why she did that. She doesn't want her only child confined to that town; she wants you to explore and see the world. I don't understand how you could choose a small town where the most exciting thing to do on the weekends is go to a football game or Jolly's, over a thriving city that never sleeps. Come on, Yemi; college is a wonderful experience you shouldn't be missing," my best friend said to me.

"Did you make the dance team?" I asked her quickly changing the subject.

"Of course, I did. They didn't know what hit them when I walked in and executed every last dance step with precision and accuracy. They better know this country girl can bring it."

"Yes, bitch! That's what I'm talking about, best friend! Is that hoe, Treasure still pushing up on your man? That's what's gone make me come to Houston, just to whoop her ass; she got us fucked up."

"Girl, fuck him and her. I dismissed his ass, and I wish that bitch would touch me, I will beat some edges onto her shit. Walking around here looking like a naked mole rat. She tried it."

"You and Matt broke up? When did this happen?"

"When that dick became for everybody, that's when. How about you, virgin scary Mary? You gave Josh that cootie cat yet?"

"Bitch, last weekend at Jollys, I let him finger me, but that's about it."

"A nigga will catch serious blue balls fucking with your ass, but I'ma call you tomorrow I'm about to hit the fraternity party."

"Bye hoe, don't do anything I wouldn't do."

"Bitch, I'm tryna get blessed with some dick by a Que dawg, I've had my eye on for a lil' minute now."

"Little nasty."

"Don't knock it until you try it, bye hoe," she said, hanging up. Since the town was so small and everything was literally within walking distance, I continued walking until I reached the only restaurant in town, The Snack Shack. I had a taste for some chicken strips and fries. Walking in, I saw Adrienne, a 17-year-old senior here in Sicily at the only high school in town. She was mad cool, and we sometimes hung out, which was surprising because I didn't like anybody but

Desiree. I've been antisocial my entire life, or at least ever since I can remember.

"Hey chick, you here for some strips huh?" she said as soon as I walked in.

"You know me too well," I said, laughing as I took money out my pockets, already knowing the total.

"You heard about that party tonight?"

"What party?"

"You know Tyron home from ULM for the summer and he throwing a birthday party for Rosco in the Jets. He supposedly brought some football friends down with him. Everybody been talking about it, you know them girls been going crazy trying to go to the next town and find an outfit."

Rolling my eyes at the mention of his name, I pretended not to care but I did. We had dated from sophomore year to senior year, so you would think he would have the decency to at least break up with me, or even call, but his bitch ass did neither. I caught the hint when I saw him on social media with his WCW hugged up inside his dorm room.

"I might pass on that one."

"Come on, Yemani; fuck him. You need to dress it up and show him what he passed up on."

Even though I wasn't even talking to her back then, this town so small, that everybody knew everybody's business. So, it wasn't a secret that we dated, then he played me that night when I chickened out and didn't give him any ass.

"Josh going to be there," she said, sealing the deal for me. *Maybe I can spin this in my favor after all, I thought to myself.*

Later on that night, I was in the mirror getting dressed to hit this party while taking shots of Patron. Thank God, I had a bottle already because the stores around here closed at 5 pm. The town was still in ancient time days and would never modernize. The adults and such were in the house and in bed by 9, and that's when we came out to play. Looking myself over, I was pleased with what I saw. Everything had to be on point when I saw Tyron's ass tonight. He was gone regret playing me like that.

Standing at 5'3', 145 lbs, I was bad as hell if I do say so myself. With my caramel, blemish-free skin, that had a touch of freckles, hazel eyes, and sandy red hair, that I usually kept sewn down in a Mink Brazilian 20-inch body wave that I did myself. The fact I walked everywhere; even though I had a car, kept my six-pack stomach, flat as ever, I didn't have a stupid ghetto booty, but I had a little poke back there. With C-cup breast, and hips and thighs for days, I was overall killing the game, and I knew it. I sucked at applying makeup, so I didn't even bother with it aside from applying lipstick. I was in the middle of wand curling my hair when my song came on, causing me to drop the curlers and bend over throwing my ass in a circle. I couldn't dance for shit, but when has that ever stopped somebody when their jam came on?

Got money, retarded

Don't want her if it don't clap when she walking

Ain't too pretty in the face, but she super thick

I loved me some Kevin Gates, and every time he came to Monroe's club Tequilas, I was always there. It was like an hour drive into the city and the farthest I've ever been outside of Sicily Island. Dancing for a few more minutes, I then picked my curlers back up and continued to do my hair. Twenty minutes later, I was satisfied with my look, so I grabbed my keys, phone, and bottle and left out my room. I could walk to the Jets, but I usually tend to drive places at night.

Not only didn't we have street lights, but the creeps came out at night, and the last time I called myself walking, they had the nerve to toss me in a holding cell because I maced somebody trying to grab on me. He had the audacity to say he was only trying to tell me something. Hell, make your presence known before you tell me anything because I stay ready so that I don't have to get ready.

Walking outside to my 2013 Jeep Wrangler, my dream car that was also my parent's graduation gift to me from some of the settlement money I assume. Jumping inside, I started the car and pulled off, heading just the short distance to the party. I didn't have to know exactly whose house it was at. As soon as I hit the block, I would be able to tell from all the cars and people out and about. Parking inside Mrs. Shaw's yard, my god mother and Desiree's mom, I cut the engine and called Adrienne to see where she was at.

"Where you?" I asked her as soon as she answered.

"I'm inside!" she yelled, trying to talk over the music.

"Walk down to Desiree's house. I'm parked down here so mufuckas won't hit my baby. You know they get on that liquor and get to acting. You know Sheriff already on my ass as it is. So I'm trying to avoid trouble if I can," I said. For some reason, people just assumed I was a problem child when really, I was just misunderstood. I didn't go looking for trouble, it just found me nor did I pick with people. That didn't mean I let people walk over me and say what the hell they wanted to me. I didn't take shit from anybody. My mom says I get that from my grandmother and hell, she might be right. My Big Momma was the type that didn't take shit from anybody. She would beat your ass then fix you a plate to eat all in the same breath. She was the feistiest, strongest person I knew and I miss her with every passing day. They say children forget certain things as time goes on, but not me. I still had a very vivid memory of my grandparents as if I had just seen them. I could remember smells, and even their touch, that's how bonded I was to them.

KNOCK! KNOCK!

Jumping, I looked up to see Adrienne knocking on my window. "Bitch, you scared me," I said, opening my car door.

"Well, yo ass was just daydreaming and shit because I called your name a few times. Let me hit your bottle before we go in there; you know I ain't take nothing them nigga offering. Won't have me bent over somewhere taking dick in every hole," she said.

"Bruh, where do you come up with this shit at?" I asked her because she always said crazy mess like that.

"VH1," she said, shrugging.

Shaking my head at her, I grabbed my patron and my shot glass, took three, then passed the bottle and glass to her. Thirty minutes later, we both walked into the party, drunk as hell. I looked around for Josh's fine ass and spotted him in the kitchen with some more dudes, passing a blunt around. Looking around some more, I saw Tyron, looking good enough to eat, sporting a pair of stone-washed denim jeans, a pink polo shirt; hugging all of his muscles, and a pair of brown Ray Ban glasses. To his left, were some dudes I had never seen before so I'm guessing they were his teammates Adrienne was talking about. Wrapped around him like a second skin clad in his leather man jacket, was the same dark-skinned beauty from his Facebook. I'm not a hater, and I'll always give props where they were due, she was a very pretty chocolate female. Smirking, I walked further into the room, commanding attention. For someone who hardly dresses up, unless I'm going to a party in the other town over or Monroe, I held nothing back as I strutted across the room in my black leather, skin tight cat suit that stopped right above my knee with slits in the thigh part. The top of the catsuit had a deep v-cut that had my girls pushed up on display. The outfit fit my curves perfectly. My soft curls set everything off, along with my ruby red lipstick. I had paired the outfit with some retro J's. Walking around, speaking to people, knowing I wasn't friendly but just wanting to be seen, I purposely overlooked Tyron. But when one of his teammates grabbed my arm, I stopped, shot him an award-winning smile and a wink, before continuing around the room with Adrienne; we were cutting up. She had on a body-hugging, body con dress with some spiked, Converse all-star high tops.

Out the corner of my eye, I saw the pissed off expression on Tyron's face when I did that, but I just kept it moving, not paying him any attention. I could feel his eyes burning a hole in me as I stood little ways off with Adrienne, slowing swaying my hips back and forth to the beat. When I happened to glance up and catch his eye, he grabbed shawty and kissed her then smirked at me. Since I was the queen of petty, I grabbed Josh, who happened to be passing by at that exact moment, and instead of kissing him, I whispered seductively in his ear, then proceeded to lick it as he grabbed a handful of my ass and squeezed it. He smacked me hard on my ass, and I know it was jiggling everywhere because I only had a thong on. For another half an hour, we slow danced to song after song, even if it were a fast song, we had literally found our own rhythm.

When he leaned down and kissed me, I almost passed out from how intense it was. Pushing him slightly back, after I felt his manhood rise, I grabbed his hand and walked with him towards the door. It was really hot as hell, and my drunk ass just wanted to catch some air, but Tyron didn't need to know that. Let any and everything run through his mind and drive him crazy. I was headed to my car, with Josh kissing on my neck when I spotted Adrienne barely standing, being walked off by some guy. *I could have sworn this hoe was right behind me and when did she get that drunk?*

"Aye, wait up," I said to them as I pushed Josh slightly and ran over to them. I noticed it was one of the guys with Tyron. Reaching them, I said," I got her, thanks though."

"I wasn't trying to try any funny shit, yo; lil momma looked like she needed some fresh air.

My moms raised me better than that," he said then turned and jogged back to the party.

"Bitch, how we drink the same thing and yo ass drunk?"

Slurring, she said, "Man, I was good until I hit the blunt while you was too busy trying to make Tyron mad, you didn't notice I had a blunt tooting it. I got it when we first came in, and that shit crept up on me, I guess," she said, holding her head.

"You drove?"

"Naw, got dropped off."

Rolling my eyes, I grabbed her and walked back over towards Josh.

"Sorry, we 'bout to roll out."

"You just got here."

"Adrienne lit; I gotta get her home. I can't leave her out here like this. You can come with me, though," I said to him, in the mood to finish whatever we started a few nights ago.

"Naw, the party jumping, I'll check you after the party," he said, kissing me on the forehead and walking off back towards the party. No, this nigga didn't just booty call me out like that. Won't nothing be open after this party over but legs and unfortunately, these gone be closed so he shit out of luck. We could have hit the Mom and Pops diner in Wisner or something but oh well.

"Can you walk?"

"Yeah hoe; I'm not handicapped. I just wanted that fine ass nigga to assist me," she said, smirking at me as she switched ahead.

Once I dropped her off, I headed home. Grabbing my bottle, I got out the car, noticing my parents still weren't back from dinner. Walking to my room, I sat my bottle down, grabbed clothes, and walked into my adjourning bathroom to hop in the shower. After I was bathed up, I fixed myself a mixed drink, made some roasted chicken cup o' noodles to eat, and found something to watch on tv for the remainder of the night. I'm not sure when I fell asleep, but I woke up to a pounding headache and somebody beating on my door. I just laid there thinking my mom or dad about to wake up, going off any minute now. Putting the pillow over my head, I attempted to lay down, but the knocking would not go away.

"Ma!" I yelled, trying to wake her up to go get it. When I didn't get a response, I threw the covers off, got out of bed, and went into their room, without knocking, which I knew they hated. When their beds were still perfectly made, I figured maybe they got a hotel in Mississippi. Walking towards the front, I yelled, "I'm coming, geez!" I said as I flung the door open, ready to go off until I saw Sheriff John and one of his deputies standing there.

"I didn't do anything, I've been here since I left a party," I said, mad they woke me up. I just knew they were about to tell me some dumb shit because for some reason, anything that happens, Yemani has to have done it. Majority of the shit I haven't even done, I'll just cop to it anyway, and I don't exactly have a valid reason why.

"We not here about that," his deputy said.

"Ok, what then?" I said, folding my arms across my chest impatiently. When Sheriff John refused to make eye contact with me, for some reason, my heartbeat sped up, and my breathing quickened. "Sheriff?" I asked with a shaky voice. He still struggled to find the words and the deputy, who was new, looked like he didn't have to heart to say whatever it was they came to say. Leaving them standing there, I ran back to my room and grabbed my phone. Running back out to the living room, I noticed they had stepped inside and closed the door. Calling first, my mom's cell phone, then my dad's, I got both of their voicemail after a few rings. I called back five more times until Sheriff finally spoke up and said something to me that stopped my heart altogether.

CHAPTER 2

I am my sister's keeper.......

DESIREE

Stepping off the plane, I walked through the terminal to baggage claim to grab my luggage. An hour later, I was walking outside and spotted my mom waving frantically to get my attention. Rolling the luggage cart over to where she was, I let it go and hugged her tightly. I had really missed my mom more than I think she knew. I just had to get away from this place, and I really had no intentions on coming back. She was supposed to come visit me for Christmas, but got caught up at the hospital she works at. I know it's the summer, but I purposely took summer classes so that I would remain eligible to reside in the dorms and not have to come home. However, as soon as I heard about what happened, I dropped the classes before they even started, and was literally on the first plane leaving out to Monroe so I could be here for my best friend. I know she's going through it right now and I honestly can't even begin to imagine her pain. To lose, not one, but two parents at the same time was enough to drive a person over the edge.

"My baby girl, look at you," my mom said as she let me go and took a step back to examine me. I don't think I've changed much since she last saw me. By the way she was staring, it was like I had morphed into a different person. Only thing different was my hair. Gone were my usual honey blonde hair, and now I was rocking honey blonde, jumbo box braids. I had never had any and decided to get some to give my hair a breather and keep from combing in it. Other than that, I was the same 5'5, 165 lbs, size ten, redbone that I was when I left home.

"How is my sister?" I asked, referring to Yemani, who hadn't answered my phone once these last few days.

"She barely holding up. I got her some sleeping pills to take that will have her out for a while. She'd been up before that nonstop, having a complete meltdown. My poor sweet baby girl, I hate this happened," she said as her voice cracked.

Ever since me and Yemani formed a friendship in kindergarten, we've been super close and so have our parents. My mother loved Yemani like she birthed her, and vice versa with her mom. She called me every day during school, making sure I was going to class and getting on me if I was slipping. I loved Momma Caroline, and it hit me hard to learn that she was gone, but I was trying to summon up all my strength for my best friend. "I hate it happened to mom," I said as I started helping her place my bags inside the back of her SUV.

Once we had them all situated, we got in the car and headed towards the place I left a year ago without a second look back. No one, not even Yemani, knew the real reason why I was so ready to leave. Of course, I was excited about college, but there was a certain person, who helped influence my decision to go to Houston versus an hour away to the University of Louisiana at Monroe, and his name is Marlo. Marlo was a real ladies man. What drew me to him was the fact that he was way older than the boys I was used to dealing with and very mature. He had a way with words that just made my panties wet instantly. All of his qualities; complete with that monster he was carrying between his legs, was enough to make his ass irresistible, him being fine was just an added bonus. He was everything a woman could want, charming, funny, he had major swag and was just overall, a cool ass person to be around. He was also my cousin, Katie's, on again-off again, boyfriend. Before judgment is passed on me, I didn't intend for things to even go as far as they went with him. We started messing around on one of the many times that they were off, and I messed up and fell hard. Marlo became my first everything. First person to ever have my heart, and the first one to break it. The first person to take my virginity and please my body. Hell, if we revealing secrets, he also was the father of my first child, but I had an abortion after he convinced me to and said this wasn't the right time for us. Later, I found out he had gotten back with Katie. I hoped like hell he moved away or died, because I wasn't in the mood to dredge up all memories and feelings. I was content with being single and ready to mingle. Besides, the town had enough heartache to deal with than to be bothered with our drama if it were to spill out. I know I'm dead wrong for my part in everything, but at the end of the day, I was a kid and he was 26. He knew better; I'm afforded a few fuck ups in life.

An hour and a half later, we were pulling into the driveway of the place I've called home my entire life. Getting out, I decided to get my bags later as I walked inside the house and went straight to my room. Opening the door, it looked exactly the same way it did the day I left. Grabbing clothes from my drawer to put on, I headed into the bathroom to wash away the hours I traveled off, today. Once I was clean, I went laid in bed because I was extremely exhausted.

KNOCK! KNOCK!

It had been two days since I got in town, and Yemani still had yet to return any of my calls, so I was popping up on her today. I had been outside her house for about 10 minutes now knocking, but she had yet to come to the door. I was literally cooking to death in this heat, and it didn't help that my tank top I had in was literally sticking to my body. Suddenly remembering that I had a key to the house, I kicked myself for standing out here, burning up and getting an unwanted tan for nothing. Walking into the house, I immediately turned my nose up at the sight and smell. Momma Caroline would be rolling over in her grave if she saw her house in the current state that it was in. It was a foul odor coming from someplace in the house, there was trash and empty containers everywhere. Setting my keys down, I closed the door and got to work cleaning up everything from room to room. A few hours later, I was exhausted but the place was spotless. The entire time I was moving around and making noise, Yemani, not once, came out of her room. Walking inside her door, I saw her with a blade cutting her wrist up. She had only succeeded in making two insertions before I ran over to her and wrestled the blade out of her hands. She swung wildly at me before

I got her to focus on her attacker. Looking strangely at me for a minute until recognition settled in, Yemani then fell into my arms, crying.

"Thank God you are here, Dezzy. I ca-ca-can't do this," she cried. I was starting to feel bad, thinking she was ignoring me this entire time when she was clinging to me for dear life. I was literally the only family she had left since she didn't fuck with her mother's family and her father was an only child, or so he thought because he was adopted.

"It hurts. I can't live without them," she said, crying hysterically at this point.

"Shhh, I'm here, sis! I'm here, and I'm not leaving you. We getting through this together, baby."

"Oh God! They gone, Desiree, they really are gone. How can I make it without my momma and daddy? Why didn't you let me die?"

I didn't have an answer for her, so I just held her in my arms and rocked her as silent tears slid down my face. I wanted to take her pain away, but I didn't know how, so I just held her until she went back to sleep. After she was knocked out, went into their medicine cabinet and grabbed their first aid kit. Following in my mom's footsteps, I was going to school to become a nurse, so I skillfully had her arm cleaned up and bandaged in no time. I, then took a brush, and brushed hair out until it untangled, then I parted it down the middle and braided it down into two big braids. Next, I gathered all of her clothes up and washed them, then went home to get my clothes because I was moving into their guest room. I was serious when I said I wouldn't leave her again. I can't believe I walked in on her attempting to take her own life. It brought tears to my eyes even trying to imagine a world without my sister. I would not want to live in that world, which gave me a window into her reality.

I was walking back home since my mom was at work and my car was back in Houston, when a car pulled up on the side of me and slowed down. Not bothering to stop and see who it was, I kept walking as I texted away on my phone, replying to Zac, this guy I had met at a party a few weeks before I came here. He was a bad boy and that attraction is what drew me to him that night. That was the only time I'd seen him so far because our schedules were both crazy. We've been playing this cat and mouse game for a while now, and I honestly was enjoying it. He was currently telling me he would come here if I needed him and it felt good to have a guy in my corner who seemed to, genuinely, care. I didn't realize how much I needed someone to be strong for me as well until this very moment.

"Desiree," a voice called out to me. The very voice I did not wish to hear at the moment. Pretending not to have heard them, I kept walking because my street was only a block away. Swerving in front of me, he cut me off and hopped out the car, looking every bit of good just like the last time I saw him.

"So, this how we acting?"

"Marlo, what do you want?" I asked him looking around, making sure no one was watching us because he surely was showing his ass right now. Even if him and my cousin were broken up, that would still be something for the town to gossip about.

"Oh, it's like that now? That's all I get is, a Marlo what you want? Shit, tell a nigga how you really feel. The woman you gave your heart to comes back into town, avoids you for a few days and you finally run down on her to only hear what you want? That's fucked up, ma," he said, pulling at my heart strings when he mentioned he gave his heart to me.

"I'm sorry, I just figured it would be best this way," I said, putting my head down trying to control my emotions. I hated the way this man had control over my emotions.

Stepping forward toward me, he leaned in to kiss me, and right before our lips connected, his phone started ringing and my cousin's picture with hearts beside it popped up before he could hide it. *Saved by the bell.* This is why me and my boyfriend really broke up. How can you give another person your all, every piece of you when someone else holds some of those parts? Coming back and seeing him just caused every old wound to resurface. Every heartache, every happy moment; I felt myself falling again. Feeling caged in, I did the only sensible thing I knew to do, I ran. I bolted down the street like the police were after me, and I was running for my life.

Making it to my house in record speed, I made a mental note to go out for the track team as I put my key inside the door. I ran inside, closing and locking it behind me as I leaned against it and let the tears flow that I wouldn't dare drop in front of him. I had been so strong for a year, and I couldn't allow him to take me back when I was so focused on moving forward. My phone began to ring as I was getting myself together.

"Hello?"

"Hey, I see somebody finally stopped playing phone tag and answered the phone," Zac said.

Closing my eyes, I tried to steady my breathing before I answered.

"What's wrong?" he asked, his voice changing from laughter to concern.

"Just being home brings back unwanted memories," I said just as Marlo started beating on my door.

"Desiree, bruh; stop being fucking childish and open up this door!" he yelled.

"You ok?" Zac asked me. I still had my eyes closed, mentally counting down, and I guess my silence angered him. "DESIREE ARE YOU FUCKING OK? IF YOU DONT ANSWER ME IM GOING TO ASSUME YOU'RE IN DANGER AND I'M DROPPING WHAT I'M DOING AND HOPPING ON A PLANE RIGHT NOW! WHO THE HELL IS THAT BEATING?" Zac yelled.

"I'm ok, I'm ok," I said more clearer and collected. "It's just an old situationship."

"Doesn't seem that old, ma," he said, still with a hint of annoyance in his voice.

"I haven't seen or talked to him since I moved to Houston for school a year ago, it's very old," I said, more confidently as I walked away from the door, heading into my room.

"What are you doing?"

"Just came from my best friend's house, cleaning up and I had to stop her from hurting herself. I just want to take her pain away," I said, my voice cracking.

"Only thing you can do is be there for her, ma and be strong for her. You got her back and know that I have your back," he said, making me blush.

"Is that right? You got my back?"

"Of course. Shit, I was ready to hop a flight to that small ass town and fuck some shit up about my baby," he said.

"All we do is talk, how I'm your baby already?"

"Shit that's more than I give a lot of hoes. Hell, they don't even ask for conversation. They see a nigga and see dollar signs. They wanna be with me because of my status and clout in these streets, money, and shit just to say they fucked me. Bitches be tryna get bragging rights off a nigga and shit. You, all you ask for is conversation. You keep a nigga talking and thinking. You ask me how my day going or if I've eaten. Hell, its been awhile since somebody genuinely asked me that and cared about what my response would be. Shit, if they do ask, hell, it's only to try and butter a nigga up and get some bread. With you, I feel like everything is genuine. You ain't tryna jump on a nigga dick, and you be shooting my ass down when I try and take you places. Hurting my poor lil' feelings; I just knew I was ugly or some shit," he said.

I couldn't do anything but laugh.

"Now you laughing at me? Just don't care about my lil' feelings at all," he said. He had a way of brightening up my day. I couldn't stop smiling as I packed clothes to go stay with Yemani. Just that quickly, he had turned my frown upside down. He was really like a breath of fresh air.

Two months later

Yemani had opted to skip her parent’s funeral, and I didn't blame her for not wanting to sit through that. She was going through enough and not seeing them was her healing process. She was slowly coming back around, even though she wasn't a hundred percent back herself yet. Today we were having a big cookout in the park just to bring some type of light in this darkness that we've all been in. Not only was Yemani affected, but the town as well. Caroline was born and raised in this town. She went away to college, got married, and returned to start a family here.

"Where are we going?" Yemani impatiently asked me as I drove to Ferriday, Louisiana. She had been putting off reading her parents will for a while, and I figured today would be the perfect day to do it while she was in a good mood. Besides, it would be the last time for me to do it because I had to leave and go back to school, which was starting in a little over a week. I still haven't figured out how I would tell Yemani or how I would even focus on school, having to leave her behind. Pulling into the parking lot, we both got out and walked inside.

"Good afternoon, how many I help you?" The cheerful secretary asked us as soon as we walked in.

"Yes, Yemani Jacobs to see Mr. Hightower," I said.

"Huh?" Yemani said, confused. Ignoring her, I went took a seat in the waiting area. Coming to sit beside me, she said, “Desiree, what is going on? What are you up to?"

"Ok look, you have to read your parents’ will. The lawyer's called a few times and sent letters. I have to go back to school, Yemani, so it had to be today. I know I'm the only person who could get you to go, so that's why we are here. It's going to be ok, sis, I'm going inside with you, and I'm right here," I said to her, grabbing her hands and squeezing them.

"Hearing this will make it that much more realer," she said, tears coming to her eyes.

"I know, baby, but you have to know what they left you to take care of yourself. I know their home is paid for, so you need to know if they left it to you and if he has the paperwork and if they left you any money for the upkeep. Everybody in town chipped in and paid these last few months but for how much more longer, baby?"

She didn't say anything, just remained quiet. A few more minutes passed before a sexy, white man mid-forties, sporting a dark blue, tailored suit walked out to the lobby to greet us.

"Ms. Jacobs," he said, walking to Yemani already knowing who she was. "Nice to see you again, I'm Richard Hightower. I met you when you were no more than 4 or 5."

After we both shook his hands, we followed him to a conference room. Taking a seat, a lady came in and offered us some snacks or beverages.

"No, thank you," we both said.

"Ok, let's get down to business since you are here to read the last will and testimony of Caroline Renee Skinner-Jacobs and Dave Markel Jacobs. To our loving daughter, we start off by saying how very much we love you. You are our blessing from God, and if we are reading this, then your father and I have gone on to be with your grandparents. Know that we love you and we want nothing but the best for you. Please try and live your life. I know it's hard to lose the four people you love the most, but we all want nothing more than for you to live a thriving, prosperous, long life. And that starts with school. In the event that we are still alive, skip this part because we will, with great joy, do it in person if we are blessed with that chance. However, if we are dead and have not changed this, then that means you have not started school. Baby, you've always been so smart; you used to walk around the house all the time trying to fix people's teeth and brush your baby dolls teeth. You've always wanted to be a dental hygienist, and we want you to get out of town and go live your dreams. Your father and I chose to start a family in the place we were raised, but that's because we had experienced life at that point. We don't want you to be there forever so therefore, you can access the 50,000 we are leaving you only under two conditions. The first 25,000 will be deposited on your 19th birthday, that will be a few days after school starts. The remaining 25,000 will be deposited to you on your 21st birthday, only if you are still in school. The day of graduation and only then will you return to get the rest of what's in the will, but it's only available to you should you choose to make it that far. To ensure that you actually make a valid effort to go to school, we have instructed our home to be vacated a week before school is to start and locked up. Donna will hold all keys and deeds to it. We love you baby, and we are not trying to be harsh with you, we just know the potential that you have, and we want you to chase your dreams. We will be with you every step of the way.

P.S. Your father wants you to know that he is also leaving his baby to you; his shop that he planning on opening., he already has papers drawn up, so your name is on everything. His only wish is that you keep it in the family to pass down to your kids. Make us proud our sweet Yemani, love mom and dad."

When he finished reading, me and Yemani were both crying. I'm not sure if I was crying because it was sad, she might finally be coming to college with me, or she had just gotten evicted out of her home.

"Since you have read the will, and it's one week before school according to their website, i'm sorry to have to tell you that's we'll have movers cleaning everything out first thing Monday morning," he said.

"Wait!" Yemani said. "I'mI'm sure they didn't really mean that when they wrote it. Can't you do something about it? Its my parent's house! They own it, no one can kick me out!" she yelled.

"I'm afraid it's nothing I can do. That's why I tried contacting you sooner."

"Thanks a lot," she said to me as she got up and stormed out. Running behind her, she was already at my mom's car and waiting on me by the time I got outside.

"Yemani-" I started to say.

"Just take me home," she said, cutting me off.

Not saying another word to her, I got in the car and drove us back to Sicily Island. Parking in her driveway, I said," I'm sorry. You know I would never do anything to intentionally hurt you. I love you and was only trying to help." When she didn't respond, I said," Are you still coming to the cookout?" Still not responding, she got out, slammed the door and went inside her house.

Sighing and deciding to give her time to herself, I backed out and headed to the cookout. When I arrived, it was in full swing. They had jumpers and slides for the kids, kiddie pools, water guns, card games, dominoes, the music was going, the liquor was flowing, and it was lots and lots of food.

"Desiree," my mom called to me. Walking over to her, I noticed someone standing behind her. When I got closer, I noticed it was Katie. *Great*, I thought to myself. When my mom moved fully out of the way, it was like time stood still as my eyes immediately went to her stomach.

"Hey Desiree," she said, wobbling over to give me a hug.

I froze up, still in shock that she was actually pregnant. Marlo had convinced me they were done when he cornered me at the store a month ago, but why would a pregnant person call a man that's not her baby father. How dare he practically force me to get an abortion, but she gets to keep her baby.

"Katie," I heard Marlo's lying ass voice say from behind me. I guess he noticed us talking.

"Marlo, the baby, look who's in town," she said, moving her hair out of her face, and that's when I noticed the sparkling ring on her finger.

"You're married?" I whispered to no one in particular.

"Oh yeah, girl, for almost a year now," she said with a smirk like she knew about everything and this was her way of rubbing it in.

He had married her. That's why he kept telling me to get an abortion because he was about to marry her. Forcing my tears not to fall, I willed myself to keep it together just as my phone started ringing. Seeing Zac's name flash across the screen caused me to instantly smile. Even if he wasn't there, he always seemed to be there.

"Hey baby," I said, purposely calling him baby in front of them. "Excuse me while I take this call," I said cheerfully.

"Well hello to you, what's going on?"

"You."

"Me?"

"You always seem to call when I need you. I saw my ex today, and he's married. I guess that's why he made me abort our baby, and she's pregnant.

She was flashing her ring to me and wanted me to cry, I think she knows," I said as I walked down the long trail way.

"First of all, don't be telling me about another nigga who knows how that pussy taste and still want you. I ain't about to sit up and console you about the shit. Second, since you told nobody about this but me, I'm the only one that can call you out on your shit. Ma you dead ass wrong. It don't matter how old you were and how naive you were, you knew enough to know you was fucking your cousin's man. It doesn't matter what bullshit he fed you to talk you out that lil' pussy. At the end of the day, you just as wrong. He didn't force you to open your legs. I'm sorry about your kid, but take that as a learning experience and put on your big girl panties and woman the fuck up. Never let a mufucka see you sweat. You keep your head held high at all times, right or wrong," he said, putting my ass in check really quick. That's why I was so drawn to him. Nobody talked to me like he did.

"You right."

"Of course, daddy right."

"Daddy huh?"

"Damn right and don't you forget it. How Yemani doing?" he asked me. He always was sure to ask me about her as well, letting me know he wanted to be included and involved in my life.

"She was doing better until I got her evicted today."

"Evicted? Doesn't she own the home? Y'all good? I can have some m-"

"No, it's nothing involving money, the will said she had to get out and accept her scholarship to college, or she'd be homeless."

"Some people come from a crackhead as a mother and an absent father. You can't do nothing but respect that. At least her parents care enough to want to see her succeed in life. That's just tough love; she'll be ok. She needs a little push in the right direction," he said. "Nigga, hold up; you see I'm on the phone. You ass just hating and shit," he said, talking to someone else. "Yeah, I'm back, baby, that's my hating ass brother. iIf the nigga stopped scaring women away, he would have one and wouldn't be all in my shit, but let me hit you back before I have to beat this nigga ass," he said, hanging up. Laughing, I walked back towards the cookout when I saw Yemani.

"I was looking for you," she said, walking up to me.

"Listen i'm,"

"Don't worry about it," she said.

"I'll talk to my mom, she is going to have the keys, so she can work something out so that,"

"How's the weather in Houston this time of year?" She asked me cutting me off.

"Why?"

"Because 'm coming with you and going to school."

CHAPTER 3

New beginnings aren't always so bad…

YEMANI

"There's been some type of mistake with my dorm. My key is not working, and it says online that me and my roommate, Desiree Adams are in building 17 of the honors dorms, room 1515," I said to the lady behind the desk at the residence hall.

"Do you have your student id number so that I can take a look at that for you?"

"Yes ma'am," I said, grabbing my phone and pulling up my notes app where I had written the number down. "1775346521."

"Give me one moment," she said, typing away on her computer. I just stood there hoping everything was ok and wishing my parents were here with me. I didn't know the first thing about what I was doing.

"What they saying?" Desiree asked, walking up.

"She told me to give her one moment."

"It's so hot; I'm ready to get in the room and shower. I hope they haven't bumped us down to those raggedy dorms or something. I can't live like that. They share a shower with four people, and the dorms are literally hanging on their last leg," she said, fussing.

"Ok ladies, it says here that you were bumped up to the campus apartments. I don't know why they didn't tell you that nor do I know why they gave you room keys for some else's room. I'll be more than happy to fix everything right now."

"Wait, how did we get a campus apartment? I thought they were strictly for upperclassmen?" Desiree said in excitement.

"Technically, one of you is an upperclassman, and both of you have the GPA requirements to reside in the apartments," she said handing us both keys. "I also took the liberty to change you guys from a four bedroom where you would have shared with two other girls to our deluxe, two-bedroom apartment. Have a wonderful semester and Yemani, welcome to our campus," she said, winking at me before calling next in line. Walking off, I wondered if my mother had anything to do with this change. Getting into Desiree's 2012 Toyota Camry, we headed in the direction of our new home for the next couple of months.

"Let's go get our things out of that hotel first before they try and charge us for another night," Desiree said.

"Yeah, you right. now that we have our keys, we don't have to be in a rush. Bitch, I can't believe we have our own apartment," I said excitedly.

I've lived with my parents my entire life; not saying I didn't have the freedom to come and go, but it would be different having our own space and not living in just a room. Best of all, it's rent free because it's included in our tuition. I was actually finding myself excited about this. *Momma, daddy, I'm doing this for you*, I thought to myself.

Two weeks later, I found myself laying across my bed, exhausted. I had just left my only class for today which was an early morning class, which I already hate. School had only been in going on two weeks, and shit was already hectic. Who gives homework on the first day of class? I thought since I graduated top of my class in high school, that college would be a walk in the park, shit, that was a lie if I ever heard one. Pulling out my phone, I saw Desiree face timing me.

"What's up," I said when her face popped into view.

"Happy birthday, bitch! Damn, you old as fuck now."

"Thank you, and bitch, your birthday next month so we old together, hoe," I said. With everything going on, I had completely forgot it was own damn birthday!

"I have another class, then dance practice, so you're on your own for the day. Sorry but we gone fuck shit up this weekend, and we can go eat tonight. I didn't forget your gift, lil' ugly."

"Bitch, you tried it. I'm a dime plus nine."

"Whatever, hoe. I gotta go love you and try and enjoy your day."

"Doing what?"

"Your car came, so go sightseeing or hit the mall."

"By myself, bitch?"

"When your mean ass ever wanted to hang with a gang of bitches?"

"Yeah, you right, you know me so well."

"I'll skip biology and fake sick if you want me to."

"Don't use me because your ass don't want to go to class. I'll be good until you get out of class, bye hoe," I said, hanging up.

I went to shower, and got my day started since a bitch was nasty 19 and single in a big city full of fine ass men. Thirty minutes later, I was sitting on my bed, wrapped in a towel, checking blackboard to see if my math teacher had posted our grades from the test she gave us the first day of class. Hell, seeing as though I had a C on the last two homework assignments, I was skeptical about my test grade. Math had always been a problem subject for me. I knew how to solve the equations, but after a while of looking at numbers, my attention span began to wonder and I marked any answer. I have to take tests in a quiet secluded area with no students, and no distractions to really pass. As soon as her home page popped up and I clicked on grades, I closed my eyes and really prayed for the first time in a really long time. Opening them up, I saw I had made an 89 on the test and I was very excited about that. Jumping up and down, screaming, I picked up my phone to call my mom and let her know how good I did on my math test that was sprung on me. I also needed to remind her that she owed me a Brahim bag and Vegas tickets. Dialing the number and letting it ring, it took me a few minutes to remember she was dead. Tossing my phone to the side, as silent tears ran down my face, I tried to keep myself from breaking down. I had made a decent grade in math and it's my birthday, all I wanted to do was call my mom and let her know about my progress.

"I need a damn blunt," I said out loud, wiping my face and getting up to get dressed. Settling on a body con dress with Gucci slides, I brushed my loose wave soft curls out of the bun I had it in and then I put on a little lipstick and hoop earrings. Grabbing my phone back up, I wanted to hit Desiree to see where I could get a blunt from, something I haven't smoked in a while, but the way my nerves set up right now, I needed one. While I waited for a text back, I went ahead and logged into my Chase account to see how much I had to spare at the mall today. I was doing surprisingly well balancing my money and I was actually proud of myself. I had also applied for work study and was set to go on an interview sometime next week. Pulling my account up, I had to do a double take when I noticed I had 25,585.64 in my account. I had 25,000 more than

I was supposed to have. Racking my brain about where the money came from, Desiree texted me back with an address to a house where I could get some gas.

Bitch, just wait on me to get out of class because if you tryna smoke, that mean your nerves bad and your attitude will be worse. Niggas in Sicily Island might let that slide, but niggas here will real life try and square up with you. She texted me

Girl bye; go your ass to practice. I'm good, I'm only tryna get some gas and go about my business.

Bitch! Yemani, did you forget I know you in real life, hoe so you can't run that shit by me? If you not tryna go with me then be careful, la baby, ok? I'm serious them niggas over that way ain't wrapped too tight.

I'll be fine, best friend but check it, how about somebody put 25,000 in my account, weird, right?

You forgot the will said you would get it?

Oh shit, yeah, I did. (sad face emoji.)

Tossing my phone in my purse, my mind was spinning a mile a minute as I grabbed my keys and walked out the door, locking it and walking down to my vehicle. Hopping into my car, I typed the address into the GPS my dad had installed in my jeep, then sped off down the streets headed towards Third Ward, as Desiree had called it. The way she was acting, they had a shoot first, ask questions later policy or some shit. I made a mental note to get my license to carry and start going to the gun range because what I wouldn't do is play with a bitch or nigga. I wasn't in my right mind either; they can get all these hard punches. Jumping into the highway, my heart sped up as I pressed down on the gas, merging into the incoming traffic. I had yet to get used to the big city, the highway, or traffic. Truth be told, the shit scared the hell out of me as the cars sped by, going damn near 100 miles per hour while I was struggling at 60. Putting my signal light on and switching to the slow lane, I tightly gripped the steering wheel before I felt like I was ok. Plugging my aux cord in my phone, I tried to focus on the fact that a bitch was 19 today. I knew once I got this blunt in my system, I would be turnt. I know my parents wouldn't want me crying all the time over them; I just couldn't help it; my best friend was gone. I loved my daddy, but I was more a momma's baby. Pushing back tears that were threatening to fall, I turned the radio up as *Kevin Gates, Intro To Luca Brasi* came on. I loved me some Gates with his sexy, crazy, freaky ass, but we would never work out. He talking about he thought it was legal to beat yo hoe and shit. Nigga if it is, it's legal for yo ass to catch this work. Laughing to myself, I started rapping along to the words having my own mini concert.

Turnin' up, we kill it all, on Instagram we flexin'

I'll steal one of you niggas, check one of you niggas

Turning on the intersection of Dowling and McGowen street, I immediately became alarmed. This place looked like it came straight out of a movie scene where they depict crime in America. I see what Desiree was talking about, still, I needed a blunt, so I shook off the fear that had crept up on me. *They bleeding like you bleeding*, I pep talked myself as I pulled into an empty lot next to the trap house, im assuming. Looking around me, I took in the scenery before me. Having not really been outside of Louisiana before, and with the limited places I choose to visit, I just had never seen anything like this before in my life. We had a hood in Sicily Island, of course, but this made our shit look like a million bucks. Before I could fully get out my car, a corner boy was on me like white on rice.

“Say, red, what's a fine ass chick like you doing over here?” he asked, leaning towards me, reeking of some odors I wasn't familiar with, but one that was very noticeable was the funk. The more he stood in front of me, the less oxygen I felt like I had.

“I just need some Reggie.”

“Reggie?” he said, looking at me like I had asked him some fuck shit.

“Bruh, if you don't gone head back to where you came from with that bullshit,” he said, turning away from me like he thought I was the opps or some shit.

“Listen, I’m new to the city and that's basically what they have in the small town I’m from. Can you just give me whatever you have, please?”

"You better be glad you fine as hell, shawty," he said, walking off. Reaching in my pocket, I grabbed $25 to hand to him when he came back. "Here," he said, handing me the weed. Without even asking him for the price, I just handed him the $25.

"Thank you," I said to him, preparing to get in my car.

"Man, this not even for you, but to each his own," he said, hitting me with a head nod and walking off. I got back in my car letting what he said marinate in my brain. I hadn't smoked in years, and when I did smoke, it wasn't an everyday thing, merely just socially. However, I needed something to numb the pain, and I always seemed to be floating on cloud nine whenever I smoked in the past. Getting inside the car, I opened the bag and inspected the weed, trying to see if it looked different than what I was used to. Not finding a difference, I sealed it back up, put it into my glove compartment, and reversed preparing to back out of the lot when

BOOM!

I connected with a hard object, causing me to hit my forehead really hard on the steering wheel. It took me all of 30 seconds to realize some idiot had hit my damn car. Holding my head, I took my keys out of the ignition and jumped out the car. I had a slew of curse words ready for whoever the hell the idiot was driving. I got to the back of my truck and came face to face with the most handsome man I had ever laid eyes on.

CHAPTER 4

I'ma die a real nigga…

MIDOS

Pow! Pow!

Putting a bullet into the nigga, sitting in my face for letting the bull shit come out of his mouth, I turned to the other niggas in the room.

"Now, y'all lil' niggas know my patience is fucking thin, so I'ma need y'all answers to be better than these niggas because my trigger finger itching," I said, annoyed as fuck that this was how I was spending my day. I wasn't a stranger to getting my hands dirty, but I was a boss, and not a worker so this hands-on shit, I rarely did lately, unless a nigga was severely trying me. Now granted, I would push a nigga shit back no problem on a daily, however if it was involving this drug shit, I had niggas directly under me that were supposed to handle this shit. Yet, here I was about to air this entire warehouse the fuck out and start over with an entirely new crew. The doors opened, and Mack, and Debo, my first and second in command, walked in looking confused.

“Midos, what's up?” Mack asked, surveying the bodies I had spread out around the warehouse.

“I might be demoting y'all niggas is what's up. Y'all just the niggas I was looking for, so how about y'all join the party?” I said, coolly to them, my English breaking a bit because I was so pissed off. I was battling with myself not to just fucking, up this AK 47 and squeeze the trigger ‘til that bitch started clicking.

“Just because I cut back on these meetings and my involvement these last few months, doesn't mean I don't know everything that goes on with my fucking empire, so which one of you bitches wanna explain why two traps short in cash and product, and Chaz and his crew, pushing shit on my streets without paying a moving fee?"

They both looked between one another like I was speaking a foreign language or some shit. A few months ago, I decided I had put in enough work and was stepping behind the scenes. I wasn't stepping down, or going legit, even though I had well over a few legit businesses. However, I was just playing the background but still supplying the streets while these niggas handled these on the front line. All that shit was a wrap after I looked over the books and realized the traps in Third Ward been short for a minute now and Chaz bitch ass still pushing shit on my streets.

"I ain't know shit about this," Mack started to say, but that was the wrong answer.

POW! POW!

I hit his ass with two head shots before he could even finish the fuck shit that was about to come out of his mouth.

Turning to Debo, I said, “What you got for me, bitch?”

“Look, man, I respect you as a legend in this fucking game but you not about to fucking talk to me like I’m some weak ass nigga or some shit. You bleeding like I’m bleeding and if I’m dying today, then let's get this shit the fuck over with because if not, a nigga got some pussy to tend to not be in here with a bunch of niggas. If you want some answers, you approach me like a fucking man; I ain't with this other fuck shit. I wasn't in charge of no books so I don't know shit about that or what's wrote down. However, I do know that I don't count money when it's initially picked up, but when it all gets to me, I know how much it’s supposed to be and if it's not that amount, I take out my own pockets and make the shit even so when I drop it off to you, your counts always correct. So, I’m not understanding what's the problem when you get all your bread. Instead of killing niggas, who don't even work at that house, go to the shit and see what the fuck is up, ‘cuz I don't even see them niggas in here,” he said.

Smirking at him, I was tryna decide if I wanted to pop this lil’ nigga or not. That was some real ass shit he just spit and he did have a fucking point; them niggas wasn't even here. I decided to let this nigga make it because he was a real one and I needed niggas like this in charge of all the shit I worked so hard to build. He wasn't about to fold like the bitches in front of me, damn near pissing their pants and shit. Feeling a vibration, I looked down and noticed it was my phone ringing, “Do your fucking job, and tighten up. Shouldn't no nigga move shit on these blocks without you knowing about it and you shouldn't be babying these niggas by replacing money with your own shit because they think they getting away with taking from me. You short, you let me or Zac know. Get the clean-up crew to get these niggas out my shit and get these bitch ass niggas back to work. I'm switching up trap houses, and drop spots. A nigga ain't about to be flossing around with my shit," I said, getting up and leaving out the warehouse. Walking outside, I jumped into my Ferrari and sped off, heading to Third Ward. "Hello?" I answered my phone because I had missed the call and they insisted on calling back.

"Midos, baby, are you coming over today?"

"Lilly, what I tell you about blowing my shit up like that?"

"I'm sorry, baby. I miss you, let me suck that big dick just the way you like it," she purred.

I can't lie; my dick jumped hearing her say that shit. She worked my nerves and I could barely stand the hoe, but she was a headologist when it came to delivering some of the best head a nigga ever had!

“I got shit to handle, I’ll hit you later on, ma,” I said, shaking my head.

I wasn't that far from my destination, so I sparked a blunt to calm the beast within. I just knew I was gone have to kill all these muthafuckas in this bitch but I was gone try not to. Turning on the street, I sped past the house, just to peep the scene out and take everything in that these niggas had going on. Turning into an abandoned house, I reversed and went back down to the trap house. Dropping some damn ashes on my pants, I slowed down because I was coming up on the house. As I looked down to wipe the ashes off, I felt a hard ass hit to the passenger side of my car.

“What the fuck!" I yelled as I stepped on my brakes, put my car in park, cut the engine and hopped out. Realizing my whip had been hit, I looked up as some dumb ass broad hopped at the car, walking briskly over to me with a mean mug on her face.

"Damn, I don't know how y'all do it in Houston, but when somebody is backing up, you don't fucking fly out behind them," shawty said to me. Even with her cursing me out, she was still beautiful. However, I didn't tolerate disrespect from anybody, so fuck how she looked, I wasn't gone let her pretty ass slide.

“Check this shit out, bitch; you seem a little fucking special so I’ma overlook that bullshit you spitting because you clearly don't know who the fuck I am, so I’ll give your ass a fucking pass. You better be lucky I don't kill you right here."

"I got yo bitch, you damn gas station working, Bin Laden looking son of a bitch. Who the fuck you take me for that I’ma let you fucking disrespect me? I don't give a fuck who you are and if this how you talk to people, I don't fucking care to know you. I’m having a bad day, so I don't need this shit. Well, I was having a good day at first, until I checked my grade in math and did awesome, went to call my momma and," her voice cracked. "I just want my damn blunt I had to GPS and drive 30 minutes to get. I don't have time for this shit, and if you kill me, well, I just don't give a fuck; I've seen everything but death anyway," she said, looking me dead in my eyes.

Looking into her eyes, all I saw was hurt behind them. I don't know why it pulled at my ice cold heart to wanna kill whoever the fuck had harmed her, but it did. Instead of chocking the fuck out of her, I had a strange need to want to just hold her close. Pulling out my phone, I made a few calls speaking in my native language, then hung up. Glancing up at her, I noticed she was looking at me as if I had sprouted another head.

"Ok, seems as if we got off on the wrong foot, how about we match one in my car and wait for a tow truck? Deal?" I asked her, extending a peace offering.

"My truck is still drivable, though."

"I know, but I'll still have it fixed. Don't worry about it; I own a few body shops," I said.

She thought about it for a minute, then went back to her truck, grabbed something, and walked back over to me and handed me her truck keys. I laughed at the mace and little pocket knife on her keys.

"So, you savage, huh?"

"No, I just have to protect myself," she said, untwisting a baggie she had in her hands.

Looking at the bag, I grabbed it and sniffed, before turning my nose up at her and throwing the shit on the ground.

"Hey, I just bought that."

"From where?"

"Shit, seeing as though I'm still in front of a trap house, I'll take the obvious guess and say here."

I know these niggas ain't pushing this shit out my damn spot, I thought as I said, "I got a rule of never smoking from a blunt I didn't roll, and never smoking weak ass shit. I got some fire ass gas in my car so let's go," I said, turning and walking back to my baby that surprising wasn't all that bad to say she was just hit.

I made sure to take into account them niggas ain't once come outside to see what the fuck the commotion was in front of my shit. They know I don't play that shit, so it was apparent none of them niggas had the privilege of keeping their lives. Making a mental note to get Debo on the shit, ASAP, as I hopped back into my car. Pushing the start button, I fired the air because it was damn near 100 degrees outside. Hitting a button on the dash, it flipped over to reveal my stash as well as another rolled up blunt. I never rode with shit in the cup holder or ashtrays like these other rookies out here. I had so many secret compartments that the police could turn my shit inside out, have the dogs sniff, and still, they would come up empty handed. Every car I drove was equipped the same way, also with bulletproof windows.

“Damn, that's neat,” she said in reference to my hidden compartment.

“That's how a boss nigga roll. Quit fucking with them lame ass niggas,” I said then immediately got mad at the thought of her chilling with another nigga. As soon as the feeling of anger washed over me, I had to immediately shake my head and hit the damn blunt because it was obvious I was fucking trippin’.

"Sorry about going off on you," she said once she got comfortable in her seat, closing her eyes as her body melted into my custom-made, plush cushions.

"Yeah, you went in on my ass," I said, laughing because shawty really said I looked like I worked at a gas station. I can't even believe I'm laughing instead of killing her. Some men in America say they don't kill women and children, but I'll push they shit back in a heartbeat about that slick ass mouth these American women have. But here is one, who was just talking shit to me and instead of checking it or killing her, I'm tryna match a blunt with her. Damn, I'm slipping.

"What was that about anyway?"

"Well, you did disrespect me. I know I'm not the first one to get mad at that bitch comment."

Smirking, I said, "You really are new to the city, that's why I'm not even going to respond. Shit, bitches be glad if a nigga give them any conversation, so they don't even care what the hell comes out my mouth," I said, truthfully because they didn't care what I called them. They sacrificed their respect for money or a chance to be near me or anybody in my circle.

"Why you couldn't call your mom?"

"Huh?" she said, looking down at her feet.

"You said you got a good grade on your math test and you went to call your mom."

"She," she said as her voice cracked and she shook her head, trying to shake her emotions.

"Just light the blunt up," she said to me.

"Bet," I shot back, respecting the fact she didn't want to talk about it. I'm not exactly the conversationalist myself, so I wasn't about to force her ass to talk. Lighting the blunt, I took a long pull of it before I passed it to her. She tried to take a long pull as well but ended up coughing uncontrollably. Laughing at her ass, I patted her on the back until she got herself together.

"This isn't any of that bullshit you had in that bag or that you used to smoking. This is pure weed straight from the grounds of Egypt."

"Egypt?"

"Yes," I said. Before we could continue our conversation, I spotted a tow truck pulling up.

"I guess that's my ride," she said.

"I could drop you off to where you need to go," I found my mouth saying before my brain could fully process it.

"You don't have to do that; I appreciate you even getting it fixed."

"You're right; I don't have to do it, I want to."

"Ok, I stay in the campus apartments. Here, I'll put the GPS in."

I let her think she was directing me someplace when really I already knew exactly how to get there. This was my town, and nothing breathed wrong without me knowing about it. It wasn't an alley or back road that I didn't know about. Whipping off the curb, I sped down the street, making a left and heading toward the highway. I should have taken the long way so I could interact with her more, but shit, I had gotten sidetracked and forgot I had business to tend to.

"This is a nice car," she said, admiring my blood red seats.

"Thanks, just one of my toys."

"One? Must be nice, oh thy bougie one."

"Bruh, did you just call me bougie? Can niggas even be bougie?"

"First, are you even a nigga? And hell, I guess they can if this just one of your toys. Back home, people lucky to have one decent car, you have toys," she said, making air quotes with her hands.

"My father is Egyptian; my mother is Italian and black."

"Egyptian and Italian? I thought it was against religion to marry outsiders in Egyptian cultures?"

"Outsiders?" I said, laughing at her choice of words. "Outside their faith, yes, culture, no. And it's not against anything. You are your own person; no one can make you do anything. However, Egyptians do strongly frown upon marrying someone who is not Muslim. But I never said he married her; I said my mother is Italian and black, and my father just like me didn't give a fuck what her religion was. Unfortunately, being the son of the king, he had no choice but for his wife to abide by the ways of the land and convert, which my mom wanted no parts of because she was a devoted Catholic. She also didn't wish to reside in the palace with my father's other wives, and instead, insisted on having her own place with me and her. That would have been fine and dandy except my grandfather, the king, found out, and refused to be embarrassed at the fact that his grandson wasn't living in the palace. He ended up giving her an ultimatum, move in or leave the country. Being stubborn and hard headed, she chose door number two and booked me and her a one-way ticket to America. She was a teacher in Egypt studying abroad, so that's the field she choose to return to in the states."

"Really?" she said, hanging on to my every word.

"Naw, bruh; I'm high as shit right now," I said, laughing hard as hell. I was higher than the fucking sky right now.

"That's fuck up. That's not funny; I was getting emotional thinking about it."

"Man, here's a little history fact for you, so you won't be out here looking slow as fuck. Egypt stopped having kings and queens in 1954. They now have presidents and shit," I said, taking another pull from the blunt before passing it back.

"I see somebody paid attention in high school," she shot back.

"Actually, I had two bachelor's degrees and a masters, so I paid attention in a few classes other than high school," I said, hitting the blunt again.

"Whatever," she mumbled, not having a comeback. "I knew you was bullshitting anyway. Only King and Queens I've ever heard of live in England," she said, accepting the blunt I passed back to her."

"Uh huh," I said. Although Egypt didn't have actual kings, my grandfather was king of the entire country in the drug world and ruled that shit with an iron fist. He was ruthless, reckless, and out of control. I don't know why folks said I reminded them of him because I may be wild, but he was on an entirely different level. This nigga forgot he was Egyptian or must have watched one too many Scarface movies because he really thought he was a mob boss. What made it even worse it that he wore a Thawb, like nigga how you regulating shit with robes on? He disliked my mother for my father those words was true and he told my father if he ever caught her on his land again he would cut her limb for limb. I never got a full explanation on his beef with her though.

"But for real though, none of that was real?" she asked a few minutes later after we had went silent for a minute.

"But no, what is true was the fact my grandfather disowned my mother and kicked her out the county,"

"How can you kick a person off an entire continent? Like how would he have known she was still there? And how is it even possible to go along with something like that?" she asked me, eyes barely open from the few puffs she had taken.

"With great power comes much respect," I said.

"My nigga, did you just quote Spiderman?" she said, busting me out.

"Shit yeah," I said, laughing.

"So, what happened to your dad? Did he become a sperm donor?"

"Naw, that didn't stop my father from being a father to me or taking care of us. It was just like he had an away job or something because he was home just as much as he was away. I also went back home to Egypt a lot and even went to school there a few years, when my mother got sick. She didn't want me staying around watching her die as she called it, but it was really because I was bad as hell and already a young boss in the making by then, so she wanted me with my father. Her sending me away just elevated my status," I said, pausing because I never really shared this much of myself with another human being, let alone a female I didn't even know. *Shit, I don't even know.*

"Go on," she said, hanging on to my every word, very fascinated by what I was saying.

"Story times over," I said, pulling into the campus apartments. "Which building is yours?"

"Building 7," she said.

Once I drove over there, she said, "Thank you," and got out the car. I drove off wondering if I should have gotten a number for her even a damn name.

"Call Zac," I said.

"Calling Zac," my car responded to me as I sped back down the highway to get back to my destination. I originally was headed to the park to check this bitch ass nigga, Chaz before I stopped at the warehouse. I got word his ass was out there selling shit on my blocks, after I specifically told this bitch ass nigga, if he want to push that trash ass shit around here, he had to pay like he weigh, just like everybody else. Apparently, me saying this meant nothing, because he turns around and slaps me in the face by still pushing that shit and I know that was some of his shit that ole girl had in her hands. So, either one of my workers was pushing it out my shit, or he had niggas posted pushing it around that bitch. I know for a fact them niggas ain't told him about Midos, because if they had, he wouldn't even be trying a real nigga right now.

My name is Amyr Jarrah, better known to the streets as Midos, and if you ain't figured it out by now, I'm the King of Houston. Anything you needed from drugs to guns; even murder for hire, I had available. I was flooding the streets with the purest Egyptian coke and weed around. I believed in everybody eating though, and I wasn't a greedy nigga by a long shot. If you didn't want to purchase work from me, that was fine. But if you wanted to move anything in my city, you had to pay a percentage fee to do so. It wasn't a damn, high ass fee because I knew people had to eat, as well as feed their workers and families.

"What's up?" Zac said, finally answering. Zac was my nigga. I wouldn't call him my best friend because that shit sounds gay even saying it. Like what a grown as man look like saying, oh this my best friend? That shit don't sound right coming out my mouth. That's my fucking brotha though, and right-hand man, as well as business partner. We went 50/50 on everything and built this shit from the ground up together. Nothing was done without the other knowing. He wasn't some flunky, and I was the boss, we were both boss ass niggas, neither role was higher than the other, even though my father supplied us with our shit.

"Headed to run down on Chaz bitch ass," I said.

"Shit nigga, you told me that damn near three hours ago? The fuck you been doing?"

“Canceled a few niggas at the warehouse, speaking of which, we need a new second in command.”

“Why? The fuck happened to Debo?”

“He just got promoted to first in command after I had to cancel Mack ass. But shit, after I left that, I went to see about traffic and money in Third Ward since the money been short over there lately.”

"The fuck you mean the bread been short over there lately? And how come I'm just hearing about this?" he shouted.

"Damn nigga, just what the fuck I said. I just found this out, hell, you know I can't be still on my off days."

"Nigga, nobody told your ass to work all day, every day like you struggling to pay bills."

"Fuck you, fruity ass nigga," I shot back. "Damn; you gone let a nigga finish or what?"

"Cry baby ass nigga, gone finish. Hell, I know you killed them niggas anyway, you got a fucking problem and your day don't seem to go right if you ain't killing some damn body. I know it's facilities that can help people like you," he said, laughing,

"Anyway, nigga like I was saying, I went over there to see about that and got into a damn accident."

“Shit, you straight?”

"Yeah, I hit this chick whip, well, shit, we hit each other car, cursed each other out, then matched one in my car while we waited for a tow truck to come. I called Pete and Barney and had them tow it to our body shop. I’ma have them sand it down, knock the dent out and repaint it," I casually said.

"Man, get the fuck out of here; this ain't April fool’s day, so yo ass is not about to trick me. What you was really doing? Letting Lilly swallow yo kids?"

"Nigga, I just told yo punk ass what I was doing, damn."

"Shit, I heard what the fuck you said, hell that don't mean I’m believing what the fuck you said. Nigga, you don't know what the word nice, mean. Since when you let bitches ride in your car? Them hoes either catching a cab or uber. Since when you let a bitch slid, cursing you out and you damn sure don't match blunts with them. Shit, you barely talk on the phone, that's why your hating ass always in your feeling when I'm talking to my shorty."

"Man, shut your ugly ass up, I'm getting ready to pull up in a few minutes," I said, cutting him off because he was right; I didn't do any of that but shit, something drew me to her, and I can't explain it exactly, so I wasn't gone try to.

"You by yourself?"

"Fuck you mean? Hell yeah and I'm not worried about these bitch ass niggas, they need to be worried about me, though."

"Yo hot head ass always running up somewhere solo; I got a bullet for your weak ass security detail," he angrily said.

"That's what your ass get for hiring the bitches, to begin with. Shit, you need a refund I ain't seen a damn detail team yet," I said in reference to the niggas he hired since I caught some hot lead a few months back. I ran down on a fool, who owed me some money and chased him into an alley before I realized it was a setup. I took six bullets and was still shooting back. If I was dying, I was gone go out with a fight. Clearly I survived, but ever since then, Zac ass called himself hiring a security team for me. So far, I haven't seen them niggas, but I really haven't been anywhere since I'm just getting back home two months ago. My father insisted I stay in Egypt and recuperate.

"You would have did better having my own security escort me around. 'Least them niggas with all of that dumb shit," I said, because my security team was the truth, but their only jobs was to be posted outside my house and accompany me to business meetings, that's it. I didn't need a nigga to hold my hand as I walked down the street. I don't care how many niggas was gunning for me; I wasn't hiding behind shit.

"When you get there, let me know," Zac said just as I turned the corner, where the park was. When I spotted the pigs, I just casually kept cruising by.

"Shit, the laws all over this place, that's what his ugly ass gets."

"Who moves shit at a park anyway? Hope they caught his fraud ass, baby chain wearing ass, stunting with his re-up money, knowing he ain't coming like that looking ass," Zac said, laughing.

"Yo, his sholl be out here flexed out like he balling, a nigga aught to run up in his shit just because," I said, holding my stomach with laughter. "What you about to get into, bitch? We do need to plan a trip to Third Ward and regulate shit that way. Them boys getting besides themselves like they forget we ain't nothing to fucking play with."

“They ass act like they forget how we put that murder game down. We stepped back not out. Shit, we definitely gone shake some shit soon and make an example out of them bitches.”

“I might just put Debo on it, and let him handle our light weight, and have him recruit some new niggas for that house. I trust that lil’ nigga fully that's why I canceled that fuck nigga and put him as first in command. His attitude reminds me a lot of our asses,” I said “But shit, what you about to do, though? Let's fall off in Onyx tonight.”

“Shit, I’m tryna run down on shawty. Her ass be tryna play a nigga; only wanting to chill near campus, and dodging me when I try and take her on dates and shit. She going out with a nigga tonight, fuck what she talking about.”

“You ain't chasing pussy but up here talking about me ‘cuz I matched a blunt with a bitch, ole soft ass nigga. Next, you gone be paying for the pussy," I said, laughing.

"Nigga, fuck you! You know I don't chase shit, but shawty, different so I'll power walk after her ass."

"Yeah whatever, but I'm tryna fall off in some pussy so I'll hit you later," I said to him, already texting one of my hoes.

"Shit as much as you ass clown them damn girls and as mean as you are, I'm surprised they even let your ugly ass smash."

"When this dick hit them guts and get to rearranging them insides, they have no objections to what the fuck I say," I told him as I hung up and drove towards one of my condos. I would never bring a bitch anywhere I laid my head, nor would I ever let one of them hoes ride in my shit. If you can't find a ride to this dick, you can't have it, plain and simple. Shit, bitches can get everywhere else, so why not? If I was in a good mood, I would send an uber for you, but that's rare occasions because I didn't care that much. I had pussy on speed dial, who would damn near walk to me; dick was just that good. From the park to one of my condo on Yorktown St, took a good hour to get to because of traffic, but once I made it, Lilly was patiently waiting outside for me, and she was in Galveston when I texted her. Bitch must have literally broken every traffic law to get over here. Shaking my head, I hopped out and walked to my door, letting us in. Still not really paying her any attention, I walked to the corner where my bar was, fixed me a drink, then walked off upstairs to get undressed and hop in the shower. I've had a long ass day, and a nigga needed to shit, shower, and fall off in something wet, in that order. Bout time I hopped in the shower, I had finished my drink, was halfway through my blunt, and feeling good as hell when I felt the shower doors opening. I had a huge walk in shower that also had a bench inside in a corner, and I was sitting down, kicked back, dick swinging as I watched Lilly seductively walk in with some type of lingerie shit, that had holes cut out in the breast part and crotch part. I couldn't understand why she had the shit on in the shower, but I couldn't deny that she looked bad as fuck in it.

Standing at 5'5, dark as midnight, with a set of perky breast that I'm positive were bought, but looked damn good sitting up like two melons, a slender waist, toned legs, and an ass that put Buffy the Body to shame that she more than likely purchased as well; shawty was the truth. A big hoe and thought I didn't know, and was more than likely looking for a meal ticket, but bad, none the less. I loved a chocolate girl, and her smooth, chocolate skin had me ignoring the bullshit she thought I didn't know about. Too busy looking at her, I didn't even notice her get down on my knees and gobble all 11 inches of my thick ass dick up, like I was 6 inches or some shit.

Sliding my dick down her throat with ease, she relaxed her jaws and started sucking on my dick like she a lollipop that was couldn't get enough of. I think I forgot to mention this bitch was hands down the best at what she did. Never have I ever had somebody suck my dick like she did, and for that reason, I would never stop fucking with her, hell I couldn't give this mouth up.

"Fuck! Suck this dick, you freaky bitch," I said, grabbing the back of her head as I started fucking her face.

"Mmmhh," she moaned as she leaned up, spit on my shit, then went down all the way, gagging a bit then releasing my dick with a pop.

When she released my dick, and started jacking it, as she gently sucked on my balls; I lost it as my toes curled and I gave in to the nut I had been desperately trying to hold onto because the shit was feeling just that good. Once she swallowed all my kids, she rubbed my dick over her chocolate nipples, causing the beast to spring back to life. It didn't take much to get me back hard. I had stamina out the world and didn't need but a 30-second pause before I was ready to go again. Once I was ready, the bitch tried to quickly jump on my dick, but I caught her ass in mid-jump and damn near broke her back how hard I pushed her ass back.

“Right idea, wrong nigga.”

“What you mean, Midos? Damn, you didn't have to push me that damn hard,” she said, rubbing her back as she got up.

“You know I’m not running up in you raw, now you want some shower dick, then say that, and I'll go grab a condom.”

"We been fucking around for how long now? I can't believe you tryna play me like a hoe."

"If it walks like a duck and quacks like a duck, whelp," I said, shrugging my shoulders at her ass. I was trying to figure out what sucker ass nigga she took me for.

"Fuck you, Midos because you know damn well you the only nigga I been with since we started messing around."

"Uh huh, you want this dick or not?"

Rolling her eyes, she just shot me a death stare. If looks could kill, I know my ass would be dead.

"Suit yourself," I said walking over to my rack where I kept sponges and body wash, and started washing my body.

"Wait, no, I'll go get a condom," she quickly said.

“You'll get what? Shit, I was born at night not last night,” I said, walking past her into my room. That bitch couldn't get me shit unless I was standing in front of her, watching her and even then, it would be a toss-up if I took it. Hoe wasn't about to poke a hole in my shit and trap me for the rest of my life. Making it to my room, I quickly opened my top draw and grabbed a magnum XXL, the black pack that I had to specially order to even fit my shit, and walked back to the bathroom. Ripping it open and rolling it on, I made sure it was tight on both sides and secured before I slid the glass doors open, and stepped back into the shower. No words needed to be spoken as I grabbed her ass up, flipped her over so that her face was pressing into the shower granite wall, and rammed my dick inside her.

“Ahh!” she screamed as I grabbed a fistful of hair with one hand, and grabbed her by the back of her throat with the other hand, and started delivering powerful and deep strokes.

"Fuck Midos, oh my Godddddd!" she screamed as I picked up the pace. Smacking her on her ass, I said,

"Throw that ass back."

She fucked up when she started twerking on my dick because each time she threw her ass back, I was catching that shit like a racket ball. Pulling out, I hit her on the ass. "Go assume the position on the bench," I said to her. She knew exactly what I was talking about as she quickly ran over and got into position. Getting behind her, I pushed her back down, making her arch higher, as I went back in. Moving my hips in circles, I felt like I was dancing in the pussy. The three blunts I faced, combined with the alcohol, had my ass acting an ass right now. She was getting all this high and drunk dick. Putting her arm out trying to push me out of her a little bit, only made me grab her arm, twist it behind her back and grab her hair as I started hitting it harder, causing her to move up.

“Naw, don't run; this what you wanted, right? Take this dick, ma. Move that fucking hand. Matter of fact, give me this one as well,” I said because she had put her other hand back, trying to push me and get away at the same time. Holding both of her arms straight out behind her back, I slid deeper and went harder as I felt my nut building up. Biting my lips to keep from moaning, I just growled and went even harder. “You wanna make daddy nut with that mouth, or you want me to continue beating that pussy up?”

“Let me suck it, please, let me suck it, daddy,” she cried out. Smirking, I slapped her on the ass twice, hit her with two more strokes, then pulled out, snatching the condom off.

“You better fucking suck it good or I’m running back in that pussy, and yo ass won't walk for at least a month.”

CHAPTER 5

You can't be hard all the time. Be hard in them streets but always show your woman your gentle side…

ZAC

"So, this what a nigga gotta do to spend time with you?" I asked Desiree as she walked across the parking lot. I was posted up against my car waiting on her to get out of dance practice.

"Zac, what are you doing here?" she asked, walking over to me.

"Shit, you acted like it was a big deal to go on a date with a nigga or give me some real quality time; other than the bullshit you be on like chilling with you on campus between classes or meeting you at the campus Starbucks and shit," I said, kinda getting mad as hell as I really thought about the lame ass shit I was allowing.

"I didn't mean to make you feel no type of way; I'm just merely trying to take things slow and day by day."

"Shit at this rate, it'll be a year before I get you alone. I already told you I'm not any of them fuck niggas you used to dealing with. Therefore, I'm not taking no for an answer so come your funky ass on so you can shower, we have dinner reservations for 7 pm," I said with authority.

Taken aback how a nigga had just bossed up on her, she just stood in place, looking at me with glossy eyes.

"Bet that pussy wet, huh?" I said, laughing and shaking my head. I never understood how some chicks get turned on when a nigga put their foot down, but they liked that shit.

Snapping out of her trance, she blushed and quickly said, "Umm no, it's not."

Smirking, I popped the locks to my car and said, "Get in and that wasn't me asking you. Make sure you lock your car."

"I didn’t drive my car because I usually walk to practice. I like the exercise," she said, sliding into my car. "And I could never be funky, thank you very much. You just used to fucking with them dirty hoes," she shot back.

Laughing at her slick ass mouth, I said,"Naw, I ain't never fucked a dirty bitch, I done hit a few ugly hoes cuz pussy is pussy, but I draw the line at a dirty one," I said matter of factly. Hell, a female’s face didn't matter to me if she was face down, ass up. I'll fuck an ugly hoe quick, but I wouldn't let the hoe suck my duck no matter how tightly I squeeze my eyes, I would just know her ugly face was staring at me.

"You got issues," she said, shaking her head, laughing. This what I liked about her, she had the same personality as me. Any other female would have gotten mad, but she didn't let much get to her, well, when she had her guard down. Her past experiences had her pushing a nigga to the side and running from what we could have. Hell, might as well say she, my girl because this the longest I've ever entertained the same female consistently and still had interest in her. We been texting about four months now and shit, that's a lot for me. I've had hoes on my team longer, but I been lost interest in the hoes, and they only cross my mind when I want to get my dick wet, but Desiree is on my mind all day every day, and I find myself texting her lil' ass a lot. Shit, a nigga don't even text but be quick to scroll to her number.

"Run upstairs and get your clothes when we get to your apartment and don't take long or I'm coming in after you, throwing you, anything in a bag and dragging you outside. Fuck around and have one yellow shoe, one red one, and a purple dress, try a nigga if you want to, Desiree," I said calling her by her full name so she would know I wasn't playing with her. I usually called her Des, beautiful, red, or something like that, never Desiree.

"Today not a good day for dinner, how about another-" she started to say before I immediately got pissed off.

"Fuck that shit; we eating tonight because all you tryna do is buy time to fucking stall again. I'm done doing it your way."

"I'm not stalling."

"Ok, then what's the fucking problem?!" I said, yelling because I was getting very agitated.

Jumping at the tone and pitch of my voice, she quickly said,

"It's Yemani's birthday, and I told her we could go eat when I left practice. That's my sister, and I'm the only family she has, and nobody else is here to celebrate her birthday with her."

Feeling fucked up and stupid, the only thing I could reply with was, "Oh."

We sat in silence for a few minutes while I kicked myself for putting my foot in my mouth. I don't know why shawty had me tripping like this on her, but I just had to be near her right now, and I didn't want to wait until another day.

"Ok then I'll take you both to dinner," I said.

Perking up and turning her frown upside down, she said," Ok, but I hope it won't be awkward for her. You know it's her dinner and all. Why don't you invite your best friend?" she said, referring to Midos, whom I had told her about on more than a few occasions.

"Ma, that nigga isn't the blind date type and he kinda not wrapped too tightly. I'll call him and ask him, though. Run up there and get dressed. The same rules apply to both y'all so don't make me embarrass you and the birthday girl. If y'all wanna be on fleek or whatever you broads call it, then it's y'all best bet not to play with me," I told her, and she scurried out the car and hurried, disappeared into her building. Her dramatic ass really ran like somebody was chasing her. Laughing, I dialed Midos to see if he would agree to this bullshit ass date.

"Yo?"

"Bruh, what you doing at this exact moment?"

"Shit, putting Lilly ass out about to kick back and chill."

"I need a huge fucking favor, man. Like you know a nigga don't never ask you for anything, but I need this damn solid."

Laughing, he said,"Is this bitch bad?"

"Huh?"

"Shit, nigga; who you think you fooling? How long I been knowing you? Shit, being that I'm your business partner, I know you not hurting so you not calling to borrow money, nor are you calling to go handle some business, so that leaves a bitch. Is she bad?"

"I don't know, but my girl bad and shit birds of a feather flock together."

"Hell naw, it's always that one ugly duckling out the crew," this clown ass nigga said. "You think she'll let a nigga smash?"

"Nigga, I don't know you act like I know the broad. What part of that's my girl best friend did you miss? Man, it's the girl birthday and both her parents are dead, so she has no other family. Des was taking her to dinner, and I popped up to take Des to dinner. She tried to cancel since she taking her friend, so I said I would take them both, and she asked me to see if you would come along so Yemani wouldn't feel bad and lonely at her own shit. Her day probably already been fucked up since her parents not here."

"Damn, when you hit a nigga with a sad ass sob story like that one, I have no choice but to say yes right?"

"Hell yeah," I said happy that it was easier than I thought.

"Shit, you lied cuz I don't give a fuck about that bitch or her damn sob story. The fuck that gotta do with my life."

"Yo evil ass gone die alone and miserable."

"I'll also have a barn house full of hoes that would put the playboy mansion to shame. I might be alone, but I'll never be without a bitch," he shot back.

"Bye, ole ignorant ass nigga."

"Don't get mad at me because you tryna get rid of this suicidal ass bitch so you can slide up in her bad ass friend. Tryna throw me Medusa and shit, just to get yo mack on. When you think about it, shit, that's being a bad friend, and I really should be the one mad because we better than that," Midos said.

"Man whatever, Ima think of something before we get to the restaurant."

"Drop your security detail, and we have a deal. Maybe throw in a new car."

"Fuck you, ole weak ass nigga. I ain't buying yo ass a car, but I will cancel them fuck boys I hired because they not doing they job no way."

"The bitch bet not be ugly either or birthday or not, I'm on her ass, text me the info," he said, hanging up.

I sat there wondering what I had gotten myself into, and praying Yemani was a bad bitch because if not, I knew that clown ass nigga would let her ass have it. His mouth had no filters at times, hell, none of the time. Another 30 minutes went by, and just as I was getting ready to get out and go get their ass, they emerged from the building, and my heart literally stopped beating. Desiree walked towards the car wearing a bad ass red dress with someone beside her, who was an equally bad ass chick, that I assumed was Yemani. *Yeah, she gets a pass, that nigga gone be happy.*

"So Yemani, how you enjoying the city?" I asked her.

"It's cool, besides these rude ass niggas that y'all have here that don't have no damn matters or home training. No offense, but I don't know who raised them. They quick to use that bitch word," she said, rolling her eyes. All I could do was shake my head because niggas here was as cutthroat as they come. If you was looking for the gentleman, casanova type nigga, Houston most definitely wasn't the city to search for his ass at.

"Well, did you at least enjoy your birthday for the most part?"

"It was ok, yeah," she said not bothering to look up. I didn't really have any comforting words to say to her being that I wasn't good at this sort of thing. I couldn't even imagine losing one parent; let alone both of them. I had lost my grandparents, but I never met them anyway, so no tears were shed over that situation, but contrary to my occupation, I still had both of my parents, alive, well, and healthy. I would lay down my life for both my ma dukes and my pops, so my heart really went out to Yemani, and I admired her strength because I'm sure I would be on the fifth floor, somewhere slobbering everywhere, totally out of it.

"Where your truck was at? I didn't see it out front when we left," Desiree said to Yemani, snapping me out of the thoughts I was having which I was very grateful for because thinking about that shit was making me want to turn up an entire bottle of Hennessy.

"I'll run it with you later," Yemani responded, looking up at her.

"Why later?" Desiree asked her until Yemani shot her a look, letting me know she didn't want to say in front of me.

Shit, it ain't like a nigga gave a fuck, but instead of voicing my opinion, I decided to remain quiet.

"So Zac, what do you do out here?" Yemani asked.

"I'm a business man," I casually said, directing my attention to the lovely Desiree. She was wearing the hell out of that dress, and I had to periodically keep adjusting my mans because he was trying to jump out my pants and attack her ass.

"Is that right?" Desiree said, looking at me with those sexy ass eyes. Picking up my glass, I took a sip of water and cleared my throat to get myself understand control. Everything about this girl was turning me on and knocking me off my square right now.

"Yeah shawty, that's right, but since we already had this conversation, then you knew that already."

"I might have needed you to refresh my memory."

"Naw, you needed to see if a nigga answer would be the same," I said smirking at her.

"Ok, you got that," she said, laughing because I had totally busted her ass. I wasn't new to this shit by a long shot. Feeling my phone vibrating, I looked down, noticing Midos texting me.

Got caught up in something important, Ima run it to you when I call you.

You on your own with your girl and ugly duckling. If I was you, I would hit both them hoes and call it a night. Shit, if you wasn't suddenly in love and shit; you would have been did this, ole soft ass nigga

Shaking my head, I replied.

Nigga, fuck you and Yemani not even ugly, she actually bad as fuck. She too pretty for your ass anyway. But I want full details on what's going on if it's involving business and not hoes. If it's serious, I'll drop what I'm doing and come with you. I'm tired of your ass playing Superman and shit and tryna sick kick a nigga out when we both supposed to be on the front line. Sending my text, I placed my phone down and focused my attention back on the girls, who were now whispering in their own little world having a side conversation.

DING!

Seeing Midos text back, I laughed out loud at this stupid ass nigga and didn't even choose to respond back.

“Damn, I guess that text real funny, why me and Yemani can't laugh too?” Desiree shot me with attitude. She was funny as fuck though. She be ignoring a nigga, turning down dates, and never wanting to go anywhere off campus, but call herself now getting an attitude. Just to see where her head was, I decided to fuck with her.

“Oh naw, she ain't say nothing too funny.”

If looks could kill, I know my ass would be dead right now from the death stare she was giving me. I had to hold the laugh in, I almost let out because her mad face was funny as hell but she couldn't have it both ways. She couldn't check me about my phone, yet ignore and push me away also. Shit didn't work that way. Desiree was either going to be my girl and get the privilege of checking me and seeing my phone, or she was gone continue this little game and get no rights to anything involving what I did and who I did it with. A nigga was really done playing these games with her. I ain't never chased a girl harder than I found myself chasing her. Crazy thing about it was, it wasn't even on a sexual level that I was attracted to her. I mean, don't get me wrong; I would most definitely beat the pussy up, no hesitation if given the opportunity. However, that's now what drew me to her. She was easy going, easy to talk to, genuinely caring and nurturing, and she really had a good heart. She real life fucked with a nigga for me; not the fame, my name, or the money. That shit was mad attractive and made me want to learn more about her and explore and see where this had the potential to go.

“Did you hear me, Zac?” Desiree asked me.

“Damn ma, I was so focused on your beauty, I didn't hear shit you said,” I truthfully told her.

“Awww, y'all so cute. I like him, best friend,” Yemani said.

“He aight,” Desiree shot back.

“What you said, though?” I asked her.

“You said your best friend 25th birthday party next weekend, and you was throwing him a huge party. I said I wanted to do something for Yemani this weekend, but I figured she could just wait and party with him. Hey, maybe they might even hit it off,” she said, looking at Yemani when she said the last part.

"What is this, bitch, black people meet.com? I'm not tryna get hooked up," Yemani shot back.

"I don't know, ma. Midos a rude ass nigga and he really not the boyfriend type."

"Good because I'm not on the market to be someone's girlfriend, especially these rude ass Houston niggas. We not gone mesh well, they mouth too much for me and I'll pop off if I feel disrespected."

Shaking my head, I said, "Nope, like I said I don't feel like you and Midos would be a fit; hell, I'm not tryna be planning no funerals."

"Yeah, I know you need your friend alive and well," she said, looking me dead in my eyes with not a fear in her soul. I liked shawty already.

Smirking, I said, "You hell, ma."

Just then my phone alerted me to an incoming text.

Can't make it. My pops just popped up at my door. I read the message from Midos

Everything straight? I said back.

I think some shit jumped off. Not sure the details, we at my house now. He said

Your house, house or one of your condos?

Naw, I'm at my house, cut your date short and swang wide, this business.

Reading over what he said, I was immediately concerned about what Pops wanted. It wasn't unusual for him to come in and out of town, but he always called and let Midos know when he would be here, so to just pop up meant something was seriously up.

"What's wrong?" Desiree asked me, studying my facial expression.

"Some stuff going on concerning one of my business. I'm not exactly sure what but that was

Midos hitting me up. I'm sorry ladies but we're going to have to wrap this up," I said, digging in my pocket and peeling off two hundred dollars, which was more than enough to cover dinner. Standing up, they both looked confused as they quickly followed behind me. Walking briskly through the crowded restaurant, I ignored the waitress asking us questions and possibly assuming we are dining and dashing. The stupid bitch would find I left her ugly ass more than enough as well as a hefty fee. The closer I came to my car the worse my nerves became. I was usually the level-headed, calm one until shit for real; then I went to another place. Not wanting Desiree to see that side of me, I tried my best to steady my breathing. Popping the locks to my Range Rover, I hopped in, started the car up, and barely gave the girls time to close the door before I whipped out the parking lot. Breaking every traffic law, it took me literally no time to arrive back at the girl's dorm room. Pulling in the parking lot, I didn't even bother parking as I pulled up to the curb. Yemani jumped out immediately, probably glad to get away from my ass whereas Desiree took her time getting out.

“Is everything alright, Zac? I've never seen you look like this?”

“Yes, shorty, everything is fine. Listen, I'll call you later, ok? I just need to go check on my brother and my business.”

“Ok,” she said, leaning over to kiss me on the lips before hopping out the car. It sucked that our first kiss was under these circumstances and I really couldn't enjoy it like I wanted it. Staying to, at least, to make sure they both got in safely, I then sped off in the direction of Midos’ home, which was about an hour from here with lots of crazy thoughts running through my mind.

A nigga ain't got time for this bullshit, I thought to myself.

CHAPTER 6

There's just something about him…

DESIREE

"What was up with your boyfriend?" Yemani said as we walked into our apartment.

"First, he's not my boyfriend," I said, pausing to take my shoes off. "Yet," I finished up.

"He's a weird one, but I like him. He's better than the asshole I met today."

Raising my eyebrows, I looked at her waiting for her ass to continue. "Bitch, when was you going to tell me you met somebody today? Where your truck at? I know you ain't got this nigga driving your car and shit?" I asked her because I knew how niggas could be and I wasn't about to let my best friend play herself while a nigga flossed around town in her shit, possibly even picking up hoes.

"Bitch, you just tried my whole entire life with that bullshit you already know me better than that," she said, giving me a look, letting me know she was highly offended.

"Well shit, hell, you are in unfamiliar territory, and the game these niggas be running is lethal."

"Shit, you must fell for that shit and had a nigga pushing your car then," she shot back.

"Ok, touché, bitch, touché. Actually, no, but fine. Ok, if your truck not with a nickel and dime boy, slanging reggie out your shit then, where is it?"

"Speaking of reggie, I asked a nigga today at that address you gave me for some, and this nigga acted like I had talked about his momma or something," she said.

I had to really look at this ignorant hoe to see if she was playing.

"Bitch, is you serious or is you SERIOUS?" I asked her ass. Hell, even before I moved here for college, I knew nobody smoked that weak shit anymore. Shaking my head at my poor friend, I continued to get undressed in the living room as I awaited the rest of her story. This was normal for us to get undressed in the living room sometimes and place our clothes in a pile to pick up when we headed to our rooms. Hell, she was a girl and my sister so shit, I didn't feel any type of way stripping down to my bra and boy shorts in front of her.

"Damn, I don't smoke; you know I haven't since hell forever, but I needed a blunt. Anyway, after he gave me some good shit, I didn't even get a chance to smoke the shit because as I was backing up, some damn idiot sped past me and we hit each other."

"WHAT!" I yelled, jumping up from the comfortable spot I had just found on the couch. Running over to her, I begin checking her over, making sure nothing was out of place, and she wasn't hurt.

"What are you doing?" she asked me, laughing.

"Hold still, I'm trying to make sure you are ok."

"I'm fine."

"Bitch, spill the beans before I get mad. Got my blood pressure all up and shit."

"It's nothing to tell. This stupid ass fine ass nigga hit me, we cursed each other out, then matched a blunt in his car while we waited for a tow truck. He offered to get the dent knocked out free of charge, and we just ran it about life. I talked about myself and," she was saying but the entire time she was talking, she had a sparkle in her eyes and a smile on her face.

“Ohhweee,” I said, pointing at her, smiling. “Bitch, you like that nigga!” I yelled.

“What? No, I don't you tripping.”

“You can't even say that with a straight face without smiling, you like that nigga. What's his name?”

She looked at me for a split second before she said, “Shit, I don't know.”

“Well, call him and ask.”

“I didn't get his number,” she said, hitting herself in the forehead.

“Yea, you gotta like this nigga and he had to be fine as fuck to make you give your truck to him; no name or no number. So how the fuck was you gone get it back smart ass?”

“Fuck what if the nigga steals my shit?” Yemani yelled, jumping up.

“That's your fault, too busy eye fucking to find out, but that's Zac’s stomping grounds in that neighborhood, so I'll have him check it out and get dude information if too much time passes and you don't have your shit.”

“I’m so embarrassed, Dezzy, how stupid can I get?”

“It's cool, best friend; you was dickmatized and haven't even had the dick. It happens to the best of us,” I said, laughing at her.

“Bitch, don't act like Zac don't be having you stuck. I saw your ass tonight, blushing and blinking your lashes so hard I thought for sure one would fall the fuck off.”

“So. The difference between us is I can admit I like his cocky, fine ass. Shit, I’m trying to keep things slow, but he definitely can get the business. You, on the other hand, mad because you wanna fuck this mystery man and scared to admit it. Sprung off conversation having ass," I said, sticking my tongue out at her. Picking up a pillow, she tossed it at me before getting up going to her room.

"I love you too, hoe, and you must be too mad to open your birthday gift. Oh well, I'll keep it," I said as she ran full force back into the living room.

"No, no, gimme, gimme," Yemani said excitedly bouncing from leg to leg as I pulled a gift from under the couch cushion. Snatching the box out my hands, she quickly ripped it open, revealing a panda bracelet with charms identical to the ones her mom wore and a piece resembling her father's store. I saved up my money to get this for her because I knew she needed it and it was my way of saying you'll always carry them with you.

“I love you so much, Des. I wouldn't have made it through this ordeal without you man for real, and I want you to know that,” Yemani said. I pulled her to me, embracing her in a hug. Yeah, she's a little rough around the edges; yeah, she can be mean as hell, but under all that rough exterior is just a sweet girl who's been through everything designed to break her but she's fighting to remain here. I loved her and admired her strength.

KNOCK! KNOCK! KNOCK!

“Who the fuck!” I yelled, kicking the covers over of me as I laid there trying to will myself to move. Glancing over at the clock, I noticed it was 7 am.

“This better be the damn police with some important ass news because if it's anybody else, they catching these damn hands!” I yelled, jumping up. Me and mornings didn't mix well that's why my classes didn't start until noon. I wasn't sure how Yemani did it with that early morning class, but more power to her.

Throwing on a robe, I wiped slob off my face as I stuck my feet into my Spongebob furry slippers and rushed towards the front. The words that were on the tip of my tongue caught as I stared at Zac, looking daddylicious in some basketball shorts and white tee with Jordan slides. I forgot all about cursing him out as I stood there eyeing him from head to toe mainly from knees to toe. Ok, I was really eyeing that third leg looking back at me and shit, I couldn't tear my eyes away from it.

“Look, lil’ nasty ass girl, when you finished eye raping a nigga, can you invite me in?” he said, smirking.

“Huh?”

"Bruh, watch out," he said, pushing past me. I stupidly still stood there with the door opened as my eyes followed him to my living room couch.

"Close the door and bring your ignorant ass inside."

Doing as I was told, I closed the door and walked to the opposite end of the couch and had a seat, making sure to cross my legs tightly.

"Why you over here so early?"

"Early bird gets the worm, woman."

"Well shit, I don't want no worms," I said, uncrossing and crossing my legs back.

"Look, I'm here to take you to breakfast, so go brush your teeth, take that hideous ass thing off your head, and wipe that white shit off your face; that I hope is slob because if not, we gone have some damn problems."

Embarrassed to the max, I didn't even say shit as I bolted off the couch and into my room with the quickness. I slob when I sleep, which I hate and can't control but shit, I didn't know it was on my face. Running to my bathroom, I got a look at myself in the mirror and damn near passed out. I was all kinds of tore up, looking like Wanda ass from Holiday Heart. My bonnet was half on and half off with hair sticking up from under it because I had taken my braids out. Slob was all on the side of my face and dried up in a white residue, and I had eye boogers.

“Bitch, you definitely can't get that nigga looking like this,” I mumbled to myself as I picked up my toothbrush to brush my teeth.

Thirty minutes later, I emerged from my room a brand-new person.

“I’m ready.”

"Damn, we was just going to breakfast, you ain't have to shit on a nigga like that ma," he said, nodding his head in approval. I played it cool on the outside, but inside, I was doing backflips because he approved, letting me somewhat redeem myself from earlier.

"Boy, I'm not even all that dressed up, I practically threw this on," I said, waving him off as I bent down grabbing my keys.

Feeling myself being lifted off my feet and pushed against the wall, I didn't have time to even process what was happening before Zac crushed his lips on mines. The kiss caught me off guard, so I was resistant at first, but his lips were so soft, and his kiss was so good, that I unwillingly found myself getting lost in it.

"Mhhh," I moaned out, wiggling my hands out of his grip and throwing them around his neck. Snaking his hands up my shirt, he twisted my nipples around his thumb and forefinger causing waves of pain and pleasure to rip through my body.

"Watch that damn boy word, ma, I'ma grown ass men," he said as he quickly released me. "Now come on because a nigga hungry as fuck and I know your ass got class soon," Zac said, nonchalantly walking off like he didn't just fuck me up with that kiss.

Touching my hands on my lips, I was still trying to piece together exactly what the hell just happened. *Get it together, Desiree,* I pep talked myself as I straightened out my clothes, finger combed my hair, picked up my purse and phone and headed out the door behind him. Locking it, I followed him out the building and to his car, which he has switched up this morning and was now driving a black on black Maserati with chrome wheels.

“You switch cars like you switch clothes, huh?” I said.

“What can I say, a nigga is a lover of cars,” he said, popping the locks to the vehicle. Sliding inside, I was immediately in love. I expected the seats to be that hot leather that most fancy cars have, but instead, they were a cream texture and very comfortable. I wasn't sure if the car came with the huge touch screen system situated in the middle, but the face had to be about 12 inches in width. You ever been somewhere where everything just looked expensive, so you kept your hands securely to yourself in fear of touching and breaking something you couldn't afford to replace? That's how I was feeling right now as I sat timidly in the seat because shit, I couldn't even afford the air freshener that even had little diamonds hanging from it.

“Dude, you have diamonds on your air freshener?” I said really tripped out about it.

“It was custom made so when it's empty; I just refill it. Midos ole extra ass gave it to me for a birthday gift.”

“I bet they real diamonds too,” I mumbled, well, at least, I thought I did, but judging from how he started laughing, he heard me.

“I figured we can just swing by the Waffle House up the street, is that cool?”

“Yeah, I’m not picky and require the Four Seasons breakfast or anything.”

“That's what I like, a simple type of girl.”

Pulling into Waffle House, we got out and walked inside.

“Good morning, welcome to Waffle House,” a server greeted us as we took a seat at a booth.

Picking up the menu on the table, I tried to decide what I would even order because I wasn't usually a breakfast person, and instead, preferred to do a meal replacement with a tasty protein shake instead.

“Shit, a nigga hungry as hell. I think I’ma get that all-star meal and add extra everything,” Zac said. He ate like a fat person when he wasn't even that big. He put you in the mind of Hosea Chanchez, who played the character Malik on the Bet series, The Game.

“I think I'll have a boiled egg and toast with water,” I said.

He looked at me like I had lost my mind.

“I know you not one of those girls who be tryna eat cute in front of a nigga?”

“No, actually I’m not a breakfast person, and I happen to like eggs and toast.”

“Well, if you don't eat breakfast, why you wanted to come? I could have ate something at your place.”

“Because you asked me and I wanted to come with you just to be in your presence,” I said, throwing caution to the wind and finally admitting I liked him more than I previously let on.

Not bothering to respond back, instead, he leaned over and gave me a long, juicy kiss that caused butterflies to form in the pit of my stomach. I was ready to stop fighting my worries, and give in to this man before I lost him because I really did like his sexy, cocky ass.

After we finished eating and made it back to my apartment, it was a little after 8:30. I don't have class until 12, so I was headed back to bed. I had invited Zac to my bedroom not for anything other than to sleep because I know how people get sleepy after a hearty meal. When I woke up at 11:30, he was nowhere to be found, so I just assumed he had long since left. Quickly jumping up to brush my teeth and wash my face, I grab my bookbag and ran into the living room but stopped in my tracks as I noticed flowers sitting on my coffee table. Picking them up, I noticed a card attached that simply: read have a good day in class today, beautiful. Quickly putting them in water, I hurried out the door and to my car to get to class. I usually liked to walk because it was good exercise, but I wouldn't make it today with how late I woke up, so I was driving. I had a feeling I was going to have a great day.

"As you all know it's our first home game Saturday, and we most definitely have to bring it, so I need you guys to tighten up on your kicks, and make sure you are sharp and executing the routine with precision," Samantha, our captain, said to us. I was currently at dance practice and still in the same chipper mood that I had been in all day.

"We ready," a few girls yelled out.

"Practice dismissed," she said.

As everyone was busy picking up their bags and grabbing water, I was responding back to a silly meme Zac had texted me.

"I saw somebody creeping out of building seven this morning; I wonder whose room his hoe ass was leaving?" Samantha said to Carla, who was standing next to me. Not one for gossip, I started gathering my things to leave because I didn't wish to be a part of the conversation. As a captain, Samantha was great at what she did, and that's where it stopped. Known for a pass around and jump off, she was always either in somebody's business or bed. She aspired to either be a professional dancer or paid hoe, I suppose.

"Who bitch?" Carla asked.

"Girl, Zac's hoe ass. I also saw him last night as well, but I can't remember with who," she said which paused me in my tracks.

"Oh yeah, that's right, he was dropping Desiree and her roommate off," she said, turning to me.

The words I wanted to say were struggling to come out as I bit down on my tongue hard as hell. I had made the dress out squad so I would be on the front-line Saturday and my mom had already booked a flight to come see me perform, so I didn't want to curse this bitch out and risk that. However, she wasn't gone try no slick shit either and get a pass.

"Yeah, he was, so?" I said casually as my fingers quickly texted him, letting him know about his hoes.

"Oh, girl don't get offended; we all know firsthand that dick for everybody. He'll throw you a lil' bag of something, but don't get to attached.

He usually spits games, gets what he wants and moves on. Since he did that walk of shame this morning, I think that's his cue to dip," she said, laughing with Carla.

"Well, I wouldn't know if the dick was for everybody or not because I haven't had it, and he didn't do a walk of shame. He did leave my house after he took me to breakfast and took me to dinner last night but I see what you mean, because he’s always asking me to be his girl, must be part of that game he be spitting," I said, grabbing my bag and walking to my car. I was done with Zac because this was the shit I wouldn't put up with.

CHAPTER 7

Mind of a maniac...

MIDOS

It had been a few days since my pops dropped a bomb on me with the information he hit me with, and I found myself sitting in my living room nursing a drink, still thinking about the unexpected visit. Well, it wasn't unexpected that he was here because I already knew he was coming, just didn’t know he was gone see me. He usually calls first. He’s always coming in town and thinks I don't know him and my ma dukes back fucking around. He didn't know I knew he'd slip in and out the country. However, when he wanted to announce his arrival, he would always call me and give me a heads up that he would be visiting me, or shoot me a text or email. For him to not do neither and just show up on my doorstep, I instantly knew when I opened the door that some shit was up. I figured maybe moms was pregnant or something because it had been quiet on my end lately other than that bitch ass nigga Chaz, and them niggas in Third Ward with the bullshit they was on. They do say it's always a quiet before a storm, and shit, they Katrina'd our asses with this one. For a mufucka to intersect one of our shipments before it even made it to its drop point, meant we was dealing with niggas on a higher level. No low-level nigga got the brains or money to pull that shit off. You needed a boat even to be out to sea, and you needed money and enough men to execute the shit.

My father usually had a few top men on the boats when they sailed over to the drop points, and he said it was a blood bath. He knew something was wrong when the boat wasn't on course, since he has a tracker on it. When he had some men take a chopper and check it out, they discovered everybody on board slaughtered, and weapons, drugs, and money was gone. Fire danced in my eyes at the thought of a war I knew was to come. It's one thing to have the balls to fuck with my shit, but to have balls enough to fuck with my father's shit, knowing who he was and the amount of power he possessed, these niggas were asking; no, begging us to kill them. They clearly didn't have shit to live for. The real question on my mind though is how did they know exactly what route the ship would be on? I can see if they hijacked the boat in the states and had a shootout near or at my drop point, but that shit had barely left Egypt, which means these niggas might not even be American. Egyptian men wouldn't even dare do something like this to the King, knowing the consequences if caught. I know my father doesn't want to hear it, but he needs to consider the possibility that somebody in his camp is a snake and betraying them. Who else would know the coordinates, how to get on and off the boat undetected and avoided the cameras.

RING! RING!

My ringing phone brought me out of my thoughts temporarily.

"What's up?"

"Boss, we have that truck finished you asked us to do."

"Bet, I'm sending you the directions on where to drop the car off at."

"Ok, where you want us to leave the keys at?"

"Shit I didn't even think of that. I guess just lock them in the car. I forgot to get shawty contact information. Wait, get her name off her insurance card in her glove box. I'll call the school and get

her name and apartment number, and put somebody on delivering them to her."

"Damn, you must like her to be doing all of Pete said.

I didn't even respond to him as I hung up. I w sick of people trying to play me out like I like the hoe. Like, damn, it wasn't even like that.

Since I used to knock this broad off at the residence hall, it was easy as hell to obtain the information needed, I even got her phone numbe up out the hoe.Shooting Pete her information, I shot her a quick text,

Sup. Hitting send I wondered if a nigga should have said more, but shit that's all I could think of to say. Her name was Yemani which was a very unique and different name, but I liked it.

"To what do I owe this visit," my mom said sarcastically to me. We were out at Pappadeaux having lunch.

"Cut it out, ma, you act like I never see you."

"You don't so that's not a lie."

"You know you're my favorite gal."

"Uh huh, I can't tell, you never come see me anymore like you used to."

"I see you every Sunday for dinner, matter of fact, I saw you two days ago!"

"You used to see me every day. I be lonely in that big house you put me in. I told you I would have been content with a nice modest home, or townhouse. I'm in that big house all day, every day by myself with no one to talk to. Would be nice if I had a grand baby," she said. Here we go again. I knew this was coming up. She wasn't damn lonely; she just wanted a nigga to get trapped for 18 years.

"Ma, we had this conversation already, I'm not ready for all that just yet."

"Son, you about to be 25 in a few days. You don't think it's time to settle down with a nice respectable young lady and give your momma some grand kids? You're not getting any younger, and I'm getting older by the day, and I could relapse any day with my condition, I, at least, want to enjoy grandkids before I go," she said.

DING!

Looking down, I saw Yemani ass had finally texted a nigga back.

Who this is?

Who you want it to be? I texted back before focusing my attention back on Ma dukes

"Don't talk like that, you are fine," I said to her but really on the inside I was freaking out. Why would she bring up a relapse? I made a mental note to get up with her doctor to see what's up. I thought we had beat cancer and was in the clear; I couldn't even allow myself for a minute to even think about my mother leaving me or even relapsing. I couldn't go through that again. I felt so helpless during that time in my life.

"Don't do that, baby, I know that look, it's nothing for you to worry about just yet."

"Ma, I love you," I said, getting choked up. My mother was my entire world, and I would lay my life down for her. Shit, maybe I would look into adopting a kid or something, if that would make her happy. I didn't see myself running in one of those hoes raw and dealing with their asses for the rest of my life. I could like adopt an almost grown child so that way, I don’t have to deal with that crying shit and moms can have somebody to talk to and shit, yeah that's what I’ma do.

"I’ma get you your grandbaby ma."

Smiling from ear to ear, she didn't say anything else just went back to eating, content with the answer I had just given her. I couldn’t do anything but shake my head at her spoiled ass. Now, I had to damn figure out this grandbaby thing, and we would be good. Ever since my mom got sick the first time, I tried to hustle and buy her everything that her heart desired. Back then, I was a small-time corner boy, and it's not like we were broke, and I needed the money because that wasn't the case, I just took pride in having my own money. My dad took damn good care of us. Shit, hustling was just in my blood, it's drew me in like a moth to a flame. When my mom sent me away, my dad took one look at my change in demeanor and immediately knew I was hustling. I thought he was going to be mad as hell especially since when he asked me why I was doing it, I responded because I was a man. After I said it, I thought for sure he was going to beat my ass because you wasn't opposed to catching an ass whooping or even dying where I'm from, for disrespect to your parents. Instead, he told my ass if I thought I was a man, then I was to get out and live off purely everything I hustled. I was just small time, and since I had a roof over my head already, the shit didn't hit me that I wasn't turning a big profit until I had to try and pay for a hotel, food, and clothes off the little money I was making. My pride wouldn't allow me to go back home, but shit, after I ran out of everything I had brought over with me, I sucked that shit up three days into being hungry, and went back to my father. I was 14. He took one look at me and summoned his maids to feed me and clean me up.

That night he dropped some real knowledge on me, then told me to finish school, go to college and get my business degree. After that, in a few years, we would revisit the topic. I graduated high school and college early and when I was 22, my life changed in a major way. True to his word, my dad showed me the game; the proper way from the bottom up and made sure my aim was on point with a gun. I could shoot a nigga between his eyes blindfolded, that's how much of a beast I was. Not to get it twisted though, I didn't jump in this thing a plug and running shit just because of my father's status. I worked my way up, because the shit I was on when I was 14, paled in comparison to the boss moves I was making now. When I decided to come back to the states and take over Houston and the surrounding areas, shit wasn't no cake walk to lock all these places down. Nothing was just given to me, nobody said, here, Midos, here's the crown, naw; I worked my ass off for it. Hearing my phone vibrate with an incoming text message, I looked down hoping it was Yemani responded back, and noticed it was Debo texting me. I glanced at it and saw it was a simple message reading,

it's handled.

I knew exactly what he was talking about, so I hit him back asking where them niggas was at.

Zac got them.

I read. Shaking my head, I said, “Ma, excuse me for a second while I call Zac real quick.

“Go on, baby, and tell my son I said hey and I’m on his ass as well about grandkids and not coming to see me. Y'all done got old and got beside yourselves.”

Laughing, I stood up and walked outside to my car because this was a conversation I didn't want overheard.

“Yo?” he said, answering on the first ring.

“Nigga, what yo ass up to?”

“Debo snitching ass,” he said, laughing already knowing that I knew what he was up to.

“That still ain't tell me nothing.”

“I wanted to play with my toys; shit, since it's been a minute. You about that gunplay and that's fine and all, but once you start slicing a mufucka up; watch how they sing like a bitch. You want to find out who been taking shit and whats been going on, hell, threatening to shoot won't get answers because these lil' niggas be ready to die like it'll earn them something else other than being on somebody shirt and niggas yelling R.I.P for a few days until they become a distant memory."

"Whatever, nigga. Your method takes too long, and I don't have that much patience, my nigga."

"Your ass just scared of all the blood and gooey shit."

"Ain't scared, just don't care for the shit," I shot back.

"Come on down here; you might learn something."

"I'm spending the day with moms, so I'ma pass on that you just tell me how it goes. Oh, by the way, your ass in the hot seat just like me, so you own moms a baby."

"A baby? Ma, tripping. I'ma buy her ass a life-size doll and call it a day. Anyway, Debo said he got word that Chaz was gone be at some damn party tonight, I told him to put some niggas on it but keep it clean and as less casualties as possible."

"You sure we don't need to personally handle this."

"Naw, he got it. That nigga cold as fuck, he cleared Third Ward out in two point five seconds. I barely got me a few to myself. Nigga kicked that bitch in and got to spraying. That's my new best friend."

"Ole gay ass nigga, I guess y'all gonna be going to get y'all nails did and shit together, huh?" I said, laughing because of his choice of words.

“Fuck you,” he said, hanging up. Laughing, I walked back into the restaurant to see if my mother was finished eating because next, I was taking her shopping.

“Ma, I know you tired by now,” I said to her as we walked in yet again another store.

“I can't find the perfect shoes to go with this outfit. Hush up, boy; beauty takes time,” she fussed. As we walked in and were greeted by a sales associate, I locked eyes with this fine ass broad, I’m talking about she was so bad I had to look twice, some shit I rarely did. As she walked towards us, I couldn’t even pry my eyes away from her; she was just that bad. She wasn't prettier than Yemani, but her body looked damn better. *Damn, why the fuck was I comparing them?*

“Good evening, can I assist you and your lovely sister with anything today?” she said as she approached us. My mother started blushing hard as fuck when she heard this and pushed her naturally long hair behind her ears.

“I know it's hard to believe, but this is my son,” she said.

“No it's not,” she said, looking from me to my mom. “But he's like grown, and you don't look a day over 21.”

“I know, right,” my mom said, smiling brightly. “What can I say; black truly doesn't crack because I’m a fabulous 25,” she said. I whipped my head around so fast to look at her. This lady was a trip, bruh, I swear.

Extending her arms towards me, the sales girl said,” Hello, I’m Angela.”

“Midos,” I said to her.

“That is not what I named you,” my mom said, busting me out.

“I knew it wasn't,” Angela said, laughing.

“It's Amyr, but let this be the last time we mention that, Midos is fine.”

“I kinda like Amyr,” she shot back with this devilish look in her eyes.

“Probably because you wanna scream Amyr, huh?” I said being mannish, quickly forgetting ma dukes was near me. Shit, she threw it out there, and I, for damn sure, was gone take the bait.

Blushing, she said, “Excuse me, I'll be right back.”

Stepping closer to her so my mom’s nosey ass couldn't hear me, I leaned over to her ear and said, “Pussy wet already, huh? You gotta go clean yourself up, don't you?” Then I turned and walked off like I didn't say anything, leaving her there and I walked to the other side where my mother had wandered off to.

“Acting just like your daddy,” she said as soon as I walked up on her.

“Speaking of him, are y'all still gone pretend y'all not back messing around?”

“I don't know what you talking about.”

“Uh huh. I came to check on you one day and saw his car in the yard. Now, this wasn't strange because he always comes to check on you when he is in town. He also calls and lets me know before he comes, so the fact he didn't call me, and when I hit him, he told me he was busy, told me all I needed to know.”

“Well, I’m the parent, and you are the child, so I don't really have to tell you anything. However, if you must know, I have needs too; I’m still young,” she started to say before I cut her off.

“Oh hell naw, I don’t wanna hear that shit. That's a visual I don't want to know. Y'all asses too old to be still fucking.”

“Says who?”

“Man, let's drop it,” I said, getting mad as I walked ahead of her to check out some shades. Shit, I knew they were fucking, but to hear the shit really fucked a nigga, fuck around and have nightmares and shit. Shaking off the thought, I looked around for Angela's ass because I was most definitely tryna slide up in that. I was trying some Panthere De Cartier sunglasses when I heard her voice behind me.

“Those look nice on you.” Turning around, she quickly slipped a piece of paper in my pocket, then started back talking like nothing happened. “I must, however, warn you; they are a bit on the expensive side. They retail for 1,175. Perhaps I can interest you in these in our brown shade?” she said with some Ray-Ban aviator shades in her hand. “These are very stylish and only retail for $150.”

She didn't know me, so I told myself not to get offended, she might have only been tryna look out for a brotha. However, the cocky me couldn't even let that shit ride. If she didn't know who the fuck I was, she was gone learn today. Smirking at her, I removed the Cartier shades and said, "I'll take the entire collection in every shade you have, with that pussy on the side."

Her eyes bucked out of her head and she damn near choked. I laughed because I wasn't sure if it was because of the fact, I just dropped damn near ten bands on some shades, or because I said I wanted that pussy on the side. I wasn't much of a betting man, but I was gone take a wise guess and say both.

CHAPTER 8

When people don't know that you crazy in real life...

YEMANI

I was headed out the door early as usual since I had been walking to class the last two days. I was still trying to figure out what I was going to do about my truck. I tried talking to campus police about filing a report, but technically my truck wasn't stolen since I willingly gave him the keys. I was going to keep the faith that my vehicle would be returned because the sexy, rude devil didn't strike me as the type that would have any use for my little ole Wrangler when he said he had many toys. Locking the door, I was debating on grabbing Starbucks, when I bumped into a guy looking as if he was stopping at my door.

“Can I help you?”

“Yemani Jacobs?”

“Who’s asking?” I asked him with a hint of attitude, immediately going into defense mode because I didn't know him. I discreetly eased my hand into my purse, clutching my mace.

“Look, I was just told to bring you your keys shit,” he said, tossing my keys to me and walking off.

“Bitch ass,” I mumbled as I bent down to pick them up because when he tossed them, they just fell to the ground.

Quickly grabbing them, I hurried out to the parking lot excited to not only have my baby back, but I was curious to know the condition that she was now in. As I rounded the corner of the building and saw my Jeep Wrangler, whom I called Koko, I literally took off running to her. On the outside looking in, you would think somebody was chasing me, and I was running for my life as I excitedly raced to my baby. She was looking good as hell, cleaned up and shining bright like a diamond. Walking over to my truck, I gave it a more thorough inspection as I examined where the dent was and noticed it had been sanded down and looked exactly like it did the first day I brought it home. Since I had my car back, there wasn't a need to go to class early, but since I was already up and dressed, I figured I would go for some breakfast.

Popping the locks on my truck, I went to hop in but stopped when I saw a card on the front seat. Picking it up, it read, *Hope the truck is to your liking.* Smiling, I got in the car as I let my mind drift back to the handsome Egyptian with a head full of curly hair that looked so soft to the touch, and full, juicy lips. He didn't look Egyptian to me, more like Iranian but I'm guessing that's because he had Italian in him as well. Whatever the case was, he was fine as hell and had hella swag. The day I saw him, he was dressed down in some jeans, Jordan's, and a Polo button- down shirt with a snapback, looking fine as hell.

RING!RING!

Glancing down, I noticed it was that same number calling me that had been texting me. Debating on whether I should answer or not, I went ahead and answered it.

"Hello?" I said with attitude.

"Damn that's the thanks I get for returning your truck in good condition, attitude? Who pissed in your coffee early this morning? The voice boomed over the phone. I immediately recognized it as the sexy demon I couldn't get out of my head.

"How did you get my number?" I blurted out. Kicking myself for asking something stupid, I went quiet waiting for his response.

"I'm a man who is in the business of getting exactly what he wants shanty."

"Is that right?" I found myself flirting back.

"Hell yeah, but listen I gotta run beautiful I was making sure you got your truck back and it was ok. Ima get up with you later," he said before hanging up.

Smiling to myself, I started the car up driving off, I headed to McDonald's to grab me an egg and cheese McMuffin before class. As I was getting waiting on my number to be called, I decided to have a seat at a table in the overcrowded, fast food joint.

Pulling my phone out to browse the web and kill time, I was just logging onto Facebook when I heard, "Say ma, is this seat taken?"

Looking up, I looked eyes with a strikingly handsome guy with smooth chocolate skin.

"No, it isn't," I said to him.

"Good because it's crowded as fuck in this bitch, and a nigga ain't tryna be standing up and shit," he said, sitting down as his cologne invaded my nostrils tantalizingly. "I'm Greg."

"Yemani," I shot back.

"Interesting name. You go to UH?"

"Yeah, this is my freshman year."

"Cool, check it; we having a party tomorrow night, you should swing by it, we need all the fine baddies in the building."

"Tomorrow? But tomorrow is a Thursday night? You guys having a party on a Thursday?"

Laughing, he said, " Yeah, most definitely a freshman." As he passed me a flyer, winked and got up. I watched him walk away for a few seconds before I gathered myself together to check out this flyer. I was slowly warmed up to Houston and all the fine ass men they had.

Looking at the flyer, smiling, I noticed it was a fraternity party. I couldn't lie, I was excited to go, because I had heard all about fraternity parties from Desiree, and they sounded fun as hell. Hearing my number being called, I quickly put the flyer in my purse as I hurriedly went, grabbed my food and was out the door and headed back to campus in record time. I was ready to get my day over so I could go find me an outfit for tomorrow night.

"Hey girl," Krystal said to me as she walked into class. We had developed a class friendship and usually always sat by each other. She also was new in town and was from Tampa Bay, Florida, here on a scholarship as well. I wasn't usually the friendly type, which was why I didn't have friends like that, but I took to her pretty well.

"Hey chick, you looking cute today," I cheerfully said to her.

"Thanks, I finally got brave enough to venture out in the city solo, because I was in desperate need of some more summer clothes and my sister so caught up in her shit to go with me," she said. She had on a cute, spaghetti strap, colorful top that flared out at the shoulder then got slender again and scrunched up, stopping right above her belly button. She paired it with some distressed, denim cut-off pants and wedges. Her 99J colored asymmetrical swing bob, set everything off. The color complimented her dark complexion very well. Krystal was what I would call a BBW but she wore her weight very well. Hell, really, she wasn't big, she was just thick as hell because her waist line was damn near smaller than mine. She just had big thick ass thighs and ass for days.

"Sister? You got family here in town? I thought it was just you? And you should have just asked me to roll with you."

"Technically, it is just me. We didn’t come here together, she came with her baby daddy, his brother and their child. We not that close but I try forming a relationship with her but something I can’t get with the hoe shit that she does so it puts a strain on our relationship. Also, I thought about calling and asking you but I didn't want to seem like I was crazy or shit, I don't know. I know we talk in class every day, I didn't feel like that meant we could hang out," she said, glancing down.

"Damn, if she doing hoe shit like that, it’s your duty as her sister to call her out on her shit.”

“Yea easier said than done. I let a lot of people slide, not just her, it’s a lot that should have been addressed whenever I find my voice,” she shyly said. I was in agreement with her about finding her voice because I couldn’t even understand not having it. Shit, I’ve always been outspoken all my life. You let anything slide and folks will start ice skating.

“Shit, you gotta find something because clearly mufuckas have run completely out of free passes now. But fuck all that, you cool, we cool, anytime you wanna chill, hit my number. I wouldn't have given it to you if I just wanted to talk in class because I would see you in class," I said.

"Well shit, since you put it that way, it's this party tomorrow that I've been hearing about all over campus, and I’m dying to go, so can you please go with me because I couldn't go alone?"

Reaching into my purse, I pulled the flyer out and handed it to her. "This party?"

"Hell yeah. Where did you get that flyer from?"

"This dude I met earlier at McDonald's gave it to me. Greg, I think it was."

"Bitch, you mean sexy ass, chocolate Que dawg, plus captain of the basketball team, Greg?"

"Shit, I guess so. Hell, I don't know the nigga, he just told me his name was Greg. He was kinda fine though."

"Kinda? You must need my glasses because that nigga can get the business any day of the week," she said, laughing as she took out her math book just as Professor Carmichael walked in. "Yeah ok, more than kinda," I said to her. As I tried to focus on today's lesson, all I could think about was getting out of here so me and Krystal could tear the mall down. This could be the start of a great friendship; I'm sure Desiree will like her as well.

"How this look?" I asked Krystal, trying on yet another outfit. We had been at the Galleria mall for damn near two hours, and I still hadn't found shit that screamed yeah, you bad as fuck. I wanted to really shut the scene down, even though it was a college party, I still wanted to make a statement, and I don't even know why because it wasn't like I was interested in a boyfriend. *You liked sexy Egyptian with that curly hair though,* I thought to myself out the blue. Shaking my head at the fact that I couldn't get his fine ass out of my head, I smiled as I went back to looking at clothes because thinking about somebody, who I'm sure wasn't in my league at all, wasn't doing anything but slowing me down. Thirty minutes later, I had found the perfect outfit, and we were headed to the food court to get a bite to eat.

"I think I’m in the mood for Raising Caine's," Krystal said.

"I’ma head to Panda Express, so just find us a seat," I told her as I walked off. Forgetting to ask her to get me a sweet tea, I turned around to tell her and bumped into a hard chest.

"Excuse me," I said, looking up into a pair of hazel eyes that belonged to the guy from earlier.

"Two times in a row that we have met today, look at that ma, its fate. If I see you tomorrow, then I’m going with my move with your pretty ass," he said, hitting with me a panty-dropping smile.

I wasn't usually straightforward, seeing as though I've only had one boyfriend my entire life; I felt bold as I said, "I’ma hold you to that," and walked off, making sure to put an extra twist in my walk.

Later on that night, I was laying across my bed, reading over my biology book when Desiree came in my room.

"When you went to the mall?" she asked, holding my bags I had dropped on the couch.

"Earlier today."

"Why didn't you text me, I would have went with you."

"You had class and practice."

"Still, I hate that you have to go places by yourself."

"It's cool, Dezzy really. Besides, I didn't go by myself, I went with my friend Krystal."

"Come again?" she said with her nose turned up.

"Krystal, this girl I met in class. We actually have two together, anyway she's cool, and she is new here as well."

"So?"

"So she cool as hell, and we went to the mall together and we going to that Que dawg party tomorrow, you wanna come?"

"First of all, I'm not even feeling this shit. I wasn't ok with you and Adrienne, but I wasn't there and hell, I ain't think you really liked her ass; you just didn't have anybody else to hang with who gone put up with you, but now this," she said with her hands on her hips. I really couldn't take her serious right now.

"Desiree, for real, bruh?" I said, laughing.

"Yes, bitch and we taking a vote and I vote no, so that's that," she said, folding her arms pouting.

"You real-life petty, man. The girl cool and you would know that if you gave her a chance. You know I just don't hang with anybody."

"I don't know anything but that I been leaving your ass alone for far too long and this the results of it. How long this been going on?" she asked like I was cheating on her or some shit.

"Bye man."

"Naw, I wanna know. How long this shit been going on?"

"Girl, if you don't take your ass on," I said, laughing because she was so serious. Realizing she didn't want to laugh with me, I said, "Today was our first day hanging out. Nobody can take your place, my baby," I said, jumping up from the bed and hopping on her like old times, causing us both to fall to the ground.

"Get your big ass off me. Damn, bitch; I'm strictly dickly," she said, laughing. Pulling my shirt over my head, I said, "Bitch, you a lie, you know you want all this," I laughed as I rubbed my breast in her face. I had a bra on though, but you would have thought I was naked how she tried to get up with the quickness. Wrestling me off of her, she got up laughing. "Your ass gay as fuck."

"Only with you, big booty Judy," I shot back as I hit her on the thigh. I wasn't gay but my best friend was fine as hell, and a blind man could tell you that.

"My man don't like me to be touched," she said, sticking her tongue out at me.

"When this happened?"

"I'ma tell you later; I'm headed to study hall, and shit how these hoes trying me, he probably my ex nigga already."

"Damn," I said, getting back on me bed so I could finish studying. I planned to get everything done tonight and all my studying in because come tomorrow, I'ma be turnt until Sunday. I had decided I would go with Zac and Desiree to his best friend's birthday party because technically I didn't celebrate my 19th birthday, so I was gone be lit.

Said little bitch, you can't fuck with me

If you wanted to

The party was in full swing, and me and Krystal were drunk as hell and turnt to the max. Desiree didn't come because they were on a strict curfew until game day, so she couldn't partake in any turn up 'til this weekend. That was crazy to me but if she liked it then hey, who was I to see any fault in it. Bending over, shaking my ass, I was really feeling myself, and this was my song. I loved *Bodak Yellow by Cardi B*. I didn't have the biggest ass, but that bitch wiggled, though and I knew it. I felt somebody get behind me, and I really started showing out making one cheek move then the other.

"You better stop that before you get fucked," a voice whispered in my ear. I leaned up and turned around, coming face to face with Greg. By this point, I was fucked up, so I simply smiled at him, turned around and started dancing again, putting on an award-winning performance.

"Get it, bitch," I heard Krystal screaming from beside me. Once the song went off and another one came on, I stopped dancing because it was a Houston song I wasn't familiar with.

"You having fun, I see," Greg said.

"Yeah, this is my first college party, and it's lit," I said just as I heard a whistle blow and a group of guys, wearing camouflage pants and a purple shirt with gold boots, come back doing some type of choreography. I had never seen anything like it, but I was mesmerized. Catching me off guard, Greg bent down and bit me on my right ass cheek before he joined in line behind the last guy. I didn't even realize until now that he was dressed exactly like the other guys as they hopped on one leg and barked like a dog moving throughout the crowd.

“What are they doing?” I yelled to Krystal.

“They stepping, you never saw a Greek show?”

“No,” I said.

“We gone have to change that, but it's nothing like a nasty dog,” she said to me, but I was too busy focused on the show finding myself suddenly drawn to the performance. Every few seconds, the guys would pick a girl up, or bite one, etc. I even thought I saw one guy put a girl on his shoulders and put his mouth somewhere it shouldn't by, but I’m sure it was all like an illusion. Although. she threw her head back as if she were enjoying it, putting on an award-winning performance but I knew he couldn't have possibly been doing what I thought he was doing. Feeling my phone vibrating in my pocket pouch,

I opened it, pulled it out noticing that it was Desiree. “Hello?” I yelled putting one hand over my ear trying to block out the sound. Realizing that it wasn't working, I hung up and looked around for a quiet place to talk. I would have went to my car but I parked around the corner, and it was just as loud outside as it was inside. Suddenly having to pee anyway, I told Krystal I was headed to the bathroom upstairs and to call Desiree back.

“Go head I'll just wait for you down here,” she said she flirting with some guy. Walking off from the crowd, I slipped under a rope which blocked the upstairs area off. It was someone standing down there earlier, but I don't know where they went to now, which was a plus for me. The further I walked, the quieter it became which was perfect to call Desiree back. I had to pee really bad first though. Walking down the hallway, I was opening and closing doors getting frustrated that neither one was the bathroom. I did, however, find a few girls in a compromising position with some guys. Reaching my hands in my pouch, I grabbed my keys because I was possibly going to have to drive to a gas station or take it old school and squat in front of my car, but I had to pee, and this damn house was pissing me off. Deciding to try one more door before I gave up, I opened the next to the last door and got the shock of my life as I saw two men standing over a guy, as one pulled the trigger. The gun must have something preventing the sound from being loud because I didn't hear a sound, but I did witness the body drop. I quickly tried to close the door back, but it was too late because they saw me. Not giving it a second thought, I turned and raced back down the hallway, making it to the stairs and taking them two at a time, practically falling down the steps. Looking behind me, I got lost in the crowd as I tried to make sure the guys weren't following me still. Not seeing them, I pushed past everyone until I made it to Krystal.

“We have to go NOW!” I said to her, shaking.

“What's wrong Yemani?” she said but I ignored her as I grabbed her arm and dragged her out of the house quickly, past everyone. We were almost out of the house when I heard my name being called.

“Yemani.” Not bothering to even see who it was, I started running, dragging Krystal along with me.

“Damn bitch, why are we running for our lives?” she asked as she ran beside me surprising me how she was keeping up. “And why are you running from Greg?”

Not answering her, I continued to, out of breath, run the block to my car. Finally reaching it, I reached down to my pocket bag to only realize it was gone.

"Shit! I must have snagged it when I tried to close that door or something," I said.

"Snagged what? Bitch, what's going on? Remind me to never let your ass drink again."

"My purse, I snagged my purse with my keys in it, and now we're going to die," I said hysterically. She just looked at me for a full minute before she said, "Yemani, you talking about the keys that's in your hand?"

Looking down, I forgot I had taken them out right before I opened the door because I had planned on coming back to the car.

"Oh, thank God," I said as I popped the locks and we got in.

"Yep, you can't have no more alcohol."

"I'm not drunk, ok I am but I just seen some fucked up shit. At least I think I did, shit, I don't know now, but I do know I'll feel better once I'm far away from this damn place," I said as I drove us back to my apartment, still trying to process the events from a few minutes ok. *Was that shit real? Did somebody just die in front of me?*

CHAPTER 9

Did a lot of shit just to live this here lifestyle…

ZAC

Ring! Ring!

Rolling over and glancing at the clock, I saw that it was 5 am. My alarm wasn't set to go off for another two hours, so I was beyond pissed.

Ring! Ring!

"What?" I asked with attitude as soon as I answered not bothering to see who was calling me, all I knew was that they was disturbing me and I was pissed.

“We got a problem,” Debo said. Sitting up now fully awake, I said,

“What’s going on?”

“Somebody fucking with us.”

“Fucking with us how?”

“A couple stash houses were hit,” he was saying, but I didn’t even let him finish before I started going off.

“What you mean, hit! What the fuck?! Niggas asking us to fucking turn this bitch into Afghanistan real quick. I don’t wanna hear anymore. How much was taken? What the fuck is we paying y’all for if y’all can’t watch our shit? You first in command and basically running shit from the front line so why is on the phone with me and not handling this shit?” I barked. Going off and going 0 to 100 was Midos’ thing but I was already woken up out my sleep, after I had just barely got to sleep, so I was on one right now.

"Aye, I know you upset and out of respect I'm tryna overlook it but my nigga you ain't gotta talk to me like that," he said. "Now about the money, that's where the weird part that's why I said somebody fucking with us because nothing was missing just a message left on each side of the house."

"What message?"

"I'm at the trap on 42nd, and the entire side of the house spray painted in big bold letters with the message saying,

ONE, TWO; FREDDY'S COMING FOR YOU.

"And Jacob hit me up, and it's a message on his as well, it says.

THREE, FOUR; BETTER SHUT THE DOOR

“And the last one just has guns and pow pow spelled out,” he said.

“One two? Is these niggas quoting the Freddy Kruger movie? Man, this a joke, right?” I asked him because I wasn’t even mad anymore.

“Shit, at first I thought it was some lil’ niggas fucking with us, but it was also a pig heart and bullet casing found at each house.”

“Pull everybody and have them get on that shit, ASAP,” I said, not really knowing how to feel about the shit he had just told me. After I hung up the phone, I called Midos a few times, and when he didn’t answer, I laid back down, trying to go to sleep, but the shit wasn’t sitting well with me, so I just stared up at the ceiling until my alarm eventually went off.

"I need everybody to be on their shit tonight. It's my nigga 25th bday, and I don't want any fuck ups. Security needs to be tighter than Fort Knox;

I don't need no bitches or niggas getting out of line because that liquor in them. Throw their asses out with the quickness," I said. Tonight was Midos' birthday party that I had been planning for a while, and I wanted my nigga to have some clean, drama free fun. Shit, it's been awhile since we just kicked back, got lit, and chilled.

"What's the status of that other situation?" I asked, referring to that nuisance.

"That's over with, however, we got a slight problem," Jacob said.

Looking at his ass with annoyance, I already knew the issue simply because I knew him and how he operated.

"Who even told yo ass to go?"

"Boss, I'll fix if I already got the information I need," he said, holding a purse in his hands.

"Shit nigga, I guess times is hard, huh? I wouldn't have chosen that color, though; it doesn't compliment your eyes," I laughed as I stood up and walked out.

I had a lot of shit to handle before the party starting with Desiree ass. I had been calling and texting her nonstop since that day I took her to breakfast but she really been trying the fuck out of me. I got an iPhone, so I see that she reads my messages and just don't respond. Instead of pressing ignore, she just lets the phone ring and ring until the voicemail picks up. Shit, I even went as far as to hit her as up on Facebook, but she never responds, then her petty ass will have the audacity to update her status letting me know she online. She was trying me, like I was some lame ass fuck boy and I didn't appreciate that shit; especially when a nigga ain't even do shit to her big-headed ass. I mean, the most I can think of is that I left out before she woke up because I had shit to do. However, at least I was nice enough to stop and grab flowers and shit. I let attitude play out this long only because I been mad busy switching up drop spots and traps, and also getting my own business together. I'm in the process of opening a clothing boutique, and I know that shit gone do numbers.

Pulling into the parking lot of my building, I cut the engine and hopped out. I had a few interviews to conduct for various positions, and I was hoping to fill them all today. That didn't mean I was gone hire just anybody to be in my shit, though; they actually had to be qualified. This wasn't about to be some ghetto, hood establishment, although I wasn't opposed to hiring black girls, I wasn't with any bullshit. Waking inside the building, I immediately developed a headache as I saw the long line of eager applicants and realized I'd had sex with more than a few of them, while I'm sure some knew of me from my clout in the streets. I would start with the clueless looking ones and work my way back. Looking at Ginger, my assistant, I took the coffee she was extending to me and told her to send the first one in.

Taking a seat, I got comfortable at the desk and started looking through the file of a Miss Veronica Chiles. All the ladies had a number, and their files were in order according to their number they took, compliments of Ginger who was the best at what she did and deserved everything I paid her.

"Good morning," Veronica said, walking in, wearing some six-inch high heels, a mini skirt that barely covered her ass with a shirt so tight on that her breasts were straining to break free.

Shaking my head, I said, "Exactly where did you assume you were going when you got dressed this morning, ma?"

"To apply for a job," she said, looking down at her outfit.

"Where? Im selling clothes, not hoes," I said annoyed.

"Excuse me? I look damn good and presentable."

"To who? A pimp? Girl, get this file back and quit wasting my time. For future references, first impressions and a dress code is essential to getting a position."

"Really, Zac?" she said like she knew me or something.

"Yes really, bye."

"Ok look, I really need this job. My momma tripping on me and my kids about getting out, and my baby daddy just got knocked on a 5 to10 year bid. I heard you would like this, so I only wore it to impress you," she said to me. I paused to absorb everything that she told me and was debating if I should conduct the interview when this hoe pulled her shirt over her head.

"That's it, get out my shit!" I yelled, pressing a button for security to come in and escort her ass out because she wasn't moving fast enough. Fucking around with her, I would be slapped with lawsuits for sexual harassment and shit. Nope; wrong nigga, I cut that short before it even begins.

"NEXT!" I yelled, ready to fucking go already. I needed a double cup of something. Three hours and about 200 applicants later, and I had a store manager, assistant store manager, and five employees to start off with. Depending on sales, I'll expand to more employees, but for now, I was fine with my starter team. Thanking Ginger, I walked out to my truck, hopped in and went to call Desiree before I realized it was game day. I would just have to stop by to catch her performance. Dialing Debo instead, I wanted to check on that earlier issue.

"What's up?" he asked when he answered the phone.

“You found out who did that shit?”

“Naw, but I think the shit got something to do with the same niggas who stole the re-up products,” he said. I was thinking the same thing that’s why I couldn’t go back to sleep earlier.

“Stay on that for me. But another thing, how the fuck was there a slip up handling that issue with Chaz?

"Shit, I don't know. I should have known not to put Jacob on shit. He good at what he do, but it's always something happening. He told me it was some female, young hoe."

"Shit, I don't care if it was an old hoe, it could even be his damn grandma. No face, no case. I want the bitch found by sundown; no exceptions. Get on that personally."

"Bet," he said, hanging up. The game was over so I decided to meet Desiree out front because I didn't do well with crowds of mufuckas, all at once, pushing and shit. My trigger finger became itchy in situations like that. Spotting a food truck, I decided to grab me some wings because them bitches be hitting, and a nigga was a little hungry.

"So this what we doing now?" I heard a voice say from behind me. Turning around, I locked eyes with this hoe, Samantha, I used to knock off from time to time. Bitch pussy was trash though, that's why I had to gone stop fucking with her. Her head was ok, but even it couldn't make up for that pussy. She could ride the fuck out of a dick, but that doesn't mean shit if you ain't got no walls.

"What you talking about, bruh?"

"You know what the fuck I'm talking about. Out here fucking with all these bitches from my school is one thing, but you fucking hoes on my squad, got my friends looking at me crazy because everybody knows how close we are."

"Bitch, you smoking that shit? When the fuck was, we ever close? Your mouth was close to my dick, that's about it. You lying telling your friends we were something that we weren't has nothing to do with me. That's on your body."

"Whatever nigga. Don't play because you already know what it is and why I saw you more than them other hoes did."

"Because you was always available and you freaky as fuck and was down to let me do whatever," I said, dismissing her accusations that she was my main bitch or some.

"That's what your mouth saying right now," she said, licking her lips at me. "When I'ma get some of my dick?"

"Shit, when you find one that's yours, you can have it," I said as I noticed Desiree walking with, who I assumed was her mother. Walking off from her, I quickly walked up on Desiree, and before she could say anything to me, I planted a kiss on her lips.

"Hey bae, you did good out there," I said to her as I pulled back from the kiss. I completely had caught her off guard, thus giving me the advance in the situation. Turning to her mother, I stuck my hands out.

"Nice to meet your big sister; you guys must take after your mother."

Smiling, she said, “Well yeah, we hear that all the time. Desiree, why you never told me you had a new boyfriend? I like him."

"Well, I didn't tell you because-" she was saying, but I cut her off.

"Because I wanted to properly introduce myself, face to face. "I’m Zachariah, but everyone calls me Zac. It's my pleasure to meet you, ma'am," I said to her, flashing an award-winning smile.

"Nice to meet you as well, young man. You seem very respectful; I like that. Just what my baby needs."

"Thank you; I was raised by a strong black woman. But listen, lovely ladies, I wanted to take both of you both to Bennigans for dinner."

"Can we go to Cheesecake Factory instead? I love their pasta," Desiree said smiling all innocently. Little did her ass know, it was her world, and she definitely could have whatever she liked.

"You got that, lil' momma," was the only reply I had.

"I need to go to the restroom, and then we can go," her mom said.

"Ok ma. We'll wait for you, and if you see Yemani, tell her we all going to eat. I didn't spot her in the crowd, but I know she didn't miss tonight. I hope not," she said kind of sad. I hope her friend ain't, not show up either knowing how important tonight was to Desiree.

"Chile please, you know my god daughter wouldn't miss this for anything in the world. If she did, it would be a good explanation as to why. I’m sure she around her somewhere.”

"Yeah, prolly with her new best friend," she mumbled, but I caught that. Her mom walked off, disappearing into the crowd.

"Let me find out you jealous because your best friend got another friend."

"Boy bye; ain't nobody jealous because I know ain't nobody replacing me."

"Yeah, yeah, yeah."

"Zac, what time you coming?" I heard from behind me. My jaw clenched, and I closed my eyes mentally trying to remain calm because I already knew Sam ass was trying to start some shit.

"Stop playing with me, bruh," I said.

"Oh, so you tryna front, huh? Make me embarrass you," she said with her hands on her hips. When I left her, she was solo; now her messy ass friends were with her, so she felt the need to show out.

"Bitch, only person would be embarrassed is your funny looking ass," I said as Desiree started laughing

"Oh, it's funny? You licking my pussy every time you kiss that nigga."

"Bitch, lie again with that trash ass pussy. Gone on, Samantha; you know I don't even do this putting on a show shit. Fuck around and make a nigga get on your ass. She ain't kissing shit but me. I ain't never put my mouth on that shit. You did swallow all these kids, though, don't forget I got videos, so play with it," I said grabbing Desiree by the arm and walking off before she could say anything else. Her and her friends had that shit look on their faces.

"See, this the shit I be talking about. That's why I been ignoring you and shit. I'm not about to be having different hoes checking me over."

I grabbed her and kissed her passionately to shut her the fuck up.

"Listen ma, let this be the last time you come at me left about another bitch. Anything you want to ask me, just ask me and I'ma keep it a buck with yo ass. I don't do this petty; I'ma ignore you shit because that's gone be when you lose me. A nigga like me is too old for the games, and I'm ready to settle down, but if you not on what I'm on and not ready for what I have to offer, tell me now so I can move around. I'm not out to hurt your heart, I'm trying to mend the shit if you let me, but you gone lose a good man pushing me away" I told her because I was heated at the fact she let that shit come out her mouth talking about that's the reason she been ignoring me. Here, I was thinking I had done something when I didn't do shit at all.

Walking off, leaving her standing there looking stupid, I pulled a blunt out my pocket because I needed something to calm me down. I don't care that I was in public, them pigs knew what was up on my end. Sparking the blunt up, I took a pull as I took my phone out and hit Midos up.

"Nigga, why you always calling me and shit? Nigga tryna have an eightsome before my bday at midnight and shit."

"Man, what the fuck is an eightsome?"

"Shit, I'm hitting eight bad bitches at the same damn time," this fool said.

Choking on smoke from laughing at this fool, I said, "Nigga, only you would think of some shit like that anyway. I know your wide nose ass better be at this birthday party tonight, shit. Got my ass running around town all week setting shit up for you, nigga, you and all eight of them hoes coming."

"Shit, hell yeah, I'm coming because I'm tryna leave with eight more, fuck you mean."

"Man, yo old ass need to think about settling down before your dick ends up falling off. Anyway, we meeting up to pregame or what?"

"Hell yeah, meet me at my condo downtown in about two hours."

"Bet," I said to him as I circled back around to where I left Desiree. Noticing her mom had joined her, I told Midos I would see him in a few hours and hung up. It was still pretty early, so I had time to take the girls to dinner and get ready for the party. It would be way past 12 before we fell off in that shit anyway, knowing our asses.

Putting my blunt out, I walked back over to where they were standing at.

"I didn't see her anywhere," Desiree's mom was saying when I walked up.

"Her phone keeps going to voicemail every time I call," Desiree said with a worried expression on her face.

"I'll go get my truck, ladies and meet you back here so you won't have to walk," I said, interrupting their conversation and walking off, thankful for any excuse to leave. I didn't want to hear about the shit because then I would be forced to give my opinion on the matter and people hate to hear the truth. Yemani comes from a small ass town, population in the low hundreds. She's never lived anywhere else hell, and I've seen it happen plenty of times, when girls come to college and get a little freedom they can't handle it. She prolly somewhere face down, ass up bussing it wide open. I hate to say it, but that's what usually happens when they are introduced to the big city for the first time. Now she still wrong for not showing up tonight, or showing up and leaving, not saying anything to Desiree, that's fucked up on another level. I didn't, however, think anything was wrong with her. Hopping in my truck, I pulled around to the front and Desiree, and her mom got in, and I sped off, heading to the restaurant. An hour and a half later, I found myself back at Desiree's apartment. I had convinced her to come to this party with me, so she was at her place getting dressed.

"Yemani was telling me about some crazy shit that popped off at this party she went to Thursday night. She sounded really shook up about it but was unsure if it really happened or if she was just that drunk," Desiree was saying from inside the bathroom. I was currently laying across her bed, flipping through channels on tv while texting

Midos, telling him I might just meet him there since I got my shawty with me.

"Her and Krystal came in the house afterwards, drunk as shit going on and on about the party and Greg, the captain of the basketball team," she said, still rambling. This was the result of two mixed drinks tonight. She went from sad and worried to angry, I guess.

"Bae, listen, I'ma go get my clothes then come back here and get dressed. Quit worrying about Yemani. Her and this Krystal girl, prolly just out chilling. She doesn't have family, and you are her only friend from what you tell me, so shit, she just exploring. Put yourself in her shoes. You really the only person she has left, whereas you have your parents, your friends on the dance team, and me. Who she got? She just out being a regular 19-year-old. Lighten up," I said, walking out of her room and towards the door.

"I won't be gone long," I said as I opened the door just as this chick was preparing to knock.

"Oh, I'm sorry. I didn't. I was. Ummm, is Yemani here? I've been calling her and her phone messed up or something. We were supposed to meet and go to the game together, and she stood me up," she got out all in one breath.

"Who you?"

"My name? My name is Krystal," she said, rotating between looking up at me and down at her feet.

"Who are you talking to?" Desiree asked as she walked inside the living room looking beautiful in a black mesh dress. I temporarily forgot the chick was even standing there as I took in her beauty. That dress fit her like a glove and complimented every curve on her body. My dick was bricking up just by looking at her, so I knew I couldn't let her wear that shit. I would kill a nigga just for looking for long. Hell, I would kill a nigga if I thought that they were thinking about her fine ass.

"Who is it, Zac?" she said again, walking closer. Snapping out of my thoughts, I stepped to the side to allow ole girl in.

"I don't know, but I'll see you in a bit," I said, turning to leave.

"Wait, that's her. Krystal, what are you doing here and where is my sister?"

Hearing this, I stopped in my tracks because all I've been hearing all night was that Yemani was with Krystal, yet here Krystal was having also gotten stood up by her. Either she was out thotting and bopping, or something really happened to her. She knew in the city, so she can't have any enemies, so it has to be door number one.

"I don't know where she's at. She never showed to meet me for the game, and her phone has been going straight to voicemail. The last time I spoke with her, she said she was going to meet Greg for coffee at Starbucks, and then get dressed."

"This is so unlike her. I'm not going to this party; I'm going to look for my sister," Desiree said.

"Didn't you just hear, she with Greg probably getting broken in properly," I said annoyed because I had been saying this all along. Feeling my phone vibrating, I picked it up and answered it.

"Talk to me."

"We got that package. Roughed her up a bit, but we wanted to wait for you guys to finish it."

"Damn, y'all act like y'all can't take a shit without me and Midos. Where Debo at?"

"He the one told me run it by y'all what was to be done. He brought the bitch to us."

"So y'all basically didn't do shit and still ain't doing shit?" I said pissed off because this was something else a nigga didn't have time for on top of Desiree's hoe ass friend.

"I'm on my way," I said, hanging up. Dialing Midos, I waited until he picked up.

"Oh shit, you sucking daddy dick like it's yours," this fool said into the fool.

"That's some gay ass shit to say," I said, hating because I wouldn't mind some sloppy toppy right about now.

"Nigga, what yo no pussy getting ass, want? If you want to join in, just say that, damn. Keep calling me interrupting shit."

"Man, you fuck with them hoes that a leave yo dick burning, I'll pass. Shit, let's not act like Lilly ain't smashed damn near every available dick in town," I said. "But shit, I'm calling cuz they got that issue waiting for us."

"Ok. No face, no case, is it handled?"

"Naw, we gotta go down there."

"Fuckkkkk! I'm killing a few of them niggas for this shit," he said, pissed off. I could hear him pushing bitches off of him then the phone hung up.

"Listen, I gotta bounce," I said, turning to Desiree because I had bigger shit to deal with right now.

"But what about Yemani?"

"I'ma make some phone calls and see what I can find out, so, baby, don't worry about nothing. This my city," I said, kissing her and quickly walking out. I wanted to pop this lil' bitch, get dressed, and be tuning up within the hour.

Pulling up to the warehouse, Midos was already there smoking a blunt, sitting on top of his car, high as fuck.

"Why you ain't in there getting this shit over with?" I asked him.

"Shit nigga, it's my birthday, I figured yo ass would handle that hell," he said jumping down, passing me the blunt.

"Man, come on," I said, hitting it long and hard. Walking inside the doors, we mugged the sorry ass niggas, who were standing around looking clueless as we walked to the corner where ole girl had a bag over her head and was tied up.

"Take that bag off so we can get this shit over with," I said, pulling my gun out. Once they pulled the bag off, I got the shock of my life when I saw who it was.

"Yemani," we both said at the same exact time.

CHAPTER 10

Shit just got real…

MIDOS

Realizing the naked girl tied up and seemingly unconscious was the same feisty girl I couldn't get out of my mind, And who had me hitting her up all day everyday like a bitch, I immediately became enraged, and I didn't even know why.

"What the fuck!" Zac yelled quickly untying her, picking her up, and carrying her out the room. I assumed to our office, which has a couch that turned into a bed since we sometimes slept here.

"Who touched her?" I asked as more niggas walked in. They didn't see our initial reactions, so they had no idea this wasn't the time to get smart.

"The hoe put up a big fight, so I had to show her ass who the boss was," Richard said, laughing and giving Jacob a high five.

"Did you touch her?" I repeated.

"Like fuck the bitch? Naw, I ain't break her in properly yet. I wanted to though since she said she was a virgin and she would die before she lost her virginity like this. Bitch just assumed them niggas wanted to fuck cuz that's the first thing came out her mouth. I mean, shit, she fine but she ain't all that. Wasn't nobody initially on that since she brought it up and hell, a nigga like me ain't never ran across a real-life virgin, but the stories I've heard, make me wanna take it for a test drive myself. Her ass a rowdy one because she literally started beating them niggas asses, throwing blows like a nigga. I'm talking about shawty was catching their asses with some mean ones, and they stupid ass was letting her do it. Them niggas need to be ashamed of themselves, getting their asses handed to them by a chick. Shit, I hit the hoe one time, and she dropped. She fell so hard that she hit her head pretty badly on the concrete floor, that's why she's unconscious. I hit her ass a few more times for the hell of it, and stomped her the fuck out. I was in the process of getting me some pussy before I killed her right before y'all showed up. Hell, y'all want next? It is almost your birthday, might as well bring it in with some pussy, or y'all can gone get out of here. I know the party tonight. I honestly don't even know why they simple asses called disturbing y'all, boss, my bad. We got this, trust me; the hoe not walking out of here," Richard said, still oblivious to the fact that he was a dead man walking.

My eyes had fire in them as I reached into my pants and drew my gun with the quickness. Squeezing the trigger, I caught Jacob between the eyes three times and shot Richard in his legs bringing him to his knees as he yelled in pain.

"Arghh!"

The rest of the men had looks in their eyes as if to say, we don't want no problems. Everybody knew when I pulled my gun out and dropped one body, a lot more where going to follow.

"Aye boss, none of us touched her," Mark, one of my men, said. I paused and debated if I wanted to kill his snitch ass as Zac came running back into the room at full speed with his gun drawn ready for whatever. He was looking around lost as hell.

"What's going on?"

I heard him, but I didn't hear him as I felt myself blacking in and out; I was just that mad. Crazy thing is, even I didn't fully understand or know why I was on the verge of flashing out because I barely knew the chick, but each time a mental image of her tied up, naked and beaten flashed into my mind, my blood began to boil.

"Yo aye, I'm mad too but shit what you kill these niggas for? They following orders; no face, no case. Shit, I don't know what the fuck I'ma tell Desiree because she been worried all damn day. I don't even know what the fuck Yemani ass was doing here. Hell, I barely know the broad, but I knew her hoe ass was up to no good. Clearly. Wait, how you know her?" he asked me.

"First let that be the last time you disrespect her and I won't say the shit again. How you know she a hoe, if you barely know her? And I know her because she's the chick I told you about that I hit and matched a blunt with.We been textn and talking on and off"

"Shit, it all makes sense now. You said you hit somebody truck, the day I took them out for Yemani birthday, somebody had hit her truck. Small world. Shit, she got your nose wild open, and all yo ass did was match a blunt with her; unless you got the pussy."

Ignoring him, I got back to the task at hand, having made up my mind what I wanted to do with Richard's ass. I couldn't just shoot him; I had something special for his ass.

"Pick his ass up and carry him to the table," I barked to the men. Turning to Zac, I said," Where your toys at that you always tryna get me to play with?"

He looked at me for a second before walking across the room to another corner, tapping the wall three times, it slid open revealing a box of some sort. Entering a code, the box slid open, revealing different types of knives and swords.

"Have at it," Zac said to me as I walked over and grabbed a chainsaw, a butterfly looking knife, and a blade.

Walking back to a crying Richard, who the men had tied up to the table, he said, "What I do wrong, boss man? What the fuck a nigga did? You said no face, no case, so I roughed the bitch up. Bruh, I got kids, please don't do this," he cried, pissing on himself as I dangled the knife in front of him trying to decide what I wanted to cut first. I was usually a shoot to kill type, but something inside of me snapped when I saw Yemani laying there, beaten and tied up.

"So you said you hit her with a powerful lick and she dropped to the group, right? Did the lick feel like this?" I asked him, completely ignoring his pleas as I sliced a finger off as he yelled in pain.

"Fuuuuuccck, boss! What a nigga do to deserve this?"

"Was it this hand you touched her with?" I asked, still ignoring him as I put the knife down and picked up the blade. I would have grabbed be chainsaw, but I figured that would give me a cleanup, and I wanted him to feel everything so I cut into the palm of his hands, not stopping until it was halfway severed off. "Or did you use this hand?" I asked as I then turned to repeat the process with the other hand. His screams fell on deaf ears as I felt myself go to another place. I picked up the knife and was about to start carving his ass up when I heard,

POW! POW! POW!

Followed by his head exploding. Looking up, I noticed Zac had gave the nigga three shots to the dome.

"Fuck you do that for?" I asked him.

"Because Edward Scissors Hands, yo ass was going slow like this a science experiment, forgetting a nigga just dropped 50,000 on your ugly ass for this party. Now come on, so we can take Yemani home and let Desiree clean her up.

Shit, we found her like that, that's our lie and we sticking to it."

"Naw, I ain't letting her out of my sight. I'm taking her back to my house, it's guards at the gate and-"

"Wait… pause; you taking a chick you barely know to your main house? The house you lay your head and only women been to is your moms and Barbara? That house?" he asked, looking at me as if I had lost my mind. "Nigga, you must have had one too many drinks, or you gotta lay off that Egyptian shit you be smoking," he said, feeling my head.

"What the fuck is you doing?" I asked him.

"Nigga, I'm trying to check your temperature like they do in movies and shit to see if yo ass alright because I know you gotta be sick. You not in your right mind right now, clearly with the shit you just let come out of your mouth."

Shaking my head at him, I just walked off out the room and into the office, where he had laid Yemani on the couch and covered her with a blanket. Picking her up, I walked with her outside with him hot on my heels.

"So you gone take her to your crib and then come hit this party?"

"I don't know if I wanna leave her."

"Nigga, it's your 25th birthday, like Boosie said if you make it to see 25, nigga, you an OG. We got these streets on lock right now, and aside from finding out who hit our shit, we done eliminated all our problems, that's worth celebrating. Look you like her, cool; make sure them niggas watch her. The dudes I hired at your gate some thoroughbred niggas."

"Yo ass said the same thing about the weak ass security detail you hired, but I have yet to see them niggas."

"Aye, them niggas came highly recommended from my nigga Danger, and if he say they good, I know they good."

"Shit, good and non fucking existent. Speaking of Danger, I'ma have go get up with his ass soon; I heard he making big moves in Dtown."

"Hell yeah, him and Killa wrecking shit down there."

"Might look into expanding that way," I said as I made it to my car, popping my locks so I could lay Yemani on the back seat of my Lamborghini as best as I could. She was really knocked out. Either, she was a hard sleeper, or she had a concussion. I made a mental note to have my on-call doctor meet me at the house; I wasn't gone go out until I made sure she was good. I didn't need her going to sleep permanently. Jumping into the driver seat, I said, "Give me an hour to get her straight then I'll be there. Tell yo girl that

Yemani with me so she can stop worrying. It's no way I'm leaving her outside like that."

Shaking his head, he said, "I never thought I would live to see the day when Amyr Jarrah was concerned about someone else."

"Fuck you, nigga; I be concerned about your ass, ma dukes, and my pops."

"Shit; we don't count, I mean outside of us," he said, getting into his car.

I didn't bother to respond to him as I pushed the start button and my car roared to life. Pulling out from the warehouse, I headed home with a lot of thoughts running through my mind as I occasionally kept glancing in my rearview mirror, checking on Yemani. *What are you doing*? I asked myself as I pushed the pedal to the metal, speeding down the intersection. This girl had me all off my square and acting out of character, and I barely knew her ass and hadn't even smashed yet. Still, I felt a strong need to protect her with my life each time I caught a glimpse of her rising chest, indicating that she was breathing. Looking at her gorgeous, yet, bruised face, caused my nose to flare and anger to course through my veins, making me want to bring Richard's ass back to life just to kill his ass all over again.

"Aside from a mild concussion, she's fine," the doctor said as he began placing things back into his bags to leave. "I left some medicine for her on the nightstand to take because whenever she decides to wake up, she'll have one hell of a headache. She needs to only take two pills every three to four hours, and she'll be fine, just will be cranky from the pain."

"Naw her feisty ass cranky anyway," I said, laughing, recalling the first time I met Yemani and how she went off on a nigga.

"Well, you have something on your hands," he said, laughing as he headed towards the door.

"Tell me about it doc, but good looking out, coming through to check on her for me."

"I do what I'm paid to do," he said as he opened the door, preparing to leave.

"Aye doc, you said only give her two pills every four hours but if her crazy ass gets to tripping, what will happen if I slip her four?" I said, laughing.

"Then you'll need to call me back and I'll charge you extra for my troubles," he laughed as he walked out the door. Closing the door behind him, I walked back into my guest room where I had brought Yemani and checked on her one more time before I walked around to Barbara, my housekeeper. Hell, I don't know why I even needed one when I was rarely here, but she kept the place looking magazine-ready at all times.

"Hey Barbara, make sure you check on her for me and call my phone if anything happens or she wakes up. And make sure-"

"Chile, go get ready for your party and quit bothering me. I done raised seven kids and four grandkids, it's nothing you can tell me about taking care of a sick person. She'll be fine. When she wakes up, I got just the thing for her that will make her feel better than that medicine will. That's what wrong with you, young folks, too dependent on these new age medicines that don't do nothing but something make you sicker. We didn't have all that mess in my day."

"Just give her the medicine," I said. She just waved me off.

"Chile, your girlfriend will be fine now, go," he said, pushing me toward the stairs.

"That's not my girlfriend," I felt the need to correct her.

"Could have fooled me. I don't see any more damsels in distress being carried in and I've been around for a long time. Don't forget I used to change your dirty diapers."

Aside from moms, Barbara was the only other consistent woman in my life. My father had hired her when my dukes and I moved back to America. When I was sent to live with my father, once my moms got sick, they let Barbara go. When I got my own home and my moms kept pressuring me to hire a maid, Ms. Barbara was the first and only person who came to my mind. Shit, a nigga wasn't about to have some random hoe snooping around my shit or tryna fuck. I trusted Barbara and she knew all about the crazy life I lived. She wasn't a stranger to the doc stitching me up or walking in on me cleaning guns, or counting money that was to be transferred to the stash house.

"Does your mom know you have a girlfriend?" she said, when I was halfway up the stairs.

"No, she doesn't because I don't have one so don't you go gossiping about false information," I said to her as I turned around and looked at her. Throwing her hands up in surrender, she just laughed and walked off.

Walking upstairs to the master bedroom to shower and get dressed, I decided to keep my attire simple since I didn't plan on being gone all night. Walking to the wet bar inside my room, I fixed myself a drink and walked into the bathroom to hop into the shower, once again back in the spirit of celebrating my birthday even if I was going to be brief. I would turn up super hard another day. Thirty minutes later, after stepping out of the shower, I walked into my closet to get fresh. Glancing at the clock, noticing it was 12:45.

"Happy Birthday to a real nigga," I said, downing the entire drink and saying fuck the glass. A nigga was 25 and thankful to see this day because I honestly didn't feel like I would make it. Shit, as much as niggas tried to take me out, making it to my 25th birthday was something I was proud of, that's why this night was so important to me at first. Now I just wanted to speak to everyone, kick it for about thirty minutes, then come back and sit with Yemani for a while. As soon as the thought popped into my head, I had to turn the bottle I was drinking up and take it to the head because I, for damn sure, was losing it. Where the hell were these thoughts coming from because they wasn't me at all. I barely even knew this chick and I was giving up my birthday and all the freaky shit I had planned for her. *Get it together man*, I pep talked myself as I got dressed. This was definitely gone be a long ass night and a birthday for the books.

Walking into the party, the shit was an all-black and gold theme. Shit was lit as fuck. Zac really showed love and went all out for a nigga.

“The man of the hour just walked in, y’all show my nigga, Midos some love on his birthday. Officially an OG now, son, I salute,” the DJ said as the crowd went wild and everybody started yelling happy birthday. Flashing lights damn near blinded me as everybody was trying to get a picture of me or with me, the shit was on some real-life, celebrity status. I’m the type that was rarely seen but always felt, so when I did step out, shit was something to see, I guess. Looking dapper as hell, I posed for about maybe a hundred damn pictures as bitches was coming out of the woods wanting me to snap it up with them or get on their snap chat. I passed on that shit because I didn’t do social media, that’s how niggas got caught up putting their entire move on a damn social site then claim somebody working with the police or folks following them. My nigga, if you posting guns and weed, then tagging your location, ain't nobody working with the fucking laws, you snitching on yo damn self. Then will post their location or go live, then have the nerve to say niggas stalking them, tryna take them out. I can't fuck with no fake ass pussy shit like that. Zac ass love it and eats that shit up. He forever posting pictures and shit but have the nerve to call me a pretty boy.

"My nigga, clean as hell," Zac said, walking up to me. That nigga had jumped fresh quick as hell.

"Shit, don't act surprised, my nigga; I been doing this shit," I said to him as my eyes landed on a bad ass redbone with some big ass titties. "Bitch bad on the low," I said eyes never leaving her. She felt a nigga checking her out that's why she was trying her best not to turn around, but her friends had already peeped me looking and was more than likely telling her.

"Who?" Zac asked, turning around to look. "Man, don't yo ass have Yemani at home while you out here checking for other hoes," he said.

I don't know how I had forgot just that fast.

"Man, we not together, we not even on that level, we cooling. Hey, what can I say, I'ma dog ass nigga and I can admit that," I said, serious as hell. "Besides, I can only disrespect her if that was my girl. Until I have a title, or I'm married, I'm fair game to be take advantage of," I said.

"Nigga, you seriously need help," he said, laughing. "Come on, you gone love what a nigga got you," he said, walking off. Following behind him, I couldn't help but stop and slap her on that fat ass and whisper in her eat,

"When you want a real nigga to beat it up, come find me," then licked her ear and kept walking as casually as I had stopped.

Shaking his head, he walked into an area that was roped off for me and my entire crew. As security let us in, I walked in, dapping everybody up. When I spotted a black king chair, I lost my fucking mind. “My nigga, you got me a fucking king chair?” I said, pumped.

“Shit, now everybody knows who the king of Houston is,” he said just as two half-naked girls came walking up; one, carrying a crown, and the other one, carrying a king robe and a bottle of Grey Goose.

“My nigga, just remember half this shit when my turn comes,” Zac said.

“Man, I love you, dawg, real talk,” I said to him.

“I love you too, homie. Now enough of this shit, let’s turn the fuck up,” he said just as *Lifestyle by Rich Gang* came on and everybody went crazy and started rapping along with the song. This really and truly was my shit for real.

I've done did a lot of shit just to live this here, lifestyle

We came straight from the bottom, to the top, my lifestyle

Nigga livin' life like beginners

And this is only the beginnin'

"So I got some information for you. Not on who stole y'all product, but who spray painted the houses," Debo said, putting pancakes in his mouth.

"Yeah, who the fuck did that shit because I was ready to go on a killing spree," I said."

"Is it some bitch ass nigga we know?" Zac asked.

"Naw, I don't y'all know dude," Debo said.

"Well shit, who?" Both me and Zac drunk asses said at the same time. I didn't mean to get drunk, but I'm glad I ended up coming to my party because that shit was dumb wild. It was truly a birthday for the books.

"Nigga named Brock. Apparently, he had been asking around the streets about Chaz and stirring up trouble here and there," Debo said. We were all at Ihop, throwing back food before I headed home to check on my house guest.

"Why that name sound so familiar?" I said because I had heard it before a while ago, just can't think from where. "I can't put my finger on it."

"Shit, I ain't never heard of the nigga but what's up, what he do?"

"Word on the streets is that he on some retaliation shit for what happened to Chaz, apparently that's his baby brother or was his baby brother," Debo said.

"Well, his brother was a bitch ass nigga and disrespected me one too many times so if he know like I know, he better suck that shit up and charge it to the game. It's consequences when you out here in these streets thuggin," I said.

"I'ma get on that shit, don't worry," he said. I let that shit run in one ear and out the other. I wasn't in the least bit worried about a damn Brock, shit if he came this way with that bullshit, he was gone wind up going to be with his brother. Dapping them niggas up, I got up to go home to check on the mysterious Miss Yemani.

CHAPTER 11

Mommy and Daddy, I need you…

YEMANI

Stirring out of my sleep, I opened my eyes expecting to see the tan ceiling I had grown accustomed to. Instead, I was looking at a beautifully designed high-rise ceiling. Jumping up too quickly, my head immediately began to pound as my hand went out to my forehead as glanced around the spacious yet unfamiliar room. *Whose bed is this*? I wondered as I pulled the sheets up over my exposed body realizing that someone had undressed me and I was currently only in long t-shirt that wasn't even mine.

Glancing around, I tried to think back to the last thing I remembered to try and piece together how I ended up here. Suddenly, I heard a voice directly outside of the room door. With no time to really think or process everything, I hopped up from the bed and ran to the adjoining bathroom, locking the door and frantically searching for something to defend myself with. I didn't know where I was, how I got here, or who the voice belonged to, but I wasn't taking any chances. As I stood in the cold bathroom clad in nothing but a t-shirt, I caught a glimpse of my reflection in the mirror and gasped at the vision I saw starring back at me. As I moved closer to the mirror, examining the bruises that littered my face, flashes of me fighting a bunch of men flashed across my brain. However, as quickly as it came, it left.

"Think Yemani, think. How did you get here?" I said aloud to no one in particular. The last thing

I, for sure, remember was walking to my car after leaving Starbucks. I was headed to meet up with Krystal so that we could go to the game together and, I don't know what happened after that. My mind was drawing a blank.

"Yemani?" I heard my name being called as the door to the room opened.

Why does that voice sound familiar?

“Where the hell is she?" I heard the voice say in frustration. It sounded as if he had begun looking for me as I heard doors being opened and closed.

"Barbara, I thought I told you to watch her?!" I heard the voice yell.

"Shit," I mumbled under my breath as I heard footsteps getting closing to the bathroom. Looking around, I didn't see anything I could use to protect myself, so I grabbed the top to the toilet and gripped it tightly preparing to protect myself by any means necessary. Hearing the doorknob twist a few times followed by fist beating on the door, I backed up a bit, bracing myself for whoever was coming through that door.

"Yemani?" I heard before seconds later, the door was knocked down.

"Ahh!" I yelled, charging forward, preparing to hit the intruder with my ready-made weapon only to pause when recognition of the intruder set in.

"You," I said, pointing at him while still gripping the lid of the toilet tightly. Even though I had been daydreaming about running into him again, ever since that day we met, I still wasn't taking my chances just in case he was a crazy ass nutcase.

"What the hell are you doing?" he asked me.

"Me? What the hell are you doing? You the crazy ass nigga who just kicked the damn door down."

"I was trying to check on your ungrateful ass. Shit, a nigga thought some had happened to you but clearly your slow ass in here playing in toilet bowl water and shit," he shot back.

"I'm not playing in nothing, you could have been on some other shit, so I was gone fuck you up with this top," I said. Laughing, he just looked at me for a split second before he said,

"I'm not one to hit a female but if yo ass would have hit me with that shit, a nigga would have knocked your lil' ass out."

"And we would have torn this bathroom the hell up because if you think I'm just gone let you hit me, then think again," I shot back, placing the lid back on the toilet. I figured I was good because if he was here to harm me, he would have did it by now.

"Where am I? And why am I here?" I asked him as I walked past him back into the room. This whole altercation really had me drained and my head was killing me. Getting back in bed, I propped myself up on the headboard, making myself comfortable. “My head is killing me,” I said.

Reaching on the dresser, he grabbed some medicine and poured some water into a glass from a pitcher, I just noticed was sitting on the dresser.

“Here, doc said you would have a headache,” he said, holding the medicine out to me.

I looked from him to the medicine back to him. “Nigga, you got me fucked up if you think I’m taking that bullshit. You not about to poison me or drug me and have your way with me. I be watching Criminal Minds so you can’t try that shit on me.”

“With the way this dick be fucking over insides, I highly doubt I have to drug a bitch to have my way with her.”

“Who you calling a bitch? Haven’t we been over this already? Disrespectful, ugly ass nigga. And the only thing that chicken nugget fuck up is the mood when girls realize they been catfished,” I shot back, really not believing anything I just said, but he didn’t need to know that

Smirking, he said, “Don’t let your mouth write a check your ass can’t cash. Because I promise you this not what you want,” he said, licking his lips at me.

The way he said that caused a flutter to form in my stomach and shoot down to my center, causing me to squeeze my lips tightly together. Embarrassed at the way my body was acting, I cleared my throat and said, “What’s the medicine for?”

"For you to take for your headache, what else would it be for?"

"Hell, I don't know. It doesn't look like aspirin to me."

"Look, you want the shit or not, old, big-headed ass girl because a nigga patience not that fucking great. Shit, I'm just tryna help yo ass out," he said, putting the medicine back into the bottle and placing it back on the dresser with an attitude.

See, this why y'all can't be together, y'all both some hot heads and be done killed each other, I thought to myself. *Wait... where the fuck did that come from and why the hell you thinking about being with this crazy ass nigga!* I screamed at my thoughts in my head.

Dude just looked at me half annoyed, half intrigued.

"What's your name?" I asked him out the blue, realizing I didn't know his name but he apparently knew mines.

"Midos."

"Midos? I know your momma didn't name your ass that, ole wanna be gangster."

"Wannabe?"

"Yeah, I never saw a thugged out Egyptian/ Italian before well, except on tv with Scarface and even he wasn't thugged out. You must had some black friends growing up, so you thought you was down to?" I said.

"Man, get the fuck out of here. You funny as fuck you know that. Type of shit is that?" he asked, laughing. "I fucked a lot of black hoes, does that count?"

"There you go again being disrespectful," I said, rolling my eyes at him.

"Shit, me? This the second time you've disrespected me in a major way and found yourself still breathing. I'd say an angel was watching over you because I've killed people for less. The first time you called me a gas station worker, now a wannabe gangster. Ain't shit pretend about me, and you'll find that out sooner than later. It's cool, you not the only one that thought shit was sweet with me based off my skin color. The difference between you and them niggas, is they not around to tell the story," he said with so much seriousness that I couldn't help but believe him. *Who the hell was this crazy ass nigga?*

Deciding I was gone leave his ass alone for right now, I got up and grabbed the medicine and got back on the bed as I carefully read over it. It seemed like legit medicine, and I didn't have any more options at the point because the pounding in my head was getting worse, so I took two pills and swallowed them whole before I got up and drank some water. Getting back into bed, I said, “So you wanna explain to me what I’m doing here, Midos?”

“You don’t remember what happened?”

“Duh, if I did I wouldn’t be damn asking you.”

Clenching his jaw, he said,” Say; watch that fucking mouth and how you talk to a nigga. I ain’t one of them fuck niggas you used to. Shit, I ain’t have to help your stupid ass. This my birthday and instead of fucking bitches until I passed out, I enjoyed my party, and rushed back home to check on you.”

I almost felt bad until I remembered I was half naked, with bruises all over my body. A thought suddenly popped into my head, and I raised the covers looking down at my body trying to, I don’t know, see if I had been touched. I forgot he was in the room with me as I raised the shirt up trying to get a better look. I didn't feel any different, so maybe I had nothing to worry about. But how else would I explain why I was naked?

"Nobody touched you," he suddenly said, snapping me out of the mini trance I was in. My face turned red as I realized my breasts were exposed to him and hell; basically, every other body part, since my dumb ass felt the need to lift my shirt up. Feeling like I could literally just die right there, I quickly dropped my shirt and pulled the covers tightly around me as I remained silent, trying to process my next words

"You all cute when you blushing," he said, laughing.

"Fuck you," I huffed still embarrassed and upset.

"What I tell you about that mouth? You not gone learn until a nigga show you, huh?"

Rolling my eyes at him, I said, “If nobody touched me, why am I not wearing the clothes I left the house in? And where exactly am I at?”

He looked at me intensely for a few moments his facial expressions not giving any indication anyway that he knew the answers to my question. Just when I gave up thinking he wouldn’t answer, he started talking.

“I found you like that at my warehouse. I got a call that a package was at the warehouse ready for disposal. You saw something you shouldn’t have seen, and it almost cost you, your life. When we got there, you was already naked and beaten,” he said giving me the raw truth. “I brought you back to my place because I didn’t trust letting you out of my sight even though I know, wouldn’t nothing happen to you because I already have the word you are not to be bothered. Niggas would rather kill their own mommas than to go against me,” he said.

Tears stung my eyes, but I willed myself not to let them fall. I'll be damned if I let this nigga see me crying. I barely even knew people in the city so I didn't possibly know what I could have seen that would have made them want to kill me. Just thinking about how I could have died, really had me shaken up. Shivering, I tightened the covers around me as I tried to rack my brain to remember what exactly I could have seen. Then it hit me!

"So it wasn't the alcohol, and I really did see dude," I whispered.

"Huh?" he said, looking intensely at me.

"I-I, nothing. What, where are the men who did this to me?" I asked, looking around. I suddenly felt exposed and so alone. I wished my daddy were here to protect me. He always made things better. "Why did they have to leave me like this!"

I cried out emotionally as the tears I tried so hard to hold in, came spilling over.

“They dead; you don’t have to worry about them or anybody else harming you for that matter baby girl,” the handsome Egyptian said to me. At this point, however, I wasn’t even crying about that. I was alone in a new city, being targeted by God knows who, and my parents weren’t here to protect me. That thought alone caused me to cry even harder. I could act as tough as I wanted to, but the truth of the matter is I was broken and all I wanted was my parents.

“They’re really gone,” I cried.

“Yes, they gone and they won’t even harm you again,” dude said as he reached out and grabbed me into his arms.

I realized he thought I was still referring to the men who hurt me, while I was referring to my parents. I opened my mouth to tell him otherwise, but when he grabbed me into his arms, I lost all train of thought as I clung to his warm body and held on for dear life. His embrace felt so heavenly that I didn't want to let go. It's crazy how just from this simple hug, I felt like everything was going to be ok. The way he gently but firmly held me, made me feel so protected and complete. We stayed like that for well over a few minutes until he finally pulled away. I was so caught up in the moment that when he pulled back, I leaned forward refusing to let go.

"Damn, you holding tight to a nigga like you don't want to let go," he said, laughing.

"I don't," I mumbled, not caring how it made me feel. I really wasn't ready to give that feeling up just yet. He didn't say anything else as he kicked his shoes off and climbed into bed with me, scooping me close into a spooning position and laying down with me wrapped up in his arms.

"A nigga never did no soft ass shit like this before so if you tell anybody, they'll never find your body," he threatened me. Usually, I would have a slick ass comeback, but I was exhausted, and this felt so good that I felt my eyes getting heavy as I drifted back to sleep. I thought I felt him kiss my forehead, but I could have been imagining things.

CHAPTER 12

Well damn…

DESIREE

"Fuck," I moaned with my eyes closed. I was currently laying in my bed sleep but having the best, wet dream of my life. After Zac reassured me that they found Yemani and she was fine, I still couldn't bring myself to go out and party until I physically spoke to her. What kind of friend would I be if I was out getting drunk while my best friend laid up injured? I gave Zac my key, so after his friend's party, he could come back here because I wouldn't dare ask him to miss it. The wonderful feeling I was experiencing right now felt so real as I thrust my hips forward as I was met with wave after wave of pleasure. Grabbing onto the sheets, I kept my eyes closed, not wanting the dream to end as I pictured Zac eating me like I was his last supper.

"Mmh Zac, baby, that feels so good," I moaned, reaching down and grabbing ahold to his head. The feeling at the moment felt so real that I didn't want it to ever go away.

"Open them legs wider for daddy," I heard him say, but the voice sounded very clear, too clear in fact. Pausing my movements and opening my eyes, I sat up to see a very real Zac in between my legs, head first, thoroughly enjoying himself.

"Wait, Zac! What are you-" I was in the process of saying until he put his entire mouth over my happy place and begin jabbing his tongue inside of me as if it were a miniature penis. My eyes rolled into the back of my head as I held his head in place and thrust my hips off the bed into the air so he could be a good boy and eat everything. And that's exactly what he did as he wrapped his arms around my thighs locking me into place so he could execute his tongue assault. The feeling was becoming unbearable as I tried to back up a bit.

"Uh huh, where you going?" he asked me as he paused, and flipped over, taking me with him so that now I was sitting on his chest and he was laying on his back. Looking down into his handsome face with his mouth glistening from my juices, I had the sudden urge to kiss him. Placing my mouth on his, I shared a tantalizing kiss with him, tasting the sweet essence of myself on his tongue. Raising up, he pulled his shirt over his head and tossed it on the floor.

"I'm still hungry," he said to me as he effortlessly lifted me up off his chest and placed me back onto his waiting tongue. Grabbing hold of both my ass cheeks and giving the right one a hard smack, he lifted me slightly and said, "Ride daddy's face." This was low-key my favorite position of all time, so he didn't have to tell me twice. Earlier, I was caught off guard when I realized my dream was actually happening. Now that I was fully aware this was real; I planned to put in work. I started riding his face like my life depended on it. He was so skillful with that long, devil tongue of his; that I almost paused and asked that nigga to marry me, that's just how good it was. He was eating me so good I already had my bridesmaids, wedding color, theme and kids' names picked out, it was just that crucial.

"Fuck Zac! Oh my God!" I moaned as I gyrated my hips back and forth on his face, trying to will myself to hold out a little longer on this explosive nut I felt building up in the pit of my stomach.

"You taste so fucking good," he said to me before he dove back, in this time attempting to suck my soul right out of my body. I felt his hands moving beneath me, but I paid no attention to him as I focused on stalling this orgasm for as long as I could, but found myself losing the battle quickly.

"Don't hold that shit in, let it go," Zac breathed into my pussy walls, causing me to become even wetter. The harder he sucked, the harder it became for me to hold onto this nut.

As I felt myself soaring higher than a kite, finally giving in to the pressure that had been brewing, my juices begin flying from my body like a busted water hose. Like a fat kid at the buffet, Zac didn't let anything go to waste as he stingily caught every last drop, unwilling to miss anything. Just as I was experiencing a high like no other, the glorious feeling was snatched away from me, and without warning, I was lifted up off his face and placed down onto something thick and hard. Gasping at the initial thrust of his dick inside of me and the fact that I was still coming at the same time, my eyes rolled into the back of my head as I rode the waves of my first orgasm and was quickly thrown into another one at the same time. I've never in my life experienced anything even remotely close to this, so I was in pure bliss right now.

"I told you, you fucking with a grown man," Zac said, smirking as he sat up completely, grabbed one of my legs placing it over his shoulder allowing for an even deeper penetration as he started thrusting rapidly into me.

"Ahh, baby, fuck, I, JESUS," I yelled, failing miserably at forming a sentence. This nigga was fucking me into the middle of next year and worst of all, I couldn't run or really move, I just had to hang on tight for the ride. Trying to match him, stroke for stroke as best as I could not to be outdone, he grabbed my other leg and placed it on his other shoulder so now I was sitting in his lap, legs spread-eagled with both my legs dangling over his shoulders.

"That's it, fuck me back," he said, leaning forward and grabbed one of my nipples and snaking that monster tongue across it before sucking it into his mouth, causing a shudder to run down my spine. "Fuck girl, this mine now," he said before he leaned forward and captured my lips into the most passionate, french kiss I ever had at the same time as he slowed his strokes down to slow but deep thrusts. It's like he went from fucking the shit out of me to making love in a matter of seconds I'm guessing to show me that he was capable of both and to get his point across. With the way he just handled me tonight, he need not tell me twice. Shit, we went together the minute he snatched my soul, fuck all that; a bitch can catch a fade behind that shit. Slapping me on my ass cheeks, he grabbed hold to both my hips and started plunging into my pussy at a quickened pace. The shit hurt so good that I quickly felt yet another orgasm hit me as I throw my head back and rode the waves of ecstasy. We switched positions back and forth all morning until I lost count of how many times I came. I only knew one thing, I could barely move afterward, but I went back to sleep very satisfied.

"Zac," I said, shaking him awake. It was around 8 am and we had really just went to sleep an hour or two ago, because we had woke up again and went at it for another round. I couldn't get enough of him if I tried. I was acting like a crackhead, and he was the fix I needed. I also didn't hear any complaints from him because apparently, he couldn't seem to keep his hands or his mouth to himself.

"Huh?" he said in a sleep induced state. All that shit his ass was saying to me the other day about early bird gets the worm mess yet here he was damn near dead to the world right now.

"Zac, wake up," I said a little louder as I shook him harder.

"You want to get it up, and you gotta show daddy what that mouth do because you done wore him out," he said with his eyes still closed. At the mention of giving him head, I paused and licked my lips, contemplating doing just that to that beautiful tool of his, he called a dick until I snapped out of it remembering why I was waking him up.

"Later, right now I wanna know where my sister at?"

"I told you she with Midos, she good now go back to sleep," he said, turning over and pulling the covers over his head.

"Well, why isn't she answering her phone then? I know Yemani; she wouldn't stay gone with a complete stranger and not answer the phone. She don't know that nigga like that. Hell, I don't even know that nigga. For all I know his ass could be an ax murderer, I never met him to say differently."

"She do know him, somewhat. They hit each other car, and he got her shit fixed," he said with his eyes still closed.

They hit each other? I thought, pondering over what he had just said until it hit me and I knew exactly who he was.

"Oh that's the fine ass nigga that hit her that she couldn't stop thinking about," I said excitedly because this was a small world.

Hearing me say that, his eyes popped open, and he jumped up so fast, you would never have known his ass was just sleep. "Fine ass nigga? Say bruh, you just tried my whole life with that bullshit," he said and had the nerve to be mad.

"I'm not calling him fine; like how the hell could I do that when I never met this nigga. I'm repeating what she said," I told him in a matter of fact tone, indicating he should have been well aware of that.

"Uh huh, let me find out."

"Find out then because it's not shit. Now where Midos stay at because it don't matter how he looks, I know my best friend. She most definitely would not spend a night with a random nigga."

"She had coffee with one," he mumbled.

"So she didn't spend a night with him and she damn sure didn't give up her virginity to him, so what?" I said defensively. He wasn't about to do my best friend.

"Look, she with Midos, she good," he said as he got off the bed, stretching before walking into the bathroom.

Since he clearly didn't understand the fucking question, I hopped up and walked out the room going into Yemani's room to use her bathroom and wipe up a bit. I was on a mission, so a hoe bath was gone have to get it for now. After I had brushed my hair into a bun and handled my hygiene, I walked back into the room to see Zac putting on his shoes.

"Oh good, we bout to go over there."

"Go over where?" he said.

"To Midos' house."

"I told you she good, she with Midos."

"And I told you, I don't give a fuck 'bout all that and I need to see her since she not answering her phone."

"I ain't about to go barging in this man house this early."

"Shit, I'm sure he up since the early birds gets the worm. I'm positive Yemani up because she a morning person," I shot back.

"Ok he having a cookout later on; it's like a birthday tradition his Ma dukes does so I'm sure

Yemani will come, and you can see her then, ok?"

"Negative. I wanna see her now," I said folding my arms across my chest.

"Listen, ole hard headed ass girl, I keep telling you that-" he was saying until I cut him off.

"Pussy is off limits until you take me and you won't see what this mouth do and like Gucci man said, I most definitely can do some tricks with my mouthpiece," I said, smirking at him.

"Like I was saying, I keep telling you to come on so you can meet me in the car," he said, finishing up his sentence. He knew better because had he not taken me; he definitely would have been cut off. Ok, I'm lying; that dick was amazing, but I would have held out for a minute on account that I love Yemani, my old best friend more than my new best friend. Smiling from ear to ear at the thought of seeing her, I grabbed my phone and my keys and eagerly walked outside and got into the car as Zac switched his phone from Bluetooth back to his headset, I guess so I wouldn't hear his conversation.

"Bruh, I'm headed over. No. Man, she wanna see her friend. No. Shit, yeah, I know, but hell, I wasn't about to get cut off cuz yo ass wanna be on some other shit. Fuck you. I ain't pussy-whipped; I whips pussy, you better ask about me," he said, all into his conversation to notice the sideways look I was giving him. After he hung up, he said, "See, your impatient ass couldn't even wait 'til the cookout had to come now and shit. Now you gone have folks clowning me like I'm weak or something all because you forced me to bring you."

"I didn't force you to do anything."

"Shit, threatening to cut me off is forcing my hand. I'm even bringing you to my nigga house where ain't too many souls been. Hell, I'm surprised he wasn't really mad. I guess he knows I'm serious with you so sooner or later you would have came. I hope you not on no bullshit because I would hate to have to kill your pretty ass. Midos like a brother to me and I'm super overprotective so I hope me bringing you here doesn't come back to bite me in the ass," he said with a serious expression on his face. I didn't know whether to be scared; he threatened to kill me, offended that he would contemplate killing me, curious as to what Midos was into that he would need to kill me, and super horny because he sounded so sexy when he was serious.

I remained silent, lost in thought the rest of the ride. About an hour and a half later, we were pulling up into the wrought iron gates of this breathtakingly beautiful mansion sitting back off the road. A guard came out to the car and did a walk around, inspecting us while he wrote something down on his clipboard. *What type of black nigga; that isn't a celebrity or actor really has a house this big with guards at the gate, all presidential and shit? I wonder what he do because clearly whatever it is, it's made him a lot of benjamin's*, I said, having an entire conversation with my thoughts something I tried to will myself not to do, but couldn't help it. Just as the guard was finishing up, I sat up from my position I was slumped over in and locked eyes with him. Noticing me seemingly for the first time, he wrote something on his clipboard before picking up his radio. Talking on his walkie-talkie, he walked back to his post and sat down; I'm guessing to get permission to let us in since Zac had me with him.

"Nigga, if yo dumbo-looking ass don't open this fucking gate," Zac said, growing impatient with dude. Usually, he was good about keeping his cool, but this morning, he seemed unusually cranky. Maybe he's always cranky in the mornings, and I never noticed it since we never woke up together. The look he was giving dude was enough for his ass to quickly open the gate without any further delay.

As soon as the gate was wide enough for his white on white, Audi A7 coupe to squeeze through, he whipped inside the gates, driving down the spiral driveway leading to the huge fairly mansion at the end. I had never in my life seen anything like it. The home looked like it came straight from a magazine, it was so gorgeous.

"Close your mouth, you drooling and shit. Bad enough you slob in your sleep," he said, laughing at me.

"I can't help it. I've never seen anything this big before; like look at the size of this place."

"I can't stand a liar."

"Huh?" I asked, turning to look up at him in confusion, wondering just what the hell he was talking about. I know he wasn't trying to imply that I've been here before or something. Opening my mouth to go off, he beat me to the punch.

"Lying ass, gone sit up there and just tell a bold face lie that like. I ain't never seen anything this big before," he said, mimicking me.

"I haven't," I said still confused.

"You saw this dick earlier," he shot back, sticking his tongue out at me.

"Bruh, I hate you, I really do," I said, laughing at him. I loved how playful we were with one another. Not only was it a breath of fresh air having a man who acted just like you did. It was also a plus, when it was your own man.

“Boy, whatever.”

“Boy? I think we both know that’s a lie. I already proved I’m a grown ass man, but if I have to prove it again, I don't mind doing so," he said, flashing me a devilish grin.

"You so mannish," I laughed as I opened my door eager to get out and not only see my best friend, but see the inside of this damn house. Beating him to the front door, I rang the doorbell and waited impatiently for someone to answer. A few minutes later, the steel doors swung open, and a man stood there with a mug on his face, glaring at me like I had did something to him.

"Midos, why yo ass always looking like you ready to murk a nigga? Shit, that's prolly why ole girl ready to leave, yo ass stay on go," Zac said, putting his hand on the small of my back ushering me into the huge mansion. Shit, at least Yemani got one thing right about dude; he sure was fine as hell, but that stank ass attitude had to go because if not, I'm positive they gone eventually kill each other if they ever get together.

CHAPTER 13

I ain't shit to play with…

MIDOS

"You been begging me for this dick, so you better stop running and take this shit," I said almost out of breath as I rammed my dick forcefully in and out of Angela, the chick I had met at the mall that day. She has been blowing my phone up nonstop since that day and this the first time I'm actually fucking with her. It had been a few days since I brought Yemani to the house and shit had literally turned my entire world upside down. I had to step back and realize who the fuck I was. I wasn't on that soft ass, lovey-dovey shit. I don't love these hoes, and I don't trust these hoes and wasn't shit gone change. I think I was drawn to her because I been fucking shit up for her since I met her.

First with her car, and then with the beating and shit since I'm the one told them niggas, to find her and finish the job. Granted, I didn't know it was her at the time but shit in this business, shit bound to go left like that at any minute. No face, no case has always been the motto to live by. Shaking off thoughts of her from my mind, I focused back on the task; digging deeper into Angela's pussy tryna fuck up her insides. Each time she backed up a bit tryna run, I was pulling her back down, blessing her with every inch of this dick. Her shit was so wet and gushy, the sheets were soaked, my shirt was soaked, and she was squirting everywhere.

"Oh my God! Midos, baby, you so deep; I can't take it. No," she said, shaking her head from side to side, looking distraught. I just smirked as I hit her with a few more strokes before I pulled out. Bitches be talking all of that shit, sending freaky memes and ass naked pictures, talking about what they gone do when they see you. You finally come and see what all that talking be about, and they can't back up all that mouth. Shit, I don't know about other niggas, but a nigga like me was working with some serious and on top of that; my ego stay on 1000, so you can't just tell me what you gone do to me and say I ain't ready for the pussy because I'ma take that shit like a challenge and go in for the kill the minute I see yo ass. Females stay writing a check they ass can't cash when I get to rearranging them guts. They be letting my skin color fool them. Shit, fuck all that. I'm 'bout square business this way. Stroking all eleven inches of my dick up and down while I looked down at her naked body, her face went from contorted to relived as she sat up and stared at me for a moment. I made a mental note to delete her number. It's one thing to not be able to take the dick, that's fine; only a few could, but shit to do all that damn whining after you begged for the shit was a complete no in my book. Shit, we hadn't even been fucking that long. Bitch better be glad we was at her shit and not mines because I would have straight put her childish ass out of my shit.

Closing my eyes blocking her face out, I stroked my dick faster as Yemani's beautiful face popped into my mind with that banging ass body of hers. She wasn't overly stacked, and she barely had ass which I wasn't used to, but her shit still was bad as fuck. Feeling Angela's ass lean down and put her mouth on my dick, on instinct, I reached out and grabbed her head as I begin fucking her face, still thinking about Yemani. I don't know what this broad was doing to me and why she was invading my mind. It was bad enough she was still at my house invading my space, which I wasn't complaining about, but I literally couldn't get her out of my head no matter how hard I tried. Imagining that it was her blessing me with some sloppy head which actually wasn't bad, I pumped deeper and deeper until I felt my toes curling and my nut brewing.

"Fuck girl," I said, biting my bottom lip hard as fuck, trying to stop myself from moaning out like a bitch. She couldn't take the dick when I was murdering the pussy, but she damn sure didn't have a problem taking it in her mouth as she gobbled my shit up like a damn snack.

"Hmmm," she moaned out.

Not wanting to hear her say shit and ruin the mood, I stuffed more dick down her throat as I tightened my grip on her head and started fucking her mouth rapidly until I bust all my kids down her throat.

"Fuckkkkkk!" I said as I pulled out and fell back. Looking at me with evil eyes, she jumped up and made a dash for the bathroom. Not bothering to ask her what that was about, I grabbed some napkins off of her nightstand wiping my dick off. Tossing them in the trash, I pulled my pants on, making sure to retrieve my gun I had discreetly removed and placed under the bed when she wasn't looking and started grabbing the rest of my shit preparing to leave. As I was picking my keys up, having just put my shoes on, the bathroom door open and she walked out with a towel in her hand, I guess for me to wipe myself with. Seeing me with my keys in my hand, she placed her hands on her hips and mugged me.

"Really, Midos?"

"Really what?" I said as I picked my phone up.

"You disrespect me, then you just gone try and leave?"

"A. You disrespected yourself by constantly blowing my shit up all day, every day to come fuck; not come take you out, not come chill, but come fuck. A nigga finally come through to this little ass place you call an apartment and you instead on delivering all that shit you was texting me; you came with some good but wack sex. B. I ain't trying to leave, I am leaving. Deuces," I said, chucking her the deuces as I walked out.

I don't know who the fuck she took me for talking about I disrespected her and then I'm tryna leave. Bitch got the nerve to portray herself as bougie in public and on social sites but be carrying on like that when nobody around.

Shaking my head, I walked out of her apartment and made a left, going down the stairs and over to the parking lot, popping the locks to my G-wagon and hopping in. Before I could start my car up good, this bitch was already calling me. Not bothering to answer, I declined the call and immediately blocked her ass. Pulling out the parking lot, I headed home to grab my stuff, so I could dip out to Egypt. I was headed home for a few days to see my brother Chance, my favorite cousin Dubie, and my pops. I haven't been that way in a minute. Besides I needed to get another shipment because we starting to run low as fuck on them pills that be selling out like crazy and I was gone personally pick the shit up this time, because I didn't have time for the shit Gibbs getting stolen again.

As long as I been in charge of shit, a nigga had never tried me like that. They done tried to run up on me and rob me, shot at me; actually shot me, etc, but them niggas ain't never dropped their nuts to actually fuck with my product. I was most definitely going to get to the bottom of this shit so I could see about that. Niggas prolly thinking shit sweet or I done went soft since I ain't went crazy, killing everything moving yet. I knew the longer I waited, the more comfortable they would be to try their luck again, and that's where they was gone fuck up at.

Pulling up into my driveway half an hour later, I put my car in park, not even bothering to park in the garage and got out the car. Walking inside my house, I heard loud music blasting like it's a party going on.

"What the fuck?" I said as I walked further into the house, pulling my gun out as I walked further into the house. Barbara had went to visit her kids last week and as far as I knew, Yemani was still locked away in her makeshift room. Ever since my birthday when she went on and on about somebody being gone, she had really retreated into herself. She came out her room and stuff, but she wasn't the shit talking person she normally is. Her loud mouth ass friend came over the next day, and they kicked it inside the room, but Yemani didn't come out after she was gone.

Since Zac and Desiree had apparently made it official, well; he said it's official, I don't think she agreed to the shit, but anyway, she was always at his place. I suggested to Yemani that she just stay here until she felt better because Desiree wasn't at their apartment. She agreed, and then a day later, when she said she felt better, I suggested she stay here until I straighten an issue out so that I knew she was safe at home by herself. I was really bullshitting, but I wasn't gone tell her that. I can't tell you why I didn't want her to leave, but I didn't. As I got closer to the kitchen, I realized the music was coming from there. Pushing the door open, I saw Yemani standing at the stove with a spatula in her hand, clad in some shorts that had her little booty looking good as hell and a muscle shirt on singing along with *Brandy's Missing You;* all off key and shit.

Though I'm missing you

I'll find a way to get through

Curious as to why this was her choice of song, I put my gun away as I just stood there watching her as she rotated between stirring the food, and auditioning for American Idol. It was apparent she needed a minute to get herself together and shake back because she seemed very vibrant today and the scene before me caused a smile to form on my face as I silently watched on. Doing a big finale soon was how she noticed me standing there, causing her to jump and grab her chest. Walking over to the radio, she turned it down.

"Damn, you scared me. So, your weird ass was just gone stand there like a creep watching me?" she sassed.

She's back, I thought as I smiled to myself.

"Says the same weird ass girl, who singing into a spatula, sounding like a cat being murdered or a hyena dying."

"I don't sound that bad," she said, poking her lips out. I paused to just stare at her for a few seconds before I said,

"You right' you don't sound that bad. I'm sorry for playing them like that because your ass most definitely sounds worse."

"Fuck you, Amyr."

"What I tell you about that Amyr mess?" I said, angry as fuck that Zac had slipped up and called me Amyr, jokingly in front of her, and now she refused to call me anything else. Even though my name sounded good as fuck rolling off her tongue, the shit still pissed me off.

"I don't like Midos. It sounds like some medicine I'd take if my stomach cramps up."

"I cramp stomachs up; I don't cure cramps. I'm usually the cause of them. Shit, I've even knocked a few periods on."

"Yo big head, little body ass always talking about that lil' chicken nugget dick. You don't be doing nothing but making bitches cry for wasting their time."

"Keep thinking that. I can't take somebody who ain't never felt a dick seriously, but I'd advise you to google me because it's not a bitch alive; whether they hate me or not, can fix their mouth to say Amyr Jarrah supplied weak dick or working with anything less than a monster," I said, cockily grabbing hold to my dick for emphasis.

Rolling her eyes at me, she turned back around to finish cooking the food. Checking my watch, I saw that I still had time to spare, so I ran upstairs to take a quick shower and make sure I had everything I needed. By the time I came back down to the kitchen wearing some grey sweatpants and a white tee, Yemani was sitting at the table, eating. Looking up as I walked in, her fork missed her mouth completely as her eyes instantly went to my dick. Smirking, I walked past her to the fridge to grab some water. Sometimes you just have to whip it out to show a mufuckas you ain't shit to play with. She wasn't gone keep playing a nigga with that chicken nugget shit. How her eyes bulged out of her head damn near, I think that joke has officially been retired.

Clearing her throat, she said, “You want some food?"

"Already tryna cater to a nigga and ain't got blessed yet," I couldn't help but say.

"Nigga, yo ass want some food or not?"

"Naw, I only eat Barbara cooking," I said, pulling out a chair at the table however and taking a seat.

The food she cooked which was some spaghetti, green beans, and dinner rolls looked ok, but it didn't scream; eat me, I'm good. Barbara usually cooked me spaghetti with sweet corn and cornbread. Shit always hit the spot. Now that's the only real way I'll eat spaghetti if I have cornbread.

"Well, why Barbara ain't here cooking for you?" she said with an attitude.

"She usually here all day every day, but she been on vacation and a nigga really been starving. I miss her ass more than I thought she banned from leaving me again," I truthfully said.

"You an ole disrespectful ass nigga. If the bitch here every day and I been here every day that mean, you been had me in a house you share with another bitch. See, you city niggas wasn't raised right because back home niggas ain't that damn crazy," she said, going on and on. It took me a second to realize she thought Barbara was my woman and not my housekeeper, cook, and second mom. Pulling out my phone, I checked my email and responded to a few of them.

"Oh, and you just gone be on your phone and ignore me like a bitch?" she said angrily as her chest rose up and down rapidly.

"Listen bruh, watch your fucking mouth when you talking to me. I done already told your stupid ass once before and this the last time I'ma say the shit. You not about to keep playing with me like I'ma lame ass fuck nigga or some shit. You, not my bitch so I don't owe you shit, but if you must know, Barbara is my housekeeper and old nanny, and you did meet her; she took care of you before she left," I said, getting up and leaving out the kitchen before I ended up choking her little ass up. It's good we wasn't together because I'm certain with her mouth nigga be done beat her stupid ass up.

Stepping off my private jet, getting into the car that was waiting for me, I fell back into the seats powering my phone back on. Replying back to everybody but Yemani, I then tossed my phone and just gazed out the window taking in the raw beauty that Egypt had to offer. Contrary to what is displayed on television with the Egyptian tombs and pounds and pounds of sand, it was so much more than that. It was a beautiful plush and thriving country. My father lived in Cairo, which is actually the capital of Egypt and the largest city in Africa also nicknamed the victorious city. Pulling into his huge estate; that made my mini mansion look like a Barbie Doll dream house or some shit, the driver came around and opened the door, and I hopped out, walking past at least 35 armed men until I reached the front door. My father was a very powerful man, so people were always gunning for him, they would never catch him slipping though. If they made it past all this shit, then that had truly earned the right to kill him, hell. His shit was locked down tighter than Fort Knox. Walking into the house, I headed down the long spiral hallway until I eventually made it to the immaculately designed living room that appeared to come straight from a home decor magazine.

"Aleumu Amyr," *(Uncle Amyr)* My five year old niece Ain said as she ran towards me, grabbing my around my legs and hugging me tightly. I loved this little girl like she was the child I never wanted. It's fucked up to say, but it sums it up perfectly. I don't want children, but if I happened to have one, I would love her unconditionally and I would be the proudest man in the world if I had a junior. The world just couldn't fuck with two of me at the same damn time.

"Eayan kayf al'aemam 'ukht almufadilat tafeal sayidatan jmyl?" *(Ain, how is uncle's favorite niece doing, pretty lady??*

“Walakun em 'iimi aibnat 'ukhtuk faqat.” (*But uncle, I’m your only niece,)* she said to me.
I still spoke to her in Arabic because she hasn’t learned English yet. Before I could respond to her, another door opened and her father, my baby brother Chance, and my pops came walking out. Ain’s nanny called out to her to come with her upstairs.
“Son,” my dad said in his broken English as he embraced me into a hug. He always hugged me as if he hadn’t seen me in years when in actuality, I just saw him a few weeks ago.
“Brother,” Chance said as he hugged me next.
“What’s been up, man?” I asked him because unlike my dad, it’s been months since I’ve seen my brother.
Although we grew up on two different continents, we were surprisingly very close. I would nut up quick behind him and I often times had to stop myself from running to Egypt when something happened to him. I remember one day

I caught a 26 hour flight here because this kid in his class had beat him up. That shit had pissed me off. Even though when I got in town, it was 3 am in the morning. I still waited patiently until school opened to beat that lil' niggas' ass. I had to make an example out of him and let niggas know shit wasn't sweet and they wasn't about to play with my baby brother like that, like it wouldn't be any consequences.

I remember asking my father why he didn't have the same reaction when he got mad after finding out what I had done. He replied that he was raising men and not bitches. Men fight back when attacked and bitches cry. If I didn't think I'd be chastised for correcting him, I sholl would have let him know that I wasn't sure what classification of bitches he was referring to because the ones in America not gone get hit and cry. You hit them and they'll square up with your ass. Shit, some will even call themselves trying to fight a nigga, hell. I understood the method to his madness but I still didn't respect his decisions in regards to Chance. However, it took for one mufucka to come up missing for all that shit to be cut short. No lie, before his wife, I would have bet all my money this pretty boy ass nigga was gay. He just extremely clean with feminine ways, shit, I had my suspicions and I think Pops did as well that's why he let his ass get beat up like that. Trust me if he would have stepped in, all that shit would have been dead game.

"Where Dubie ass at?" I asked them. We were currently sitting in my dad's den having a drink relaxing. That food I just hit was so damn good that a nigga was halfway fucking sleep.

"I don't know. I haven't heard from him in a minute," Chance said.

"It's your cousin, you know how he is. He'll eventually pop back up," my father said.

Dubie was the son of my uncle Edjo, who was my father's brother. His only brother actually. They both were kind of like the black sheeps of the family. Granted, we were a crime family that was heavily into drugs and anything else illegal, so imagine being a black sheep to that type of family. Let’s just say like father like son. Although Dubie was raised by my father after his father lost his mind, he still seemed to grow up truly his father’s child. Edjo’s trouble days were over before they even really started. He went from laying niggas down, to dressing stuffed animals up. He literally had lost his mind. They say when you have a traumatic experience that your brain can't handle, your mind switches off. That's apparently what happened because this nigga is crazy as fuck. One time I went to go see him and fucked around and moved his stuffed giraffe out the chair, and this nigga damn near lost his fucking mind.

“I didn’t realize how late it was,” Chance said, glancing at his watch. “I have to get Ain home; I will talk to you later brother. Father, I shall call you when I get home,” he said, excusing himself from the table and walking out the room, putting an extra twist in his walk. *Yep, this nigga sweeter than sugar but that's still my heart,* I thought but still shook my head.

"Let's take our drinks out on the balcony, I have something important to discuss with you," my father said to me. Attempting to study his face to see if I could figure out what it was he wanted to talk to me about, I downed my drink, refilled it, and walked out onto the balcony with him.

"Listen, son, I'm-"

"You not sick or no shit like that?" I blurted out. I'm not sure why that was the first thing that came to my mind. I guess because it was still weighing heavy on me that my mother could possibly relapse although her doctors assured and reassured me that she wasn't.

"Why would you think that?"

"I don't know."

"Well I'm not sick, but I am getting old. I've did everything I could, trained you, rode you extra hard, and pushed you to this point because I'm ready to step down. I'm tired, I'm still young enough to enjoy the fruits of my labor, and I want to spend the rest of my life with your mother while I still can."

"Ok, so who you had in mind to take your place?"

"My firstborn son of course, as it has always been. Well, Edjos should have taken over instead of me, but you see the state he is in."

"I don't want your crown; this is your legacy, not mine. I'm making mine back in the states. Give it to Chance."

"Chance! Son, Chance wouldn't last two days in this world."

"You really don't give him enough credit. I think he would surprise you if you took the time to be as hands-on with him as you were with me," I said, still trying to progress the fact that he wanted to step down and hand it all over to me. For a split second, I let myself entertain the idea of running both Houston and this entire country. I was already getting a headache just thinking about it.

“Just think about it, son.”

“I just did, and it made my head hurt. I’ve got a good thing going in America. Something I’m proud of. Something I’ve built on my own. You inherited all of this. Not saying you haven’t worked hard to build it up and keep it afloat, but it was passed down. Houston wasn’t handed to me. I earned it,” I said. “What if I help work with Chance?”

“Like ask yourself do you even believe Chance is built for this? I may not fully understand him, but he’s my son, and I would die if he were ever seriously hurt. An ass whooping never hurt anybody; you can go to sleep and live to fight another day. With a bullet, there is no other day; you just go to sleep.”

Deciding to change the subject, for now, I said, "What's the status on them niggas that's stole our shit?"

"Still no word, it's like they disappeared into thin air. Not a trace or piece of evidence, but I'm still working on it," he said. "Well, I'm about to retire to my room, just do me a favor and think on what I said tonight. This empire has been in our family for generations; you are our last hope, son. You know Dubie nor your brother have the needed capacity to run this entire thing," he said, before turning and walking off, leaving me with a mind full of thoughts. One thing was for sure; this definitely wasn't how I imagined things would go when I decided to come home.

"Bitch, I figured I would find you here," I said to Dubie, dapping him up as I took a seat at the bar. I loved my little brother to death; even though we came from two different worlds, but me and Dubie were just alike in a lot of ways. He was a hot head just like me, and I know with a little training and discipline, we would really shake some shit up in this underground world.

"Shit you know this my spot," he said laughing. Even though he's never been to America, he learned to speak English fluently.

"What's been up bro?" I asked him.

"Shit you know me, same ole same ole. Trying to stay out of trouble and keep my head above ground."

"You good?" I asked him because he was fidgety a bit but I chalked that up to his probably using again. Back in the day we were at a party, and somebody gave us a blunt but I declined it, and he hit it. I learned at a very early age to never smoke from shit I didn't roll up or seen getting rolled because passing on that blunt saved my life. Turns out it was laced with coke because dude who's blunt it was, was a functioning addict and could handle the shit. A 16-year-old child could not. It took a few years to get him clean once we found out what was going on, but I guess he was relapsing. I hoped not, because he had been going so good.

"Yeah, I'm straight shit just tired of pushing these nickel and dime bags like I'm some corner boy or some shit."

Last time he was caught using the very product we pushed on the streets, pops demoted him from his position and had reduced him to pushing small stuff like weed and not even in big ounces. He went from moving weight to moving baggies.

"Damn that's tough," I said. "If you ever want to come to America, you know I'ma lookout," I said to him. "I can find something for you to do."

He looked at me, and I thought I saw something flicker in his eyes, but I was gone faster than I could blink. "You always looking out, brother," he said dapping me up. "Well, let me get out of here and go check on my pops before I have to check in. Your dad treats me like a crackhead and has me checking in every hour on the hour to make sure I'm not using like I'm a child. If I miss check-in, he cuts down the amount of weed he gives me. How quickly he forgot who the rightful owner of this shit is, to begin with," he said with a growl on his face, that he quickly replaced with a smug expression.

I couldn't pinpoint what was going on with him because the last time I saw him, he was singing a different tune and had a whole different attitude. Shaking the feeling off, I said, "I'ma roll with you to see Uncle Edjo. How he doing? Last time I saw him, he had an episode. He getting better?"

"He's doing as well as a man could do that is reduced to having the brain of a child. I used to have hope that he would snap out of it, now, I just have hope that he will live to see my children be born."

"Word, you got kids? Shit, moms been pressuring a nigga to have kids but that shit is dead game."

"Hell yeah, my girl pregnant with twins."

"Shit, double trouble."

"Shit, more like double murder charges. They both girls; I'm in for the fight of my life because I know they gone give me a run for my money," he said, laughing as his eyes lit up at the mention of his kids. I was happy he was out of his stump that he was just in a minute ago because that shit was weird as hell. *Must be the effects of that crack*, I thought as I followed behind him.

CHAPTER 14

Roses are red; violent are blue, I guess I kinda like you…

YEMANI

"Are you even listening to me?" I asked Desiree because she was currently looking down at her phone with a huge grin on her face.
"What?" she said, finally putting it down and looking up at me. We were back at our own apartment for the first time in a long time. Zac had a business meeting to go to, and she didn't want to stay at his place by herself. I was still at Midos' house, but I came here to be with her until she decided to dip out again. I was happy

that she was happy, but I needed her to help me fix my problems now.
"Desiree!"
"Look Yemani, you've been singing this same tune for a few days now, and I've told you over and over again to just apologize to him. I mean, I don't see why you care since according to you and I quote 'I don't like that stupid ass, dog ass, shit talking nigga. We just cooling nothing more, nothing less.' So again, why does it bother you he purposely reading every message you sending him and choosing not to respond?"
"Because," I said, mad because she had called me on my shit.
"Because what, Yemani? This, not a little ass boy like Tyron, that you used to dealing with. This a grown ass man, who on some grown ass man shit. He not about to let you talk to him crazy and think it's cool. Especially since you made it perfectly clear you wasn't fucking with him like that on no type of level but friends. Shit, you

gotta pick a struggle, boo. You can't not fuck with him and talk shit to him."

"That's the thing," I said, blushing as I diverted my eyes down to the ground.

"Ohhhhh," she said with her hand over her mouth as she pointed her finger at me. "You like him, bitch. I knew it," she said, laughing.

"Well, yeah I do, but I think he fuck with a lot of bitches and prolly out of my league."

"Shit, age wise; them hoes might have you beat but according to Zac, you the only one succeeded where them hoes failed cuz ain't nobody ever been in that nigga shit like that. As far as them hoes know, he got a condo."

Hearing her tell me that no other females had ever been inside his house warmed my heart on the inside. *Yesss bitch. One point for Yemani.*

"Ok, so if I'm the only one has been there, and I'm more special than them, how can I get him to like me like them?"

"Umm first off, you need to lose the fucking attitude. Less anger, more sexy. How can he know you like him if you always arguing with him and walking around looking like driving miss daisy and shit? You need to channel your inner sexy hoe."

"But I don't have an inner sexy hoe," I said in a pout.

"Every girl has an inner hoe, and the first step is admitting it."

"Ok inner hoe, what else?"

"No back talk and you need to learn how to cook since you said he wouldn't even touch your food," she said, laughing.

"That's not funny, and I can cook."

"Yea, directional food. Anything else you suck at. You gone have to feed a nigga like that. Well, I don't technically think he can classify as a nigga," she said with a puzzled look on her face as she thought about it.

"He can't," I said, laughing.

"Oh, excuse the hell out of me."

"But bitch, don't do him. His housekeeper comes back tomorrow, I'ma gone ask her for lessons. Anyway, how's it feel being in a relationship again?" I asked her as I got up from the couch to grab some popcorn just as the doorbell rang. I had invited Krystal over for a girls' night. Walking over and opening the door, she walked in with a huge smile on her face. I leaned out and gave her a hug. Even though I've only known her for a short amount of time, she's grown on me, and I have missed her. I start classes again next week, so she haven't seen her since the morning after the party. Although, after I got a new phone, I had been texting her ever since. After I explained what happened to the school, my teachers agreed to all send me my lessons every day to my email, so I hadn't missed a beat with assignments. I was all caught up and eager to get back to school to have something else to occupy my time.

"I've missed you so much," Krystal said as we broke apart. "Hey Desiree," she cheerful said as she walked over and sat on the couch.
Going from disliking the idea of me having another friend, to slowly coming around, Desiree said, "Hey girl, aren't you looking cute today."
This was true because today, Krystal was sporting a blue jean shirt, cut off blue jeans, with some blue jean slides that had a bantu bowtie on top.
"Thank you," she said.
"Now, back to what I was saying, Desiree, how's it feel?"
"I wouldn't know," she said.
"What?" I asked her.
"Girl, that is not my boyfriend. Ok, I agreed to try things out, but that was in the heat of the moment. I don't think I'm really ready to give someone else my heart."
"Ok, why you basically moved in, then? And why you can barely keep your phone out of your

hands or a smile off your face? Bitch, you love that nigga, so I don't know why you lying or who you tryna fool best friend," I said.

"What if as soon as I admit I love him, some fucked up shit happens?" she said as her entire tone changed. Clearly this was a question she had struggled with for a while.

"I don't have the answer to that question, but I do know you deserve to be happy and I know Zac really likes you."

"Who in the house, driving any car you want, coming and going as you please, fucking his fine ass whenever, and got these hoes all in their feelings? How many times I saw him post you as his WCW and will check a bitch, quick, who try and come for you only? Girl bye. If they ain't love, bitch, I don't know what is. That nigga loves your ass to death, so no need to keep trying to run from it," Krystal said, reaching for the popcorn I had sat on the table. We both just turned and looked at her. Once she realized we

had stopped talking and was just looking at her, she said," I- well, I was just saying. I-I. I didn't mean anything," she said as her voice trailed off. "Listen, I'm sorry."
"Yeah, sorry for holding out on us, bitch, you right about all of that you said. Our ass starting to rub off on you," Desiree said, laughing. "Shit, Zac ass do be checking them hoes left and right, though. He don't play that coming for me shit."
"And I think that's so sweet," I said.
"Girl, now when you gone quit playing and give Midos some ass," Krystal said, getting on me next. I looked at her with bugged out eyes. I don't know who this new outspoken person was, but I liked it.
"Shit, baby steps; she gotta admit she likes his ass first, that's the easy part. Hell, the giving him some ass part gone be the struggle," Desiree ass said.

"Girl, as fine as he is, combined with all the rumors, I don't see what the struggle would be? Krystal said.

"What rumors?" I curiously asked.

"Well, not even rumors; more like known gossiping facts," Krystal said. "The salon I go to get my hair did is always full of bitches talking about Midos and that anaconda dick he working with; that's been known to fuck your whole life up," she said, making me quickly think back to when he walked into the kitchen with those grey sweatpants and I almost choked on my food when I saw it just casually resting on his knee chilling, like how you doing.

"I take it fucking up insides is a good thing?" I asked. I was embarrassed at how sexually clueless I really was.

"Hell yeah," they both said at the same time.

"Bitch, what nigga rearranging them insides? Spill the tea, hoe because I knew you wasn't

glowing and acting brand new for nothing," Desiree said.
Blushing and looking down, Krystal said," Debo."
"Bitch, I know you fucking lying," Desiree screamed, jumping up.
"Who is Debo?" I asked in confusion because I felt left out this conversation.
"Bitch, if you gone get yo man, you need to start being more observant of things going on around him. Debo's crazy ass is their first in command."
"Hey, don't do my baby. He not crazy, just a tad bit misunderstood," Krystal said.
"How did this happen?"
"I don't know honestly. We just met by fate one day and clicked instantly," she said.
I had to give that hoe the side eye because she quickly forgot I knew her when she was quiet, shy and reserved. That doesn't sound like the same person that would instantly click with a crazy mufucka.

"Ok, well not instantly, but we did have one thing in common that day we met at the store. We both bought the same thing, hoy cherries, beef jerky, and white grape swisher sweets."
"What you buying swishers for?" I asked her shocked that she even smoked.
"Shit, the same reason he was buying it, so I could roll up and get my mind right. What Boosie said? Smoking on purple ease my mind," Krystal said.
"I hope you knew not to smoke no damn Reggie," Desiree said, calling me out.
"Ohh bitch, you tried it," I said, laughing. Looking at the horrified expression on Krystal's face caused me to laugh even harder.
"Bitch, you came for my entire life with that shit. I wish a bitch would try and give me some Reggie," Krystal said, seemingly appalled. Trying to talk through the tears that were rolling down her face, Desiree said," This ignorant bitch asked a nigga in Third Ward for some Reggie."

Turning to look at me, Krystal said, "Bless yo heart."

I was feeling some type of way at this point if even Krystal, who was just a lame nerd a few weeks ago, knew more about this than me. Shit, it wasn't my fault that's all we had in town. I think. Hell, that's my excuse and I was sticking with it. After they had both calmed down laughing, Desiree said," So the other day a commercial came on advertising some new ride at Six Flags and I jokingly said to Zac that it looked cool and I've never been to Six Flags, and he should take me, and he agreed. So you bitches need to get your niggas involved so we all can make this a fun trip.

"Bitch, you know I don't do heights," I said.

"I'm down," Krystal said.

"But I'm in," I quickly said. I be damn if I'm left behind while everybody having fun. "How I ask Midos to go?

"First, cook him a good dinner," Krystal said.

"That hoe can't cook," Desiree said.

"Oh baby, that's not good," Krystal said.

"I can cook directional food, bitch," I shot back.

"Ok, he has a black housekeeper, so that means he eats soul food and not that Muslim stuff," Desiree said.

"Bitch, what's Muslim stuff?" I said, laughing.

"Shit I don't know, none American."

Shaking my head at her ass, I got up, going into the room and grabbing my laptop. I was going to research some good recipes that wouldn't be that hard for me to make.

Walking back into the living room, Desiree said, “I hope you research how to find your inner hoe because when you almost kill him, trying to cook, you gone need a plan b to fall back on."

"Shit, you can't cook nor seduce him? " Krystal said, laughing.

"Fuck both y'all. Desiree, your ass cannot cook either, why you laughing?"

"Shit, but I can ride the fuck out that nigga dick and make a simple meal that, that nigga will gobble up because he so drained of energy from me working him out," she said, shrugging.
"You hoes need prayer. I can throw down in the kitchen. My big sister taught me," Krystal said.
"Well, we'll have cooking lessons later because that nigga comes home tomorrow. Right now, she needs a decent recipe and tips on seduction," Desiree said.
"I don't need help seducing a nigga. I kept Tyron around for years and was this close to fucking Josh," I said.
"Umm, you chickened out on fucking Tyron and haven't talked to him since, and you only let Josh finger you. Both of them under the age of 20. Midos, a grown ass man who won't go for any of that shit. You can't start shit you not prepared to finish dealing with a grown ass man, sis," Desiree said.
"Sholl in the fuck can't," Krystal said, agreeing.

"I don't think I'm ready for sex yet, we barely even on good terms," I said.

"Nobody is telling you to fuck the nigga. I mean, if you trying to seduce him just to get him to like you more and go on a trip then that's for all the wrong reasons, and it won't guarantee make him like you more. You only get one chance to lose your virginity, so make it count," Desiree said to me. Letting the advice they both gave me marinate in, we chilled for the remainder of the night.

The next day, I woke up early to go back to Midos' house so I could tidy up the place and be there when he got home. The Dallas trip was in a week, and I had plans on enjoying my time there with Midos, hopefully as more than friends, but I wouldn't rush anything. I was giddy with excitement just as the thought of seeing him today. I actually did miss him while he was away, and it really hurt my feelings that he just read my text and didn't respond. I did need to work on my mouth, and I was gone try very hard to watch what I said to him. Deciding to head to the mall and get pampered up and made over a bit, I jumped into my truck and headed in that direction. Desiree was still sleep because she was the type that didn't like waking up before noon unless she had to, and Krystal was laid up with Debo, so I was on my own.

To relax my nerves, I popped my aux cord into my phone and turned my Pandora station onto Gates. I was a huge fan, and his music always seemed to relax my nerves, which is weird because it's so crazy and violent sometimes, but it always did the trick whether I was happy or sad, it was my goto music. As Gates' *Posed to Be in Love* came on, I rapped along with the song, reciting it word for word as I let my drug of choice take over and ease my mind.

Hearing my favorite part come on, I turned the music up loud as I could and spit the verse hard as hell. “No understanding; I’m ignorant, you gonna probably say that I’m tripping. Throw the left hand; you duck that one, this right bitch won't miss you. Beat a bitch like Chris Brown, go back to jail, no question. No surrender, no retreat, park the whip, hop out on feet. Me and her brother juuged together, he bet not get in my business.”

I was at the red light top let down, all into the song when I heard horns honking from behind me. Honking my horn back at them, I pulled off down the street, then a few minutes later pulled into the huge parking lot of the Galleria. Parking, I got out and headed inside. My first stop was to Sephora to grab more makeup; then I was off to Victoria's Secret.

"Hello, welcome to Victoria's Secret," the friendly staff said as soon as I walked in.

"Hello," I said back as I immediately went to the PINK section to pick through a few new panties.

After I had successfully picked out five new pairs of boy shirts, I ventured back on the more sexy side of the store, hoping to find the perfect panty and bra set to do the trick.
"Do you need some help?" A sales associate asked me after I had been staring at different items going on an hour.
"I'm embarrassed to say," I said to her.
"Nonsense, I've heard it all. Nothing is embarrassing."
Hesitating a bit and kicking myself for not forcing Desiree to get up with me and help with this sort of thing, I reluctantly gave in and told her my dilemma. "I'm looking for something that says, I like you but I'm not desperate to lose my virginity just yet so let's take things slow, and another one that says ok I'm ready."
Chuckling softly, she said," See, that wasn't hard at all. You are actually in luck because our fall collection just arrived and looking at you, I have the perfect I'm not desperate to lose my virginity

outfit in mind," she said, walking off in the opposite direction. I stood there unmoving, looking nervously around at the confident faces shopping as I waited nervously for her to return.

"Here we are," she said as she came back moments later with a handful of stuff.

"This color will look amazing with your skin complexion. Might I make a suggestion on your hair? I think a sexy asymmetrical bob would look amazing on you. Maybe a light brown with honey blonde highlights," the sales associate said to me as she handed me a lace pink bra that looked more like a sports bra that had matching lace boy shorts. Next, she handed me a pink silk robe.

"This is your 'I'm not desperate to lose my virginity I just want to let you know what I'm working with outfit.' You put this on with this robe and that hair and let it accidentally fall open. Trust me that will for sure get his attention. It's sexy yet casual at the same time. Now moving on

to your ‘ok I’m ready’ look," she said, this time handing me what looked to be a black lace barely finished piece of fabric with holes all in it.
"This one is torn," I said to her.
"It's a bodysuit with slits on the sides, a see-through breast area and a crotch-less bottom area," she explained to me. I was still clueless as I tried holding it up to my body to get a visual on how it would look on me.
"Trust me this will blow his mind. You just the right amount of breast and body to pull this off. It will definitely let him know without any words needed, that you are in fact ready," she said. I still wasn't confident, but she was gorgeous and seemed to know exactly what she was talking about, so I was throwing caution to the wind and trusting her judgment. After I paid for everything and thanked her again, I went to get a manicure, pedicure and my eyebrows did.

Two hours later, I emerged from the mall feeling confident and rejuvenated. On top of getting a manicure and all of that, I also got a bikini wax. I was going all out. As I was driving back to my apartment, I spotted a beauty salon and made an illegal turn in the middle of the street as I whipped into the parking lot. I always only wear long weave, but keeping up with my transformation, I was going to try a bob. *I hope all my hard work pays off,* I thought as I pushed the door to the salon open.

CHAPTER 15

I like a challenge…

MIDOS

"Yeah, I'm just getting home now, Ma," I said to my Ma dukes as I pulled up to my house and parked.

"I heard you went home to see your daddy, how it go?"

"What you mean, how did it go? Was something supposed to happen?" I asked her.

"No, I mean, did he ask you?"

"So you knew about the shit?" I asked, getting kind of heated. Now I feel like both of them was on some other shit.

"Yes and no. He briefly talked to me about his wishes to step down, and I thought it was a good idea. I may not know how much longer I'm going to be on this earth, but I do know I don't want to live the rest of my days out with him."

"Man I talked to your doctor already, you are in remission."

"Doesn't mean I can't die of old age," she shot back. "Anyway, when he told me, I just assumed he would be passing things down to you because hell, his other son he had with that wench is a scrawny, timid something. Poor thing would get himself hurt. I often wondered about him until he had that beautiful little girl. At least, he gave his mother a grandbaby," she said starting that again.

"Ma, don't start, didn't I tell you I was gone get you a darn grandbaby," I said, slapping myself on the forehead because I had gotten so busy and forgotten all about the shit. Shit getting so crazy out here; it's hard to remember everything. I was for sure gone find her a damn grandbaby to talk to this week so she could get off case about it. A nice, 17-year-old boy would be good. Well naw, that nigga might come with issues, and then I would have to bat his stupid ass up. A girl would be better so they could go shopping together and shit.

"I heard even Dubie got twins on the way, it's just me that can't be great," she said. I had tuned her out, and she was still talking.

"Woman, you will have that grandbaby next week. But listen Ma, I gotta go," I said, opening my car door.

"Next week? How, Amyr? You gone steal somebody child or something?" she said.

"Steal somebody's child? Why the hell would I do that? Man, I'll finish discussing this with you later, I'm just getting home and I'm tired. I will talk to you later, love you."

"Ok son," she said, sounding sad. "I love you."

“I’ll get you that grandkid, mom. Love you, bye,” I said, hanging up the phone and getting out of the car.

Walking into my house, I was somewhat relieved to get home. I had so much shit on my mind that I wanted nothing more than to relax and laze around a few days. I had no desire to take over Egypt when I was content with my current status, but if I didn't do it, then who would? The empire has been in my family for decades, and I would hate to be the reason we fell from grace. Walking upstairs, my mind was full of thoughts as I placed my bags on the floor and grabbed some gym clothes so I could get ready to go workout. When I was stressed, I hit the gym or fell off in some pussy. I didn't have time for a clingy ass bitch right now, so my built-in gym it was. Changing into basketball shorts, a white t-shirt and Jordan's, I walked downstairs and headed down a hallway, which when opened led to an additional set of stairs that led to my downstairs gym.

Jumping right on it, I immediately started hitting the iron hard before I moved on to push-ups, and ending with running the treadmill. After going hard for 45 minutes straight, I was done. Walking back up the stairs into the main area of the house, I was headed for the kitchen to grab a bottle of water when I walked past Yemani, coming out of the hallway bathroom clad only in a silk robe, looking sexy as fuck. My dick immediately bricked up as I took in her body in that robe, what stood out to me was the sexy new hairstyle she was sporting. Shit looked so good on her that I almost bent her lil' ass over and gave her all this pressure.

"Midos, I didn't know you had come back home."

"So, no Amyr anymore?" I asked just to fuck with her. I think I liked to push her buttons sometimes.

"Umm no, naw, I know you don't like it, so I was giving you a pass today," she said fidgeting around. She went from putting her hands on her

hips, to folding them across her chest, to dropping them down by her side.
"Yo ok, shawty? Yo ass tweeking and shit. You ain't been smoking none of that bullshit as weed or nothing, huh?" I asked her.
"What?" she said, laughing. "No. Course not. Why would you say that? You funny, hahaha. You jokester you," she said, hitting me on my shoulder as she began laughing.
"Bruh, you wigging," I told her as I left her standing there as I jogged up the stairs to start a shower. Half an hour later, I emerged feeling slightly better as the smell of food cooking brought me back downstairs. Barbara had called me and told me she would be back this week, so I was hoping she had gotten here early.

"Smells good in here," I said pushing open the swinging doors leading to the kitchen only to instead see Yemani cooking. *Not this again. This bitch must be tryna poison me.*

"I see what's going on in here. I get it now with you acting weird earlier and now you cooking," I said.

"You do?" she asked, turning around facing me with her robe wide open revealing a pink lace type top and boy shorts. "Oh crap; this thing keeps coming open, sorry," she said, quickly closing her robe back.

"It's so damn hot outside anyway, you really don't even need a robe. We both adults. Well, you what, 19? Well, half and adult and an adult."

"I'm not half an adult, I'm grown," she said.

"Shit, cool take it off then miss, I'm grown."

"First tell me what you think going on here," she said placing a plate of food in front of me that actually looked good, which made me even more skeptical. Pushing the plate away, I said,

"Naw, I'm good."

"But you didn't even taste it," she said.

"Yeah, because your ass not about to catch a nigga slipping like that. Gone have to come harder if you think that shit gone work on a nigga like me."

"Catch you slipping? Nigga, what the fuck is you talking about?" she said, dropping the act and reverting back to normal.

"Yo ass acting all weird and shit because you mad a nigga ain't text you back, so you tried acting nice and even cooked some shit that looked good, so I would actually want to eat it. But this was all a part of your plan to poison my ass. Even tried to butter a nigga up by stripping and shit," I said, serious as hell.

"You had to have been dropped on your head as a child because you dumb as you look. I'm not tryna poison, your stupid ass. I just wanted you to go as my date on the couple's trip everyone going on. Zac taking Desiree to Six Flags, and your first in command, Debo taking my friend Krystal. I was hoping you would take me, and I…" her voice trailed off. “I like you, I just didn’t know how to show it so I googled some shit on how to approach you and then the lady at Victoria’s Secret said this outfit would work and a different hair color,” she said, going on and on.

I walked towards her and grabbed her lips in a kiss, pulling her body closer to mines, opening her robe and caressing my hands up and down her body. I let her mouth go and attacked her neck, biting and sucking on it, trying to leave a mark. Hearing her moaning softly was turning me on even more, but I knew she wasn’t ready for that just yet, so I reluctantly pulled back.

“Ask,” I said.

Looking at me she sucked in big gulps of air struggling to catch her breath; she said, “Huh?”

“You said you didn’t know how to get me to be your date for the couple's trip, just ask.”

“Oh. Yeah right. Will you take me?”

"Yeah, we can do that, but about this liking me thing. I'm the wrong person to want to have feelings for and go falling for."

"Why?"

"Because I'm not shit, but at least I can admit that."

"That sounds like a damn excuse to me. Let me find out you afraid to like someone because you may find out that you have these things called feelings," she said.

"Feelings are for suckers. I don't like women; I fuck women. Nothing more, nothing less. You a virgin and you young, so it's no way you would agree to what I have to offer," I said.

"You don't know that," she shot back. I just stared at her for a few minutes before I backed away and headed out the kitchen.

I was trying to get away from her ass before I gave her this dick. No matter what that mouth was saying, I know this wasn't what she wanted. I had intentions on taking a cold shower, when I paused and turned towards the door, grabbing my keys and I headed out the house. This job was bigger than a damn shower, it required actual pussy, so after I jumped in my car, I sent Lilly a text, telling her to be buck naked and ready when I got there. I may couldn't fuck Yemani's world up, but I could definitely put this dick in somebody's life tonight who knew what to do with it.

"How the fuck did, yo weak ass really let Desiree talk to into something like this?" I asked Zac as we walked behind the girls, talking. When I agreed to come, I didn't agree to no damn couples' matching shirts and all this extra shit Desiree had for everybody. Zac's ass already had that damn girl spoiled rotten.

"Shit, I honestly don't even remember agreeing to the shit. I vaguely heard her mention the shit before she gave a nigga some fire ass head. I must have agreed to the shit during that time," he said, shrugging his shoulders.

"And yo ass had the nerve to go along with the shit as well," I said to Debo, pointing my finger at him. "Y'all niggas done went soft as fuck, I'm disappointed," I said, shaking my head.

"Hold up, bitch; you got a shirt on as well, so that means Yemani whipped you into going too," Debo said.

"Hell yeah. Shit, least me and Debo got some ass out the deal, I heard Yemani ain't let you pop the cherry yet, so how the hell did she get you to agree?" Zac said.

"She just asked," I said. "And wore a sexy robe and lingerie," I added in as they both burst out laughing.

"Nigga, acting like you in high school, geeked up off clothes and shit and got the nerve to call us soft," Debo said, laughing.

“Fuck y’all, what’s up with Danger and Killa? We getting up with them niggas tonight?” I asked.
“Shit, I sent a message to them to hit me up. Last I heard, Killa was off with his new chick on vacation, but Dang here,” Zac said to me, but I had tuned him out as I focused on Yemani, wiggling around in front of me with these colorful flower shorts on that had her little booty poking out and looking good. She had cut her shirt up, making it a belly shirt and paired it with a blue jean jacket that had cuffed sleeves.
"You heard me?" Zac asked me.
"Huh? What's up?" I said.
"Nigga in a trance and shit looking at Yemani, ole perverted ass," Debo said, laughing.
"Ain't nobody thinking about her ass," I said, waving them off. “What's up?"
"So what you gone do about this thing with your pops?" Zac repeated.

"Shit, I don't know. It's not my focus right now. My main focus is finding these niggas who hit my shit and Brock's, ole inspector gadget ass. I'll deal with my pops issue later."

"Brock, we will eventually find, but you gotta better chance of finding Casper than finding them niggas who hit your pops boat," Debo said.

"Naw, that's what I pay mufuckas for, you included, so I need you to have your team get on this because I expect to have them niggas soon, including Brock because this bitch is working my last nerve; steady spray painting messages like a bitch. Who does that? A nigga ain't scared of no damn message on a wall. Spray these nuts and catch this fade, I wouldn't even waste a bullet on his ass," I said.

"We gone catch him soon, but just where do you expect us to get imaginary niggas from? If it didn't come directly from your pops, I almost would have bet money on it that them niggas was lying about being robbed and just took the shit themselves. I mean, who else seen the shit besides the nigga who reported back? Where the bodies at of the men? Shit, nobody talking, the streets is quiet as fuck on that issue. Pulling off some shit like that, niggas would have been running their mouths by now. Especially if they think they got away with the shit," Debo said.

"We gone sniff their asses out one way or another. Fuck waiting on them to come to us. It's time to start shaking us shit and dropping bodies," I said.

"Now you talking my language," Debo said.

"You two crazy ass mufuckas," Zac said just as Desiree came and kissed him on the lips.

"Get a room," I said.

“Don’t be a hater all your life, Midos,” Desiree shot back.

“Hate on that nigga? You funny,” I said to her just as Krystal walked up and hugged Debo.

"Amyr," I heard Yemani call me. I've picked up on the fact that she only called me that now when she wanted something.

"What's up, baby girl?"

"Will you go on that ride with me?" she asked, pointing to a ride resembling the Ferris wheel at a state fair.

"Damn bitch, we said stick to the plan, give them a kiss then ask," Desiree said.

"Oh hell naw," Zac said.

"But baby, all the other men going with their women. It's a two-seater romantic ride," Desiree said, trying to plead her point. Instead of Yemani having a comeback to what Desiree said, she just stood looking at me.

Before I could fix my mouth and form a lie as to why I could go, she hit me with those puppy dog eyes.

"Yeah, I'll go," I found myself saying. *Wait, that's not what the fuck I wanted to say. Nigga, real niggas don't do this gay shit.*

When I looked up at her, she had the biggest smile on her face that made a nigga feel good that I was the cause of it.

“Thank you,” she said, throwing her arms around my neck, rewarding me with a kiss on the lips.

“See Midos mean ass is going with Yemani,” Desiree said with her arms folded.

“Baby, will you go with me?” Krystal asked Debo.

“Yeah, shawty you got that,” Debo said to her.

“What happened to the kiss? Y’all bitches left me hanging,” Desiree said.

“Hey, I was all for your plan, but shit, Yemani’s idea worked so I had to try it,” Krystal said laughing.

“Shit, I knew I probably would have messed everything up, so I just did what he told me to do the first time, just ask,” Yemani said, shrugging her shoulders.

“Fuck y’all niggas ain’t shit, got me going on this bullshit,” Zac said, finally giving in like

everybody knew he would. I don’t know who he was trying to fool because everybody knew he couldn’t tell Desiree’s ass no.
Grabbing Yemani by her hand, I walked with her towards the ride, leaving the others to follow behind us.
"So lil’ momma you having fun?"
"Yeah, I am. I've really always wanted to come, and my parents never got around to bringing me before they died," she said.
"I’m sorry to hear that, but listen, let's not dwell on anything sad today, today is your day to have fun," I said pulling her into me for a kiss. Ever since the first kiss, I found myself always randomly kissing her every chance I got which was a lot since I saw her every day. Every day she tried going home; I came up with a different excuse as to why she couldn't. Hell, it's to the point where I don't know my damn self why she still at my house. Shit, I miss having my space, but I also don't want her to leave. Barbara has

even taken to her, and a few times I've caught her giving Yemani cooking lessons, which was good because the poor thing needed every lesson she could get. The only person who hasn't met her yet is my moms, and I've purposely kept them apart. She was still pressuring me about this grandbaby thing, and she wouldn't understand if I told her Yemani wasn't my girlfriend. I had no intentions on getting her pregnant, but she kinda sorta lived with me. The shit sounded crazy to me so I could only imagine how it would sound her ass. I can't describe or even begin to explain my feelings for her because I was still adamant I had none.

"Thank you for bringing me," Yemani's sweet voice said, slicing through my thoughts.

"You're welcome," I said, hating how sometimes she went shy around me and got to acting weird. "Now, yo ass better not be scared and shit."

"Scared? Nigga, please. You just don't be screaming and grabbing onto me," she shot back. I knew that would get her fired up.

"Screaming? Me? Or you mean yourself?"
"Naw nigga, I mean you."
"Shit, somebody must told you wrong because a nigga loves a challenge, so put your money where your mouth is."
"Ok nigga, you on. What you tryna bet?" she asked, falling right into my trap.
"Well, I'ma let you keep your little coins, college girl, but if I win, you owe me a sexy lap dance, and if you win, I'll buy you anything your heart desires."
"A lap dance? That's not a bet."
"Hey, that's what I want. What you ain't scared, are you?"
"Shit, no, because I know your ass not winning, but when I win, I want a Brahmin bag in every color."
"And some of this dick?" I asked, smirking expecting her to blush and put her head down. Instead, she closed the gap in between us and said, "Yeah that too." Causing me to start

coughing. Walking off ahead of me, I had to adjust my dick before I followed her.
"Everyone raise your hands up and keep them up until I come back and snap you in securely," the ride conductor said as we sat down in our seat.
"I want the new fall collection," Yemani said, getting comfortable as she took her blue jean half jacket off. "I wonder he will hold this for me."
"You just confident that you are going to win this bet, huh?" I asked, taking her jacket from her. "I'll hold it."
"Hell yeah I am, and ok, you need it to have something to hold onto," she said. Smirking at her, I didn't bother answering as the attendant made his way around to us and made sure the metal bar in front of us was snapped on properly. A few minutes of making rounds, and he made his way back to his station.
"Is everybody ready to enjoy this ride," he asked.
"YESS," the crowd cheered.

"I can't hear you. I said, are we all ready to enjoy this lover's ride?"
"Yesss," they screamed again.
"Let me set the mood and get you guys up in the air," he yelled, pressing a button as *Love in the Club the remix* by Usher came on at the same time as our seats begin to lift into the sky.
"Whooo!" Yemani screamed as she started singing along with the song as she kept her arms raised in the air. While she was so into the song, I draped her jacket over her legs and my hands and moved her purse over as well so that it was dangling halfway over my legs.
"And I don't want security rolling up on us, I'm not hesitating I just don't want to rush," she said, singing along with the music that was blasting loudly as we begin to turn in the air. The ride was designed to turn couples around in the air, and I'm guessing thrust them closer together, shit I don't know. While she was too busy enjoying the ride, I slipped my hands inside her shorts and had

slipped a finger inside of her pussy before she could fully proceed what was going on. She turned her head to look at me, eyes wide as she realized what I was doing. Trying to move my hand out the way, I leaned in close to her ear and said, “If you do all of that moving, you'll make this jacket and purse fall. So you really have two options, sit back and enjoy this peacefully, or let the jacket fall and have everyone watching you because believe me when I tell you, a nigga down for either option," I said, licking her ear as I dug my fingers deeper into her now dripping wet pussy.

The shit literally had a death grip on my fingers, so I could only imagine how it would squeeze my dick. I was amused watching Yemani's reaction to what I was doing to her. She was trying her best to keep her cool and just go with the flow, but she lost it when I inserted another finger inside her and begin moving my fingers in and out of her flesh at a rapid pace. This shit was an

adrenaline rush to be so high up where the only thing people could barely make out would be the bottoms of our feet and had no clue what was going on.
I heard her moaning beside me, and she leaned over and laid her head on my shoulder shielding her face from the view; I'm sure to hide the look of passion etched across it. "Fuck Amyr! Ohh no, you. Oh my God, please don't do this. You can't," she moaned into my ear.
Ignoring her, I inserted another finger into her sloppy wet pussy and moved them around until I found her G-Spot. It was over with then because once I found it, I refused to let up on it, causing her to really lose it as she grabbed a firm grip on my shirt and went from moaning my name to screaming it very loudly. I was glad for her sake that everyone else was screaming as well, so her cries blended in with the screams of the crowd enjoying the ride. As I felt the ride descending to the ground, I quickly pulled my fingers out of her

and put them in my mouth, licking her juices off of my fingers. Glancing over at her with her eyes still closed, I was satisfied with my work. As we made it back to the ground and the ride stopped completely, I said, “Seems like I won. I’ll expect that lap dance tonight in something sexy, even naked if you prefer,” I said, laughing at her.

CHAPTER 16

Damn, I let my mouth write a check my ass might not be able to cash…

YEMANI

Trying to get myself together, I wrapped the jacket around my waist before I stood up from the ride on shaky legs as I held onto Midos and wobbled down the steps.

"That was so much fun," Desiree screamed, running up to me.

"Yea fun," I said, pushing my hair behind my ears. "Come find a bathroom with me."

"Oh yeah, good idea. I've been holding it for a minute,"Krystal said.

"We'll be back, baby," Desiree yelled over her shoulders as we all walked off. I was suddenly pulled back, and spun around into a kiss.
"You can't go wondering off," Midos said pulling back from the kiss.
"We haven't been walking with you guys all day."
"But y'all been in eye sight."
"I need to find a bathroom to, you know, clean myself up." I said.
"Or we can get out of here and you can give me my prize I won."
"You cheated."
"I don't recall you setting any rules."
"Yeah, but that should have been an obvious disqualification," I said.
"Nope; won fair and square. Now hurry back and don't talk to strangers," this fool said.
"Really, Midos?" I said, laughing at him. "A stranger can catch this fade if they try me."

"Right hook, duck and jab," he said, executing the move he was telling me to do.
"I'ma hold off on that right, but my left hand won't miss a bitch," I said because I had a mean left hook.
"Yeah, yeah, gone to the bathroom, Tyson," he said, waving me off. Turning around back towards the girls, I didn't say a word as they stared me down.
"Bitch was both y'all stupid asses just doing fight moves and shit. Y'all one dysfunctional couple," Krystal said, laughing.
"We not a couple."
"Might as well be. Nobody else gone put up with that mouth you got or put your ass in check but that nigga. And shit, well he speaks for himself. Nobody but you was blessed enough to deal with his crazy ass. You might humble his mean ass," Desiree said. We didn't have to look far for a bathroom because one was actually a few feet ahead of us.

“Urghh,” Krystal said, looking down at her phone.
“What’s wrong with you?” I asked her.
“It’s my sister. Ever since her boyfriend died, she been talking reckless. I seriously think she loosing it.”
“Damn her nigga died, that’s so damn sad. Then you said they had a baby together as well. I feel bad for that poor child.” I said.
“Hold your sympathy, bitch because this crazy, love triangle will have your head spinning. I just don’t have time to get into all of that right now. I’m with my man and girls, and just want to have some fun,” she said.
“I second that motion,” Desiree said.
“Shit, I’ma remind you again when we get home,” I said, agreeing to drop the issue for now.
"Why you walking like that?" Desiree asked me because I was walking with my legs slightly apart because I was sticky all over.

"What you talking about?" I asked her, trying to play it off as I rushed into a stall once we made it to the bathroom. Realizing I needed to wet a few paper towels, I silently cursed under my breath, hoping that they would be in a stall so that I wouldn't be forced to answer any questions. Walking out, I let out a sigh as I quickly grabbed the paper towels and wet them a little bit. I was halfway back to the stall when Desiree caught me.
"I want full details when you come out," she said.
"Fine," I mumbled, walking into the stall to do my first official hoe bath. Once I had gotten myself together, I came out the stall to find Desiree and Krystal standing there with their hands on their hips, waiting patiently for me.
"Damn, can a bitch watch her hands first?" I said, laughing at them.
"Shit, you can wash and talk," Desiree said.
"It's nothing really to tell. Me and Midos made a bet about who would scream first on the ride and

be scared. He took it as who would scream in general, so he cheated. While I was busy enjoying the music and ride, he fingered the fuck out of me, and I messed my panties up and lost the bet so now I owe him a lap dance. I can't even dance," I said as I got it all out in one breath.
"Well, I'll be damn," Krystal said. "Why didn't I think of that? Having an orgasm so far up. Ohhwee, bitch, I'm jealous. Naw, we have to go again. Wait, shit; I got jeans on."
"Bitch to be a virgin you been getting more action that a little bit. You ass better come with it with this dance," Desiree said.
"Dezzy, you know I don't know how to do that," I whined, calling her by the nickname I often used when we were younger.
"Whelp, you only have a few hours to learn. Your ass better get drunker than you've ever been and freestyle it," Krystal said as we all exited the bathroom because it was starting to fill up.

"Only problem with that idea is, if she gets white girl wasted and ends up getting dicked down, she won't remember it which will be bad since it'll be her first time," Desiree said.

"Yeah, you right," Krystal said.

"You bitches can stop talking like I'm not here," I said.

"See, we tryna help you out," Desiree said just as we walked back up on the guys.

"I'm hungry, let's go," Midos said.

"Big swoll ass always eating," Zac said.

"Yo bitch ass always hating," Midos shot back.

They joked back and forth the entire way to the two SUVs that appeared out of nowhere as soon as we walked out the gates.

"Take us back to the hotel," Midos told the driver, who held the door out for us. For some reason, we had a separate car from the others.

Once we were inside the truck and situated, he pulled out his phone and called, who I'm assuming was the others.

"Yeah, we can either order room service or eat at the restaurant downstairs," he said. "Ok bet," he said as he hung up the phone.
"So about my dance?" he said.
"You ain't shit," I said, laughing because it's clear he wasn't letting this go.
"So I've been told once or twice," he said.
"I can believe it, but I haven't forgotten. You gone get this dance," I said to him.

"So, we hitting Park Avenue tonight. I got us a VIP section," Zac said. We were all downstairs at the hotel's restaurant, eating. I guess none of us wanted room service.
"I think I need to go find some shoes," Desiree said."
"Yeah, I need to find me something to wear as well," I said.
"Long as the shit not short," Midos said to me.
“Check action,” Krystal said.

"Don't get in them people mix because yo ass better not find nothing short either, unless you wanna see me nut the fuck up and kill everything moving," Debo said to Krystal.

"Why y'all niggas so violent?" I said laughing.

"You just heard what the fuck I said," Midos said to me. Leaning in close to him, I said, "Yes daddy, I heard you."

"You better cut that shit out before I have you screaming again," he said loud as hell, embarrassing me in front of everybody.

"Shit now," Desiree said. "You ain't have to flex on my friend like that."

"You can't save her ass if you be doing the same thing," Zac said as everybody burst out laughing. All of our asses were truly dysfunctional. As we got up to go to the mall, Midos pulled me to the side.

"Here, make sure you get everything you need tonight. It's on me. You can have whatever you like," he said, singing the last part.

"That's cute, but I got my own coins," I was saying until Krystal grabbed the card from his hand.
"I'll make sure she dress it up and make it real for you," she said, pushing me out the restaurant into the lobby of the hotel.
"Bitch, you acting slow as fuck. This niggas giving you his black card. If you don't take this shit and shut the fuck up," Krystal said to me. Turning to Desiree, she said, "What's wrong with this hoe?
"That's your friend," Desiree said, laughing as we headed towards the entrance to wait for our ride.
"I see it's a lot I'ma have to school you on being with a person like Midos. His status is so elevated; you gotta just roll with a lot of shit and not ask any questions. If he gives you something, take it. Not taking it would be a sign of disrespect," Desiree said.

"So I would be disrespectful if I didn't spend his money and instead spent my own shit?"

"Exactly." They both said in unison.

"That's the stupidest shit I've ever heard."

"That's the life you agree to when you fall in love with a Houston street king," Desiree said as our driver pulled up. We piled into the car and got situated before I said, "I'm not in love with a street king."

"Bitch bye; you love that nigga down to his dirty draws," Krystal said, laughing.

"No, I don't," I protested. I don't think. Did I love Midos already?

Walking into the club, we were all dressed to kill as we walked hand in hand, towards our VIP section.

"My nigga," Midos said as we walked up on a section that was already full of niggas. One, in particular, stood up and embraced him in a hug. I know it's wrong to be checking these niggas out, but he was fine as hell. Not finer than Midos, but he was fine.

"Baby, this my homie, Danger," Midos said, introducing us. "Dang, this my girl, Yemani."

My girl, I thought to myself as I smiled hard as hell.

"Shit; you actually with this nigga? He ain't holding you against your will or nothing, sweetheart?" Danger said.

"Same thing they asked me about you," a female said, coming from behind him. I hadn't even noticed her before.

"Good to see you, Jessica. How that bad ass child of y'alls?" Midos said.

"Shit, acting just like his equally bad father," she said, laughing. Everyone started catching up on old times, and we all were kicked back having a good time. The guys were on one couch, and the ladies were on the other.

"Girl, I never thought I'd see the day when Midos got a girlfriend. You know that fool ain't wrapped too tight. Shit, I thought my man was crazy, Midos takes the cake," Jessica said.

"Im not his girlfriend," I said.

"Shit could have fooled me. He called you baby and introduced you as his girl. That nigga loves you. He prolly just like typical niggas and scared to admit it. I bet if your ass talked to another nigga, he would be dead before he could even blink twice," she said.

"That's what I've been telling her," Desiree said.

"I told her to get her nigga. You gotta be aggressive with a nigga like that. He not gone go for that sweet shit."

"You not aggressive with Zac and they act the same," I said.

"Wrong. Zac hard because in these streets he has to be to survive. His gangsta turns down when he's around me. He playful as fuck and jokes, but that's his personality. Midos crazy ass is on 100 all day, every day. At work, at home, shit the gas station, everywhere. He just got damn issues and stay on go. No use in tryna change him, you just need to handle him."

"I do handle him, that nigga don't try me," I said defensively because he didn't.

"She means y'all got this weird ass arrangement going on. You staying at his house only because he insists you Be there and y'all sometimes sleep in the same bed together. However, he still out here in these streets, fucking everything walking because yo ass ain't tightened up and checked that shit. If his ass want you at his house, then that means y'all building towards something and them other hoes need to go. He can't have his cake and eat it too," Krystal said.

"Hell naw, he can't. Danger tried me like that and I got ignorant on his ass," Jessica said.

"He not having his cake and eating it too because we not sleeping together," I said. "Well, we are, but we not having sex."

"I'm sorry, but that's the problem. Shit girl, if you not fucking your man, another woman most definitely is," Jessica said. "I'm positive he got a bitch that's ready and willing every time he calls. Men like him have a big sex drive, so I'm sure you've noticed him suddenly getting up and leaving all times of the night."

I remained silent because I never thought about it like that but now that they mention it, I did notice on some nights when we would be sleep, he would suddenly get up and leave for hours.

"What can I do to fix it?" I asked.

"I don't want to say have sex because that sounds harsh, but if you want your man to stop fucking other hoes, you gotta fuck him yourself," Jessica said.

"Shit, I just found out this was my man a few minutes ago," I said, downing my drink and pouring myself another one.

"Shit, y'all live together boo," Desiree said.

"Well whatever you gone do, you need to do it fast," Krystal said, pointing. I turned around to see some females had walked over to the guys

like we wasn't even sitting in their VIP section as well, and one had found her way into Midos lap.
"I know one damn thing, Cory, if you don't make that bitch move her damn hand, we gone have some fucking problems," Jessica yelled.
"Look bitch, if you don't want to die, I suggest you move your hand," he said, laughing like the shit was funny.
"Excuse me, ladies, we talking about niggas and mine getting beside himself, this why he not allowed to go out."
"Girl, you better go handle that shit. But let's get our asses over there cuz these Dallas hoes disrespectful and I ain't about no talking when it involves Debo," Krystal said, standing up and fixing her clothes.
"That bitch done got some dick and went gangsta, but I'm here for the shit," Desiree said, laughing as we stood up and followed suit over to the guys. I looked to see if Midos had sense to make the bitch move by now, but clearly not,

because she was still sitting in his lap and now whispering in his ear. Not even putting a chaser inside my drink, I downed the liquid as it burned going down my throat. Letting the alcohol take over, I got up and walked over to the group.
Stop letting them play with you and boss up and show this nigga who the fuck you are cuz apparently his ass must forgot since you been on some chill shit.
In mid-stride, I turned and headed down the stairs instead. This nigga wanted to play, so I was gone show him how it was done. I was getting off the bench and tagging myself inside the game.
Walking from VIP, I faintly heard my girls calling my name as I walked off the last step and got sucked into the crowd. Stopping a shot girl, I got two clear, needle things that she had that were clear and contained a red substance.
"Squeeze these into your mouth," she yelled when she saw me looking at them strangely.
Doing as I was told, I squeezed both of them

inside my mouth at the same exact time, as I heard my song come on. I wasn't much of a dancer, matter of fact, I couldn't dance at all. However, my little booty be moving when I'm in my zone. Pushing further in the crowd and slapping hands away, my head started to spin a bit as I tried to find a good spot to dance where I would still be in clear sight of the VIP. I wanted Midos ass to see me since he felt like that bitch sitting on his lap was cool. As the beat to *Cash Money's Back That Ass* up dropped, I took us bending over shaking my ass. I didn't have a lot of ass, but I knew how to throw it.

Girl you workin' with some ass, yeah, you bad, yeah
Make a nigga spend his cash, yeah, his last, yeah

Feeling somebody get behind me, I looked over my shoulder and saw it was a fine ass, dark skin nigga with dreads. The perfect candidate to make

Midos mad with. Backing my ass up further on him, I was attempting to twerk and failing miserably, so I just settled with bouncing my ass up and down. When I originally started dancing, I had eyes on Midos, but glancing back up, I didn't see him anywhere.

"Bitch, you must wanna die," I heard Desiree say loudly. I ignored her and bend down further dancing, shaking my ass as hard as I could. Everything happened so fast that I didn't even have to time process the shit before I was knocked out cold.

My head was spinning as I woke up holding my head, looking around trying to figure out where I was at. Instead of seeing the hotel, I saw dingy, old walls and a light handing over my head that was swinging back and forth and blinking rapidly like it was on the verge of going out.

"Hello," I said as loud as I could, but really it came out as a whisper. My throat was dry and felt sore, and my head was pounding.
"Oh, glad you are finally awake," I heard a voice say. Trying to focus my vision on the voice, I looked up to see Midos standing in the corner.
"Midos, I, how did I get here?" I asked, attempting to stand but falling back down.
"I brought you."
"Well, where are we?"
"My nigga Danger had a place where he takes people to kill them. His very own soundproof torture chamber which I need to really get me one of these things," he said, looking around. That when I noticed it was all types of guns, and knives scattered around the room. *Oh, shit! Shi,t this nigga about to kill me*!
Laughing as if I had said something funny, he said, "No, I'm not about to kill your ass, although I should."

"Why-why would you think I thought you wanted to kill me?" I said, stuttering because that's exactly what I thought.

"Lucky guess," he said. Walking closer to me, he dragged a chair over to me and sat down flinging his hair out of his way. "I should kill you and that nigga you tried me with. I even thought about the shit, but I decided to let that nigga live, for now. When I knocked his ass out, he fell into you, knocking you on the ground, and you hit your head really hard."

"Ok, why did you bring me here instead of a hospital?" I asked still looking around nervously because this nigga really have lost his damn mind.

"To let you know to stop trying a nigga," he said casually as he pulled a pre-rolled blunt out of his pocket and lit it, taking a long pull from it. Passing it to me, I hesitated a bit unsure if I wanted to grab it.

"Bruh, I just hit it so why would it be spiked?"

Taking it from him, I took a pull of it and let the weed wash over me while I tried calming my beating heart down. Passing the blunt back to him, I said,
"Ok, I learned my lesson," I said to him.
"I don't think you have," he said, suddenly standing up and taking his shirt off. I wanted to ask him what he was doing, but my voice was caught in my throat as I took in his ripped-up body. My mouth begging to water as he didn't stop there with just his shirt and instead, proceeded to take his pants off next, followed by his boxers until he was standing in front of me in nothing but the fresh wheat Tims on his feet. Looking at me with glossy eyes, he said, "Strip."
It wasn't what he said that caused my pussy to thump; it was the authority in which he said it that sent a trigger to my brain causing me to rip and pull at the material until I was standing before him in nothing but my bra and panties. Smirking, he walked closer to me, dick swinging

from left to right and stopped directly in front of me. I couldn't peel my eyes away from it, protruding forward like a sword ready to slice through and fuck shit up. It was long, black, and thick with veins throbbing and a slight curve in it. Reaching down and standing me to my feet, he said, "Yo ass don't understand when I say; don't fuck with me and quit trying a nigga all nicely and shit, so I gotta show you that I'm 'bout square business and when I say some shit, I mean it," he said as he grabbed me by the back of my head and pulled me into him, crushing my mouth with his as his tongue invaded my mouth. Wrapping my legs around him, I got all into the kiss as he pushed me hard against the wall. My heart was beating out of control at this point but I was in a way loving every minute of this shit as he forcefully ripped my panties off of me and stuck a finger so far up my pussy, I thought for sure the bitch was gone come out of my mouth. I was leaking juices out of control as he moved my bra to the side and hungrily attacked my nipples never stopping his finger invasion as he moved his fingers rapidly in and out of me.

“Fuck,” I moaned as I racked my nails up and down his back, moving my hips forward welcoming his finger.

“Hmmm,” I moaned not even caring about the fact that this was really happening in this fucking torture chamber killer place. I was scared, nervous, and turned on all at the same time. Lost in my own thoughts, I didn’t even notice that Midos had moved his fingers and replaced them with his dick.

“Ow,” I said, dropping my legs. Picking them back up and placing them back around his waist, he said, “Act like the adult you kept saying you were and take this dick,” he said, moving his hips in a circle slowly. It felt like I was being ripped in half with this big ass object trying to fit into this small space.

"It's just the tip in, but I wanna put more in, can daddy put more in?" he asked me, still moving his hips in a circular motion slowly. I wasn't quite sure what a tip was, but this was feeling very different from when I and Tyron had tried to have sex. The pain was slowly dissolving, and it was starting to feel good. Nodding my head yes, he said, "Open your mouth and be the grown ass woman you said you was. You know I don't play that shit. Use your words when you talking to me."

"Yes, you can," I barely got out before he pushed his hips forward, pushing all of his dick inside of me. My eyes grew huge, and my breath caught in my throat because I wasn't expecting that shit at all. His strokes rotated from slow and sensual, to hard and fast.

"Oh wow, oh fuck!" I screamed as I tried my best to keep my legs wrapped around his body. I felt like I was fighting a war and losing as he penetrated me over and over again, taking me to new heights I never knew existed. I was in heaven and hell at the same time; because it was so painful, but at the same time so very good. If I would have known sex could be this mind-blowing, I would have given in long before now.

"Fuck girl; this shit so fucking tight, grrr," Midos said as he growled at me, grabbed me by my throat, and started literally fucking the shit out of me. "What's my name?" he asked at the same time as he tried to dig a hole through my pussy into my soul.

Struggling to talk, I said, "Fuck Midos!" I screamed, feeling myself on the verge of coming.

"Wrong answer," he said, moving his hips in a circle as if he was dancing. I'm not sure what that move was called, but each time he did it, my eyes rolled into the back of my head as I felt like I was peeing on myself. Embarrassed to the max, I tried pushing him back.

“No baby, wait, please,” I said. “Oh my God! I’m peeing on myself, stop!” I screamed as liquid burst from me squirting everywhere.

“Daddy beating this pussy, you not peeing, she just talking to me,” he said not bothering to stop, but instead, speeding up, going even deeper, which I didn’t know was possible. I thought he had his entire dick inside of me, but apparently, he still had some left. Leaning forward, I bit him on his chest hard which seemed to only turn him on, even more, cause he moaned and started moving deeper and faster.

“What’s my name Yemani,” he asked me again.

“Oh my God, I, fuck,” I said.

“Wrong again. But I can be your God,” he said.

“Amyr,” I breathlessly said.

“And don’t you forget it,” he said as he suddenly lifted me up high on the wall until my pussy was eye level with his face and placed my legs around his head and drove in. The feeling was so foreign to me that I didn’t know how to really act, as his tongue invaded my happy place. Wrapping my hands inside his hair, I leaned my head back in pure bliss and enjoyed the ride. It's funny how my night turned out, but I wasn't complaining at all. I'm actually glad things turned out like they did because I couldn't even have dreamed up something like this.

CHAPTER 17

A quiet before the storm…

ZAC

"The numbers for the month are looking good, so I called this meeting to let everyone know that, not only are you getting a raise, but we are looking into expanding our business and adding another location on the other side of town in the lower areas and close to clubs and shit," I said.

I was currently having a meeting with the staff of my store, going over numbers and letting them in on my latest business decision. Since the location opened almost six months ago, shit had been smooth sailing ever since bringing me to the current decision of expanding and opening up another location. In just six months' time, we had grossed well over 500 million dollars, so yeah, I know it was be a good business move getting another store. Since we opened, I had been putting my all into this business, coming in early and leaving out late. Ever since me and Midos took a step back from business and basically let Debo run it from the front line, and we handled the business aspect of things with number and products. I had been looking into other ventures because I was honestly in a place in my life where I was done with the shit altogether.

Me and Desiree had been going strong for five months, and I know it's early as fuck, but I loved the hell out of that girl, and I couldn't imagine life without her. She was my better half, and I could see myself growing old with her and our kids. Shit, Midos ass would clown my ass for even thinking about marriage, but that's just the space I was in with her. We just clicked, and best of all, my mother loved her, and I loved her family. I still can't believe she suckered my ass into going home to Sicily Island with her to meet her family. My phone barely worked in that small ass town, and it wasn't shit to do there. Literally, shit but trees, one gas station, one restaurant. Shit made me feel bad for her having to spend 18 years there. Shit, I barely survived eight days there, but I made it.

While we were there, her cousin renewed her vows and had a big wedding that she had been saving up for. I mugged that nigga, Marlo, hard as fuck, and it took everything in me not to knock his ass out. Once upon a time, Desiree told me how they used to fuck around, and she even got pregnant by his clown ass. This nigga had a tall tee on with some dingy forces and some Girbaud jeans on when I saw him. Like I couldn't even make myself believe she fucked his clown ass. Like man, dude took the cake when I saw him with some braids going to the back and colorful beads at the end. What threw me was the fact that she actually seemed to be in her feelings the entire time we sat through the ceremony, but I could have been tripping. I asked her about it, and she laughed it off.

"Why a lower area?" Katrina, a sales associate, asked me.

"I don't like that idea, well, I do if we don't have to go work there," Jean said.

"Some of you will essentially have to go over and work at the new store until the new people are able to handle the pressure on their own. Y'all know we pop from the time them doors open until I have to force people to get out." I said.

"Theft might be a factor in those areas, and I don't think I'm getting paid enough to be fibbing hood bitches over a 24.99 outfit," Katrina said.

"Y'all niggas must mistake me for telling you about this, to asking you about this. This store is the hottest thing in the city right now; shit, it's the hottest thing in Texas period. We have everybody coming in from celebrities to actors, everybody. We just styled Future for his appearance on the red carpet, and we did Rihanna's last week. If I make an executive decision for my spot, Im not asking y'all shit, I'm telling y'all. You don't have to like it because you are replaceable. My email is filled with applications of people applying for positions," I said, angrily because they really just tried me that fast.

"I actually think it's a brilliant idea," Ginger, my assistant, said. "Think about it, having a clothing store right by a strip club that caters to both stripper appeal and club wear, so people who live near or around can easily get there. By every club, it's always a row of apartments or houses close by. Those people might not have cars, but they always have money," she said.

"Exactly," I said, happy that if nobody else got where I was going, she did. That's why I fucked with her the long way.

"The construction for the building will start as soon as I get everything figured out, I just wanted to run it by you guys what's going on," I was

saying just as a knock was heard on the door. Walking over and opening it, a delivery guy was standing there with a package.
"Zachariah Mitchell."
"Yeah," I said.
"Sign here," he said, thrusting a chart in my hand.
“What is it?"
"I don't know; I just deliver," he said.
"Give me the shit. A nigga ain't ask yo ass all that," I said as I snatched the shit from me. I had to calm down because I had been on ten all day. Well, really ever since we got back from that trip and Desiree's mood had changed.
"Meeting adjourned," I told them. I got up from the break room chair and walked out the door and into my office, curious to see just what exactly this was.
"Hey, you ok?" Ginger said, walking in behind me.
"Yeah, I’m good," I said as I walked over to my desk and had a seat. Times like this, I regret not

putting that minibar in here like I originally wanted to do. But this was a place of business, not a club, which was why I decided against it, but now I was rethinking that decision.

"You're not ok. How long have I been your assistant?"

I sat and thought about it. Ginger was not only my assistant for my legal affairs but a couple illegal ones as well.

"A few years," I said.

"Exactly, and I've been your friend for much longer, so again what's wrong with you."

"It's Desiree. She got my head all fucked up. Man, I love the fuck out of that girl."

"Ok, what's the problem then?" she asked.

"Shit, I don't know. I feel like I chased her so hard to finally get her and now I don't know. This the shit that I'm on," I said, reaching into my drawer pulling out a box placing it onto my deck.

"Oh, wow," she said, reaching for the princess cut diamond, cathedral pave diamond, platinum engagement ring. I had dropped 50 stacks on the ring, that's how serious I was. I guess my nerves were getting the best of me and I was creating a seed of doubt in my head about her willingness to accept the proposal. I was gone hold out another month until her birthday. I planned to whisk her away and propose on the beach somewhere.

"It's beautiful," Ginger said.

"Shit, it better be, it set me back 50,000."

"50,000? American dollars? Are you crazy?"

"In love, yeah."

"She's a lucky girl, well, any woman would be lucky to have you," she said with a far-off look in her eyes that I may have imagined because as soon as it came, it was gone.

"Or I'ma lucky nigga," I said.

"Trust your gut. What's it telling you?"

"That we on the same page and I'm tripping," I said.

"Well then, go with that and kill the rest of that shit," she said, getting up. "I'm about to go see if your manager has done inventory yet, and then I'ma run these deposits to the bank."

"Thank you, bruh. I really appreciate everything you do, if I never told you that before, I really do," I said to her.

"I know," she said, walking out the door.

Grabbing the ring, I looked at it for a little while before I closed the box and put it back inside my desk drawer where I made sure it securely locked. Picking up the box, I grabbed my keys and headed outside. Hitting the locks on my car, I hopped in my car, backed out and pulled off in traffic. I needed to go check Debo and see how shit was on the front end; then I was gone pull up on Desiree. She would have just been getting out of class. Pulling up to a red light, I got a call on my phone, and I looked down to press answer so that my car's Bluetooth could pick it up when I heard gunshots ring out. Immediately ducking down, I pressed my foot on the gas and sped off with one hand as I reached with the other hand under my seat to grab my gun. I don't usually keep it so far, but some days I keep it under my seat if I know I'm just going to work. As my back window shattered, I swerved to afford hitting a car, barely being able to see as I made a sharp left turn on the freeway. The sound of gun shots drew closer and closer as the car swerved up on the side of me as my driver side window shattered and a bullet came in hitting me in the shoulder.

"Fuck," I yelled as I stuck my arm out the window and started shooting back not really knowing who I was shooting but knowing I wasn't going out like that and somebody was gone feel me.

Making a sharp left, my arm was stinging as I pushed my feet on the gas, speeding to one of my traps. No matter what car I was in, everybody knew my car so these niggas shooting definitely wasn't gone make it out this bitch passing through here. This a spot where Debo and a lot of my hard hitters be at so I knew as soon as I made it, I would be good. I wasn't running from shit, and I can handle shit myself but them niggas real life caught my slipping this time so shit, I had to get to my team. Turning right into the neighborhood, I expected them to follow me so they could get lit up, but instead, they sped past me making a sharp left and disappearing. Slowing my car down to where Debo was posted at a corner store, I put it in park as he ran over, gun drawn, looking around.

"The fuck happened to you, nigga!" he yelled.

"Some fuck niggas caught me slipping in traffic but it's up, Debo, it's fucking up! It's game time, and these bitches gone fucking feel me behind this shit," I said, pulling my shirt off, tearing it up and wrapping it around my arm as best as I could. I would have Doc patch me up when I got to the crib. "Call the cleanup crew to rid of my car, grab my shit out first, though," I said.

"They taking it to the shop?"

"Hell naw; I'm throwing the whole car away," I said as I sat down.

Somebody passed me a beer, and I turned that shit up even though I'm not usually one to drink beer.

"What this is?" Debo asked, holding the box I got from the delivery guy.

"Shit nigga, I don't know. But I was meaning to open that shit," I said. Walking off, he came back with a box cutter and sliced it open.

"What if it's a bomb? Tim said.

"Nigga, get the fuck out of here," Jason said.

"I mean, think about it. He got the box and don't know who it is, and then he just had a high-speed chase," he said.

Shit sounded crazy, but it kinda made sense, so I backed back a bit as Debo hesitantly opened it.

Can't lie, a nigga heart rate sped up some.

We all waited on pins and needles as he got all the paper out.

"The fuck?" he said.

"What is it?" We all asked at once.

"Shit, a damn hallmark card," he said.

"Huh?" I asked, standing up, walking over to him and snatching the shit from him. Opening the card, the letters were written in big bold letters, in all caps.

Y'ALL KILLED MY BROTHER, WRONG MOVE, NIGGA BECAUSE ITS UP THERE, BITCH

What the hell!

CHAPTER 18

When you forced to come out of retirement on a nigga to let them know that shit ain't sweet…

BROCK

I had really been shaking things up these last few months. I had been tryna get me some niggas together to go to war, but each time they heard who I wanted a war against, the bitch in them showed, and they each said they wasn't fucking with it. All the niggas I used to have on my team switched up on me for a new nigga, so I was alone out here and didn't have the manpower to win this war, that didn't mean I couldn't still fuck with these niggas. Chaz was my little brother and really just a small fish in a bigger pond. I told him time and time again not to get mixed up in them niggas bullshit when they first propositioned him about moving that trash ass weight around town, but he was young and dumb and didn't want to hear shit I had to say. Shit, I couldn't really get on his case about slanging drugs when that was all I knew at one point, but at least I could smell bullshit a mile away even back then. Apparently, he was working for these cats out of Egypt, and they was trying to slowly take over territory here. Somebody must haven't told these new cats that's it's already an Egyptian running these streets, or maybe they did know, and it's an old beef between the two or some shit. Whatever the case may be, it's gotten my baby brother killed in the process, so shit, they done brought me back out of retirement. With the crazy ass lifestyle that I was living before I got knocked, I always knew it would be my baby brother burying me, not the other way around. I made a promise to my baby moms and the most high that if I ever touched them gates again, I was done with the streets.

A nigga had enough money to live off of, and that shit was good enough for me. Five years into my ten year bid, my case was overturned, and I was suddenly a free man. Packing up my family, which consisted of my girlfriend, two-year-old, and baby brother, we headed to Houston for a fresh start. I turned over a new leaf and left this life alone, but I was sucked right back in with the death of my brother. These Houston niggas ain't built like that, shit try coming to N.O and trying that rah-rah shit, nigga a get four to the dome before they could even blink. They wanted to be Billy bad ass, and I was gone be the big bad wolf and huff and puff and blow they ass the fuck up. For months, I had sat back trying to let shit go for the sake of my girl and child, since the messages obviously wasn't working, but that was my fucking baby brother, my only sibling, it was hard letting something like this go. I battled back and forth with myself about letting the police handle it or taking the law into my own hands. Six months later and the case had turned into a cold case, and I had damn near become an alcoholic because the shit was eating me up on the inside. It only took a few questions to the right people for me to know the names of everyone I needed, when news first broke of his death, so why the police couldn't do that shit was the question. I was headed home just now when I saw one of them niggas at the red light, and something took over me because the first thing that came to mind was to start spraying his shit up. What just happened in traffic was a message; I'm just getting warmed the fuck up. Pulling into the daycare, I got out to go get my daughter before heading home.

"Daddy, is Uncle Chaz coming over today?" she asked.
My baby was super attached to my little brother, and as a parent, I didn't know the proper way to tell a three-year-old that somebody was dead. I had told her that he had gone to heaven to be with God. That was the best way for me to explain it to her and I thought she got it. However, one day a few weeks ago, she started asking me was he still visiting God and how long he would be there. Would he be bring her presents back since he missed her birthday, and when he was coming to get her.
"Baby, Uncle Chaz is in heaven with God. We talked about this. Remember I said he was an angel watching down over you?"
"Yeah, but him been gone to visit God a long time, daddy. Him gotta come visit us, right?"
Hearing that shit almost brought a nigga to tears, but I had to be strong for my baby. Not knowing what else to tell her, I just said the first thing that

came to mind, "You'll see him again one day, baby."
"Ok, daddy. I hope it's tomorrow." Gripping the steering wheel, I sped down the street. Pulling into my house, I saw my girl’s little sister car. *I wonder what she doing here?*
“Baby, your tete Krystal is here.”
“Yahhh,” she said throwing her hands up in the air and kicking her legs around excitedly.
As I put the car in park and got out and got her out the car, we headed towards the front door and the closer we got, I heard arguing coming from inside as I put my key in the door and walked inside.
“Tierra, what’s going on in here?” I asked because they seemed to be having a screaming match, so I’m surprised how either of them knows what the other was saying.
“I just came to see my niece and check on your stupid ass but you still on some the same as bullshit!” Krystal yelled.

"Bitch, we good over here. You been getting some dick and done got besides your damn sel;f fucking with the enemy."
"Bitch fuck you, let's not get on fucking because if I was fucking with the enemy what you call what you were doing?" Krystal said.
Curious to know what Tierra was doing, I turned and looked at her for a response.
"Tete Krystal," my daughter said, making me remember she was standing right there.
"Hey, tete baby," Krystal said, walking towards her.
"Bitch, don't touch my child," Tierra said.
"Both y'all asses need to stop acting like this in front of my damn seed!" I yelled. Grabbing her hands, I took her inside her room and turned Paw Patrol on. Going back into the living room, I had to stand in between the two of them because they looked like there were about to come to blows.
"What the fuck!" I yelled, visibly upset.

"Yo bitch came out her mouth asking me to set my nigga up because he killed the nigga she been sleeping with for the past couple years," she said, enraged. "Yeah, I haven't known Debo that long, but I love him, and he cut for me like no one else, and he's always there for me. My own sister turned her back on me, but it was that nigga that is always there with open arms."

Still trying to process what the fuck she said, I said, "Set who up? Sleeping with who?"

She looked at me like she didn't mean for that to slip out but it did. Putting her head down, she was at a loss for words as she tried to take back what she said.

"You 'bout a stupid ass bitch, and I hope a stray bullet hit your ass," Tierra said.

"Somebody better tell me something."

"I'm sorry, I, I gotta go," Krystal said.

I was already having a fucked-up ass day, and this bitch just told me my bitch wanted her to set her dude up, and she fucked another nigga.

Pulling my gun out, she started shaking, “She, he, I,” she said.

“Baby, I can explain,” Tierra said crying.

Ignoring her, I turned to Krystal, and the name she said paused my entire soul.

CHAPTER 19

The past is the past for a reason…

DESIREE

Ding! Ding! Ding!

My phone going off with back to back text messages, stirred me from my sleep. Zac had come home last night acting like the energizer bunny, so I was up all night, showing him just how much I missed him throughout my day. Opening my eyes, I saw a few messages from a number I didn't recognize. Sitting up in bed, I read over the text which didn't really give a clue as to who was messaging me. Texting back, I said, "What's up? Who is this?"

When I didn't get a text back after a few minutes, I put my phone down and hopped up to take care of my hygiene and get myself together. Zac had long since gotten up and went in to work. He puts in long hours at the store like a worker when he's really the boss, but that's what I love most about him.

After I had gotten myself together, I walked out of the room and downstairs to the kitchen to make me some breakfast before class. Each and every time I came into this kitchen, I was always in awe because of how beautiful it was. Zac's house wasn't as big as Midos' house, but it held its own in regard to beauty and design. He went the modest route with a simple three bedroom, contemporary style home, but it was just as nice. Settling on some fruit and yogurt, I sat at the bar and ate my food in peace as I watch the tv that hung on the wall directly in front of me. Zac insisted it was there because he liked to eat at the breakfast bar a lot, so he needed something to entertain him while he ate. I couldn't take him serious sometimes, but that's why I loved him. I had just admitted that to myself last week, and ever since then, I've been off my square. It's taken me so long to get to this point of actually loving someone again and letting them break every wall down that I had, so I was scared.

Finishing up my food, I ran back up the stairs and into the room to get dressed. Grabbing my phone with the intentions on checking the weather, I saw the number had texted me back.

"This better not be one of Zac's hoes he used to fuck with because we gone have to problems," I said aloud because about a month or two ago, a bitch called herself being funny talking about how is our man treating you. I told that bitch he treating me very well, but she could pull up and see for herself if she was so concerned. I wish that bitch would have came, she would have been good and beat the fuck up.

This Marlo, the number said.

Rolling my eyes trying to figure out how the fuck the nigga found me, I quickly texted back, *What the fuck do you want and how the hell did you get my number?* Pressing send, I threw on a PINK shirt with the matching PINK sweatpants as I grabbed my keys and jogged back downstairs, stopping in the den to grab my book bag before continuing to the door. When I got in my car, I saw two texts from him.

I'm in Houston. Need to see you. Just want to talk and finally get everything out about what happened between us. You the one used to holla about closure. I'ma give it to you although all I really want is you. You was a child back then, and I felt wrong but now you a grown ass woman and we can really be together how we always wanted, just say the word. He said.

At first, I almost agreed with him about meeting up because I was curious as to what he had to say until I realized I didn't give a fuck because I had moved on, so that was closure enough. My man loved me even if he didn't say it, his actions were proof enough, and I loved him, so I was good on the extra shit. Just to fuck with him though, I said.

Ok, we can meet today at 3 pm at Chipotle, I said.

Bet, was all he sent back. Laughing hard as hell, I reversed and headed to campus.

After I left my study group, it was going on 7 pm and I was so tired that I decided to stop by our campus apartment to charge my phone up and get some rest before I drove home to meet Zac. He usually didn't get in the house until 11:30 ish, anyway so I could get a 30-min nap before I had to drive, so I headed over that way. Walking across the parking lot, I saw Samantha and her click of hoes posted outside by somebody's car. Already knowing they was about to be on some bullshit, I was mentally preparing myself for the shit as neared them.

"See, I told that nigga when you fuck with young hoes they don't know how to be loyal," she said, kicking it off.

Strike one

"Yeah naw, but that's what his ass wants, and I don't even know why," her friend said.

Strike two

"Shit, if he would have kept a real bitch on his team, I would have been trying to see about my man," Samantha said. Instead of beating her ass, I just picked up the pace, making it to my door and sticking the key in and going inside.

"Never mind; she just walked inside the apartment," Yemani said. "Ok bae, I'll see you when I get home," she said as she hung up.

"I like y'all together. Your mean ass and his mean ass are good for each other," I said, loving the smile and glow she always wore lately.

"Bitch where have you been?" she asked me overlooking the compliment I just gave her.

"Huh? In a study group in the library why?"

"Where your phone?"

"Dead bitch what's with the third-degree questions?" I asked her as I walked into the kitchen to fix me a sandwich.

"The questions are because your man was shot today and you was nowhere to be found."

"Shot!" I said panicking as I stopped what I was doing running to find my keys.

"Calm down it wasn't even a serious wound. He was patched up and sent on his way hours ago, that's besides the point. There's more," she said to me. "What do you know about Marlo being in town?"

"Shit, I know he here. He texted me about meeting up getting closure. I told his ass meet me at Chipotle, but I never had any intentions on going; I just really played his ass. How you know he here?"

"Well, he was running his mouth to some folks about being here and getting the love of his life back," she said as I burst into laughter because that was one funny ass nigga.

"I'm glad you are amused because Zac heard about it and he isn't amused at all, just a heads up," she said wiping the smile off of my face.

CHAPTER 20

Before I get in another person business again, I'ma mind my own…

YEMANI

“Baby quit,” I said to Midos as he nibbled on my ear as we laid in bed. I was trying to get up, while he kept pulling me back down.

“I have to go,” I said, laughing.

“I don’t want you to go,” he said as his hands reached down and found their way into their happy place. He knew the affects him doing that had on me, so every chance he got, his fingers were inside me.

"Baby, you need to talk to your boy. I think that's crazy how he would immediately assume Desiree cheating on him without even talking to her about it first. She hasn't had any contact at all with Marlo's wack, ugly ass."

"I'm not telling that man shit because that's not my business and yours either. Your friend needs to handle that her damn self; your ass just better not have no ex-niggas popping up in town, talking about they here to profess their love because I'm killing everything in sight. Shit, you might even catch a few bullets. I still ain't forgot about you dancing on that nigga in Dallas. His ass better not pop up," he said, laughing as he pushed his fingers deeper inside of me.

"Ahh, fuck! I, I don't even know that nigga, didn't even get a good look at his face," I moaned.

"You didn't need to get a good at his damn face. Only nigga face you need to see is mines. See, you gone lose your life, keep on," he said, kissing me on my jawbone as his hands found my throat, squeezing it with a little amount of pressure, but not too much causing my eyes to roll in the back of my head and, in the process making me cum immediately. I couldn't help. That was too much pressure for me not to react that way. He just started laughing but didn't bother stopping.

"Ohhh shit, not funny, and you gone stop fucking threatening me because I keep a tool and my man taught me how to shoot so I'll up that bitch quick," I shot back.

"Shit, you must got a good ass nigga then if he did all of that. I'm scared of yo ass," he said, kissing his way up my face until his lips found mines just as his phone started going off.

"Fuck. Damn blocking asses," he grumbled as he reached for his phone. Meanwhile, since he had got me worked up, I was ready for him to finish what he started, so I leaned over and began nibbling on his neck, rubbing on his dick until he sat up, pushing me out the way and said,

“What! Where he at?” he asked, hopping out of bed and practically running out of the room. He didn’t say a word to me at all and I kind of felt some type of way about the shit as seconds later I heard the front door slam.
“Well damn,” I said as I realized I wasn’t getting any action today. Getting up, I started to get dressed so I could meet up with Krystal. She had left a hysterical voicemail on my phone, and I had been calling her back for a few days. Finally got in touch with her and she asked me to meet her.

"What's up?" I asked her as I walked inside the restaurant.
Sorry about that, shit jumped off with my people. I'll make it up to you. A message came through my phone from Midos just as I was sitting down. Texting him back; I picked up the drink I had told her to order for me and waited patiently for her to answer. Looking at my friend, her eyes

were puffy, she had bags under them, and she looked tired and worn out.

"Bitch what is you going through because you not looking good," I said laughing, but my laughter was cut short when she immediately burst into tears. Getting up, I walked around to her and slid in the booth beside her, and I grabbed her into my arms.

"What's going on? Talk to me."

"I lost it all because of her."

"Who her?" I said confused.

"He gone leave me, I know he is, Mani."

"Debo? Why would he leave you?"

"Because I gotta tell him a secret I've been holding in before it comes to light and I know he is going to look at me suspect after I say it," she said, really shaken up so it must have been something big. I heard Midos in the back of my head telling me to mind my own business, and stay out of it, but I pushed that thought away as I grabbed her hand, trying my best to console her.

"Talk to me," I said.
Taking a deep breath, she said, “The guy that was killed at that party, we went to named was Chaz. He is my sisters baby daddy’s brother, and she was also sleeping with him. Truth be told, that baby might be his,” she said, dropping a bomb on me. I didn’t know what to say, and I felt like I should have just listened to Midos and minded my own business because I didn’t want to know this information. The less I knew, the less I had to own up to when I talked to Midos later on. He was like my best friend, and I literally told him everything, so of course, I was telling him about this.
“You definitely need to tell him,” I said. I didn’t know what else to say and really didn’t want to speak on it too much because Chaz’s murder sparked my whole kidnapping and those are events I’d rather not relive.

I feel bad for her, but ultimately, she should have told Debo before everything happened if she knew the ties between the two. Midos had briefly told me about the Chaz situation and what went on with him, so I know if I knew a little, then she most definitely knew more than me. Whereas Debo and Zac be having full conversations with Desiree and Krystal about street shit, Midos said my level of involvement and information is strictly on a need to know basis. He only really told me the little he did about Chaz because I saw it happen and kept bugging him about it.

"I have one more thing," she said.

"Hell, I don't know if I can take anymore."

"Im pregnant," she said.

"Really? I honestly think I am too because Midos has never used a condom and I haven't seen a period in a month. I've been just trying to pretend like nothing is happening because if I don't acknowledge it, then I might not make it true," I said. I hadn't admitted any of this out loud yet, but surprisingly, I wasn't as upset as I initially thought. I felt as ease and blissful. Maybe because I knew Midos was my knight in shining armor and would always be there for me, no matter. I couldn't help the smile that appeared on me face.

"What you gone do?" she asked me.

"Step one: take a test. What you gone do?" I asked her.

"I already made an appointment yesterday with the abortion clinic. Will you go with me?"

"Damn bitch; just dragging me in deep into everything. We would you want an abortion? That's only going to add to your problems, boo, not solve them."

"Debo not gone want me after I tell him this, and I'm sorry, but I couldn't stomach the idea of being a single mother," she said as more tears slid down her face.

I was in a very awkward position. Like how do you tell your best friend you don't want to be

involved in her drama or that you don't agree with her decision to get an abortion? The answer is simple; you don't. Rather I agreed or not; I was going because this was my friend and I would be here for her during this trying time.
"Yeah, I'm coming," I said.

"Krystal Tindal," The nurse said, calling her to the back. I opted to wait in the lobby for her because I couldn't take watching the process, no matter how curious I was to know exactly what went on. After getting a bottle thrown at my head though, on the way inside and having to have Krystal practically drag me inside to keep me from running over and beating they ass, I damn sure wasn't coming back. The bottle came from angry protestors screaming at me about going to hell; like bitch make sure the person even pregnant first before you go off on everybody. Well, I probably was pregnant, but shit, this abortion wasn't for me. The thought of having a baby was scary, yeah, but the thought of starting a family with my man overpowered that fear. Half an hour later, I was still sitting in the lobby thumbing through a magazine when I decided to go ask the receptionist where the restrooms where. As I was walking to the desk, I got the bright idea to ask them if they offered pregnancy tests here. I figured I would kill two birds with one stone.

"Excuse me, ma'am, do you guys do a pregnancy test?" I asked

"Yes, we perform an initial test first to make sure you are in fact pregnant before we can administrator the abortion."

"Would it be possible for me to get one?" I asked her because I would rather a doctor tell me I was pregnant than to try and read a damn pregnancy test myself.

"Sign in and have a seat. The initial consultation is free. Fill out this paperwork and consent form,

and we will proceed with the test once we get a positive from the test," she said.
I barely understood half of what she was saying, but I knew I would get the pregnant test administered, so that's all that mattered to me. It didn't take long after I filled out my paperwork that my name was called to go to the back. That place looked colorful in the lobby, but once you stepped to the back, the entire mood changed. Gone was the colorful designs, and smiling faces. They looked mean behind them doors and the color scheme void of life, kinda what they hoped to accomplish with you when then they took life from you. Going into the room, I sat down and was given a cup to pee while I waited for a doctor to come on. After turning in my pee, I walked back to the room I was put in and sat on the bed, trying to calm my beating heart down. I was so nervous, but I would be happy, either way, with the results. We barely been dating four months even though I've known him for six

months, I still think that's too early to bring a baby into the situation. But on the other hand, if we are pregnant, I would be overjoyed to start my own family.
"Calm down," I said trying to pep talk myself. As I heard the door open and saw the white coat, I laid back on the bed and closed my eyes.
"Are you ok?" he asked me.
"Yes, I'm just nervous. Listen, I'm not tryna be rude but let's not beat around the bush. I am, or I'm not?" I said because I had a feeling he was about to talk around the question, seeing as though before I laid down, I saw a clipboard in his hand.
Laughing, he said, "Ok, Miss Jacobs, you are 12 weeks pregnant-"
Before he could even say anything else, the door opened up, and I assumed a nurse was coming in until I heard a voice that caused a chill to run down my spine.

“Get the fuck up and let’s go,” Midos said. his voice dripping with anger.

CHAPTER 21

The heart wants what the heart wants.....

ZAC

I hadn't sleep at all since the day them niggas had caught me slipping and down on me. Well, not niggas since it was only one nigga at the house. It took some time, but I finally got an address for his ass and me, and Debo was posted up outside the house now. I was all fucked up right now. I was fucking with Desiree, and I almost fucked Ginger today. I haven't seen or talked to Desiree since everything happened, so I had yet to hear her explanation. I had been stressing 'bout her feelings for dude since we left her city, so shit hearing that he said that shit about getting her back, caused me to lose it. The shit had me all off my square though, and I couldn't shake her from my mind no matter how hard I tried. Worse of all, my personal life was starting to fuck with my business life in a major way. I came to work drunk, hit on customers, didn't turn my permits in for the new building, so all construction had stopped, then I came on to Ginger. I'm glad she actually a good girl and turned a nigga's advance down. Instead, she let me sleep on her couch when I showed up to her house, drunk one night and as soon as she opened the door, I attacked her. I never truly had a girl best friend, but she's proven to be one that I'm thankful to have been blessed with.

"You ready to do this?" Debo asked me.
"Hell yeah," I said, checking my clip before I got out the car. Running down the street to the house, we went around back and kicked the door in,

running in, guns drawn ready to lay everything down breathing. I usually wasn't the guns type, but tonight I was gone use this bitch because I was in the mood to fuck with my knives.

"I got upstairs," I said to Debo as he moved around rooms downstairs. Walking upstairs, I kicked the first door in that I saw and walked in seeing that it was a little girl's room. I then kicked in the other door, and it had the be this nigga's room. Walking in, I checked under beds and looked inside closets. No one was here. Fuck. Walking back downstairs, I noticed Debo starring at this photo in the living room hard as hell.

"My nigga, you good?" I asked him because he literally was looking at this picture hard then a bitch. Suddenly looking up, he walked over to me, looking like the devil himself as he thrust the picture frame in my face. His sudden movements caused me on reflex to point my gun at him.

"The fuck you doing?" he asked me, pointing his shit me as well.

"My bad, my nigga; it was a reflex. You damn near threw the shit at me," I said, lowering the gun.

"Man, look at the shit and tell me that ain't who it look like. I know that's not my bitch on that picture," he said.

Studying the picture, thinking this nigga was tripping, sure enough, it was Krystal smiling, holding a little girl who couldn't have been no older than one or two. Looking back up at him, I didn't say anything, so I guess my silence was confirmation enough as he started fucking the entire living room up. While he was doing that, the front door open, and on instinct, we both pointed our guns and lit whoever the fuck it was up. After we stopped firing and the smoke cleared, we looked on to see a woman laid out with blood pouring out of her, rapidly.

"I wonder who that hoe is," Debo said.

“I think his bitch,” I said, looking down at her. I figured she was dead until her eyes popped open. “Shit, the bitch still breathing?” I barely got out before Debo shot her in the head.

“She dead now,” he said, walking past me out the front door.

“Fuck that,” I said as I turned and went back the way we came. He was tripping hard, but I couldn’t blame him. We both we stuck with some bitches that couldn’t do right.

CHAPTER 22

Some shit just ain't adding up…

MIDOS

"How is he, mom?" I asked as I rushed into the hospital. I got the call my pops had caught some lead just as I was dragging Yemani out of that abortion clinic. My day just went from bad to worse. My cousin, Dubie had took me up on my offer to work for me and him, and my Uncle Edjo had moved to the States, and I had let them stay in one of my condos. I'm not sure why Dubie had brought Uncle Edjo with him, but he did. Anyway, he hit me earlier telling me that some niggas had rolled up on him and jacked him.

Took everything down to the shoes on his feet. None of my soldiers had ever gotten jacked before, so the shit blew me that they would have waiting until my family come to start dropping they nuts. Then once I got that situation cleared up, and made sure he was straight, Lilly desperate ass sent me a picture of Yemani going into an abortion clinic. Shit, I didn't even know she was pregnant and clearly, her intentions weren't to inform me either since the first thing that she wanted to do was run to a damn abortion clinic. That shit was foul as fuck and really had me looking upside her head. See, you try and change for these hoes and this the shit they get on. The more I thought about it, the most the only explanation that came to my mind was that she was cheating on me, that's why she was so quick to get rid of it. Shit, because by now she knows all she has to do is talk to me about anything and this wasn't no different, but no, her sneaky pussy ass had to do this shit.

"He's fine. The bullets missed any major arteries."

"Who knew he was at your house? I asked her.

"Nobody."

"Where was his security detail at?"

"I don't know. I think he left them at the hotel."

"How far up your driveway did he get before shots rang out? Where was your guard at that are usually at the gates? How did they get in?" I said, firing out question after question at her. I was trying to piece this shit together because it wasn't adding up to me.

"I don't know son, I just don't know," she said, falling in a chair and crying.

"I'm sorry, momma," I said, reaching out and pulling her into my arms. I let a tear fall, as well as I just held her. Everything was hitting me at once and shit I got choked up. Even thugs allowed to show emotion every once in a while.

"It's ok, baby," Yemani said, rubbing my back. I had forgot I made her come with me since she was already in the car. Had I not been mad at her, I would have welcomed her attempts to comfort me, but that old Midos was seeping back in, and I was on some fuck hoes type shit. I don't love these hoes, I don't trust these hoes always been a nigga motto, and I should have stuck to it.

"Who is this son?" My mom said once she stopped crying and got herself together. They had never formally met, and now I'm glad.

"Nobody," I said.

"Really, Midos? Nobody? No fucking body?" she said, pissed. I knew she was on the verge of going off, but I didn't give a fuck.

"What's going on?" My mother said.

"Hello, ma'am. I'm Yemani, Amyr's girlfriend, and baby momma," she said.

"You're having my grandbaby?" my mother said smiling excitedly.

"No ma, you not. That ain't my baby."

"You got me fucked up," Yemani said. "Who baby is it then, Midos?"

"What I tell you about that fucking mouth," I told her, snatching her up and dragging her outside with the intention of finishing the conversation, but as soon as I grabbed her up, she took off swinging wildly at me.

"You better calm your stupid ass down before a nigga knock your dumb ass the fuck out," I said, slamming her ass hard as hell into the wall.

"You better not put your hands on that fucking girl, and she is pregnant," my mother said, cursing me out; something she rarely does.

"I wasn't getting an abortion, you stupid bitch. I was only getting a test to see if I was pregnant. I had no intentions of aborting your baby."

"Well, why the fuck were you there then?" I asked because obviously the hoe took me for booboo the fool or some shit.

"I was with Krystal," she said.

"Whatever, bitch, then go back with Krystal's ass then and get rid of that shit. If it is mine, a nigga don't want it anyway," I said, not meaning that but just angry at everything going on around me.
"We are going to have to ask you guys to leave if you can't keep it down. This is a hospital, not a zoo," a security officer said as he walked over to us.
"A zoo? My nigga, did you just fucking; you know what, never mind, you got that, but I never forget a face so I'll come see about that later," I said to him. Leaving Yemani standing there crying and ignoring my mother calling me, I walked off going into my father's room to check on him, the only thing that really mattered to me at this point.

"So you don't know who shot you?" I asked him. My pops was finally awake, a few days later and the doctors said if his vitals stayed this way, he could be released in a day.

"I never said I didn't know who shot me," he said. "I just need to confirm that it was them that actually had me shot, so I got a plan put in motion, and I'ma sit back and watch it play out," he said, eating some of his soup. "This crap is awful; I can't wait to be released so I can have a decent home-cooked meal. Speaking of home, I need to talk to you about something," he said.

"What's up?" I asked him.

"I'm going to ask your mother to marry me. My biggest regret in life was not making her my wife. That's my better half, and she deserves more than this creeping around we are doing. What's your thoughts on that?"

"I'm all for it. I thought it was an age limit on marriage and wedding though but I guess not," I said.

"Well, if it is an age limit I know, I haven't reached it because I'm still young," he said laughing.

"Shit in dog years," I said.

“On a serious note, son, your mother makes me the happiest man on this earth. I love her past the moon and the stars. If you ever in your life, find a love like that, someone you can’t sleep without, eat without, or be without, you better marry her because a love like that only comes once in a lifetime,” he said, giving me something to seriously think about.

“I gotta go handle some business, old man, I’ll get up with you later,” I said, dapping him out and leaving out of his room, stopping to dap his men up on the way out.

Picking up my phone to call Yemani, I dialed the number, then hung up. It had been a few weeks, and I’ve had time to calm down, so it was time to revisit our conversation again, because it wasn’t adding up with the version I had in my head. I wanted to talk with her; to listen this time. Last time, I was talking with anger and in attack mode and I’m starting to realize the error in that, but my pride wouldn’t allow me to call her. Each time I tried, I didn't go through with it. With both of us being stubborn, it might be days, weeks, or even months before we ever talked again.

"So you saying you saw Krystal's picture at the house?" I said to Zac. We were currently headed over to my condo to holla at my cousin, Dubie about some shit and to see if he remembered anything from that night any faces and just check on him. I hadn't got up with him since that day because I've had other shit to deal with, but he's been blowing my phone up left, and right, so I decided to run down on him today.

"Shit yeah, that was her ass."

"You sho my nigga?"

"Hell yeah, I'm sure. That was her ass, my nigga; cheesing hard as hell like she was on a Hallmark card," he said

"Shit," I said, cursing. If that was, in fact, her ass on that picture at that house, then that means it's likely her ass could have been the one at the abortion clinic and Yemani just went with her because she can't say no to her friends.

"What?" he asked as we pulled into the parking lot of my condo.

"I royally fucked up, that's what," I said, cutting the engine and getting out the car. Walking to my condo, I almost used my key to just walk in, but out of respect for them, I knocked.

"Nigga, knocking on the door of your own shit? How that go" Zac asked.

"I let them live here, so I gotta treat it like it's somebody else's shit, so yeah I knocked," I said as the door swung open.

"What up," I said, dapping Dubie up and walking into the house.

"Sup," he said. "What are you doing here?"

"I came to holla at you," I said to him.

"'Bout what?" he asked nervously.

"Damn nigga, you good?" Zac asked the million-dollar question.

Laughing it off, Dubie said, “Yeah man, I’m straight. Just tired is all.”

“Shit don’t work yourself too hard,” I said.

“I’ll be right back, I left my damn phone upstairs,” he said, getting up and jogging upstairs.

“Hey, now I didn’t want to say anything, but I think your cousin back using again,” Zac said.

“Why would you say that? Shit, he straight, he not on that shit anymore, he just having a hard time. Everybody knew he was a crackhead so the shit can’t shake him for nothing. He just wants a fresh start and clean slate,” I said.

“Ok, my nigga, my bad my bad,” Zac said throwing his hands up in surrender. “But he left his phone upstairs, but it’s a phone right there on the counter,” he said pointing to a phone. I looked and sure enough it was one.

“Shit I got two phones, you got three phones, so what’s your point?” I said.

"Nothing my nigga I'm dropping it," he said just as Dubie ran back down the stairs.
"I'm 'bout to head out, but Ima get up with you later on cuz ok," he said.
"Damn you rushing me off and shit," I said as Zac stood up.
"I'ma meet you in the car," he said, walking out.
"Here I come," I said because I wanted to really ask Dubie what was up. If something was going on, or he was in trouble, he needed to know that he could tell me.
Once Zac left, I said, "What's up, Dubie? What you suddenly in a hurry to leave for? You in trouble or some shit?"
"Naw, my baby moms just hit me up, so I gotta go see what's going on," he said at the same time as the door opened and my Uncle Edjo walked through the door, looking normal as hell. Gone were the stuffed animals, the snot in his nose, and the pants pulled up like Steve Urkel. This nigga looked normal as fuck to me like he was in his

right mind as he walked in tall as opposed to his usual slump.

"Uncle Edjo?" I asked in total disbelieve. I hadn't seen him like this since, shit I can't remember, but it's been years. Hearing me call his name, he paused in mid-stride like a deer caught in head lights. It was too late to slouch or and ruffle himself up again because I had already seen him acting normal. I just knew my eyes had to be playing tricks on me.

"Oh, I meant to tell you that it's a miracle; Pops feels like he's back to normal, the doctors said," Dubie was saying until Edjo interrupted him.

"Save it, Dubie, your cousin not going for shit else after he's seen me. What the fuck have you done? You've ruined our plans. Why is he here?" he asked, directing his question at Dubie.

"So nigga you been faking this entire time? Type of punk ass shit is that?"

"Not this whole time, but I've been better for a while."

"So you just had gotten so used to pissing and shitting on yourself and playing with Barbie dolls and shit that you have to keep that role up, huh?" I said, laughing because that the only fucking thing I could do at this point. This was some unbelievable shit.

Pulling my gun out, I pointed it at him.

"Let's cut the conversation. You played retarded for a reason, so shit, what your motive was?"

"That's easy; I want back what's rightfully mines."

"And that's where I came in at, huh? Since I was next in line for the throne?"

"Bingo. While you been playing checkers, I been sitting back slobbering on myself, playing chess. Know how much shit people say around a person when they think they too retarded to understand what's going on?"

"And who better to help you with your plan that your junkie son? Shit, I wouldn't be surprised if you been feeding him drugs all along, half unknowingly, and the rest willingly," I said looking at a man I've known my entire life as if I were seeing him for the very first time in my life. Hearing a gun cock from behind me, I already knew what time it was.

"So, y'all niggas had it all planned out, huh?" I said, laughing hysterically at this point.

"Yeah," Dubie said.

"Y'all forgot one small detail, though," I said, still laughing.

"What?" They both asked.

"We been caught on to you niggas, this why a worker can never outshine a boss," my father said from behind Edjo, before he pulled the trigger, catching him three times in the head. I used this as my opportunity to catch Dubie off guard and deliver a kill shot to the head.

"Damn, I was on my way back and y'all asses killed them without me, that's fucked up," Zac said, walking in the doorway.

"How did you know it was them?" I asked my pops.
"Because only person I had told that I was coming to see your mother was Edjo, and he did appear to be following my every word at the time. But I knew that I had to be tripping because I couldn't be possible, but then I remembered I was at his house when I was on the phone speaking about the shipment that I was sending to you and discussing routes and other important information that I didn't think nothing of at the time because he was deemed psychotic. I don't even know if that were true now that I think about it," he said. Calling the cleanup crew and a funeral home, I made the proper burial arrangements because that was still my Uncle and cousin.
"I'm 'bout to get up out of here," I said to my pops because I just felt drained at this point. Walking outside, headed towards my car, Zac

was busy texting away on his phone. Once we got in the car, I said,

“What you about to get into?”

“Shit, I’m about to go get my girl man. I love that girl,” he said.

“Shit, finally because I was tired of ugly ass mopping around here looking like a lost puppy.

“Nigga, fuck you; you need to go get Yemani. Life is too short for that shit. You know you love that fucking girl, you just don’t want to admit it.”

“Naw, I’m cooling, I ain’t with that love shit. Besides, lil’ momma not fucking with the kid right now, no way.”

“Aight nigga, fuck around and a nigga with pull a Russell Wilson on you and Future your ass,” he said, laughing but that shit got me to thinking about that as I started the car up.

“Naw, she knows better,” I said, but it didn’t sound too convincing or confident.

CHAPTER 23

What's done in the dark will always find the light....

BROCK

After Krystal dropped that bomb on me the other day about Tierra and who she was possibly cheating on a nigga with, I packed me and my baby shit and I went to a hotel for a few days. I went from denial, to rage in a matter of seconds. After all I had done and the many sacrifices I had made for both of their asses; they wanted to do this shit to me. If I'm honest with myself, I knew something foul was going on a while ago, a nigga just didn't want to admit that shit. I always had a suspicion that she was cheating, I just never wanted to believe it. Now that the cat was out the bag, I was gonna get down to the bottom of this. Going home knowing that she wouldn't be there, I started snooping around inside our room, looking under beds, looking inside shoe boxes, pulling out drawers, really fucking the room up like a mad man. I was looking for something, anything that could tie the two of them together. I had almost given up until I looked inside the last drawer which was her panty drawer and found a diary hidden deeply beneath everything. Getting comfortable on the floor, I started reading it and the more I read, the more mad I became. This bitch was really having an affair with my baby brother, but that wasn't the kicker, her ass actually loved the nigga and was planning on robbing me and running away with him. The shit that paused me was when she said they could finally be a real family, him, her and their daughter. I must have read that page a million times before it processed in my head.

“What are you doing?” She asked me walking into the room that now looked like a tornado had hit it.

“You lying dirty bitch. You fucked that nigga in my fucking bed?” I yelled as I lunged at her.

“What are you talking about baby?” She tried to say as if she was totally clueless to what I was saying.

“How could you? I took you from the slums of your mothers one bedroom crack house and gave you everything. Anything I’ve ever done was for you to make sure you was straight and you fucked my kid brother? My only family I had left? Really bitch?” I asked her as my hands found her throat as I squeezed until her face began to turn blue.

“You better pray she’s mine, I said as I released her and stormed out the house. Since Krystal had agreed to watch baby girl tonight, I had free time to kill as I drove aimlessly around town until I settled at a bar. Walking in and heading straight to the bar, I said, "1800 on the rocks, no chaser."

"Tough day, huh? Yours sound about like how my day has went." A voice said beside me. Glancing to my left, I saw a bad ass broad sitting beside me nursing a drink of her own.

"I'm pretty sure your day couldn't have gone worse than mines shawty," I said to her as I focused my attention back on the bartender. Once I was given my drink, I downed it in a few gulps and asked to be given another.

"I'm Angela," she felt the need to say.

"Brock," I said extending my hand out to shake hers. I spent a few hours at the bar getting to know Angela and ended up bringing her back to my hotel with me. The next day, I woke up and decided I was getting the fuck out of dodge. I was waged a war with some niggas trying to defend the honor of a nigga whom I thought was my family, only to find out he was a fuck nigga. I was prepared to die for a nigga who had fucked my girl and could possibly be the father of my daughter. That shit was too much. I knew it was only a matter of time before they pulled my information, so I wasn't taking any chances.

"Will I see you again?" Angela asked beside me as I jumped up and started getting our stuff together.

"Probably not," I said being honest because I was getting my baby out of here and never looking back. Fuck the blood test, that was my child and couldn't nobody tell me differently.

Noting the sad look that graced her face, I said, "Its nothing like that, I just have to leave town Ma some shit jumped off and I gotta get my lil shorty and go. I'll hit you up though once I get settled, maybe you can visit a nigga," I said lying because it was no way I was telling anyone where I was going. I was familiar enough with the game to know that's how niggas got caught. Running their mouth, pillow talking to a bitch.

"I'd like that," she said smiling from ear to ear as she got up and begin getting dressed. Once I had all our bags packed, I carried everything to the car, kissed her good bye, and headed to get my daughter. I had no intentions of going back to the house I shared with Tierra, so the things we left there would have to be replaced. I thought about telling the hoe to watch her back since I had started a war in these streets, but then I said to hell with her ass. Dirty bitch deserves anything that comes her way.

"Daddy, where are we going?" My daughter asked as we got on the highway.

"To our new home baby."

"We getting another home? Can I have another room this time a princess one?" She asked.

"Sure baby. Anything for my princess."

"Where's mommy?" She said.

Thinking long and hard about how I was going to choose to answer that, I said the first thing that came to my head.

"She's gone to visit Uncle Chaz in heaven."

CHAPTER 24

There's always a rainbow after the rain…

YEMANI

"Almost a year ago, I couldn't even come to your funeral, and I'm sorry; I just wasn't in a good space, you guys. I know you're probably disappointed in me for missing something like that, but you know my heart. My life has been a beautiful mess since then, though. I finally completed my first year in college. I've take all of my finals a few weeks early, so I decided to come home. I thought I was gone have to stay in a hotel in the next town over, but I managed to actually sleep in my own room. I still haven't mustered up the courage to go into you guys room, but I figure that required baby steps. Speaking on baby steps," said as I rubbed my hand over my growing belly. "We are having a baby. Your first grandchild. I'm fatherless and depressed some days, but I'm pushing through. You guys raised me to be a very tough and can weather any storm that life throws at me. I'm stronger than what I give myself credit for, and I've survived that which was supposed to break me and still remained standing tall. My heart hurts right now," I said as my voice cracked. "It really hurts right now, but I know this too shall pass. Each day gets a little better, and each day, I find myself getting back up again because I had fallen so low, I didn't know what that meant to get up. Hurting on the inside but I'm holding my head up on the outside, I know I'll be ok. Well, your grandchild is hungry, so I'm going to go, but I will be back tomorrow," I said to my parents' grave as I placed the flowers on them and walked off. I had been home two weeks, and it took me this long to finally come to their grave for the first time, but I'm glad I did.

As I got in my car to drive to my Godmother's house to eat, I said a silent prayer, thanking God for allowing me to fit into these jeans today. I know it's crazy, but after my nasty break up with Midos, I was depressed awhile, but I've snapped out of it. But every day, I have to tell myself what I'm thankful for, and then say a silent prayer about. What I was thankful for today was being able to put these jeans o because I haven't been fitting into my clothes. It's been past time to go shopping for maternity wear.

"Ohh that feels so good," I said to Tyron as I had my eyes closed and my head thrown back in pure ecstasy. The way he was working those fingers felt like magic. My body was so tired, and this was exactly what I needed. As he massaged my feet. We were currently in my room, and I was laying down with my feet in his lap as he massaged them while we watched Love and Hip Hop Hollywood.

“I can’t stand this hoe Hazel E,” he said.

“Shit me either, her ass so super wack with that bad ass surgery she got. Bitch, needs refund, like she seriously jacked up.”

“Bitch, look like she can audition for IT,” Tyron said as we fell out laughing.

It felt good to have our friendship back because at one point, we had gone to a very dark place and I couldn’t understand why. It wasn’t until I cornered him at the gas station and asked him what happened to us and why he talks to everyone, but me. Come to find out he felt guilty for making me feel like it was my fault, we broke up due to our horrible sex experiment gone wrong, but it was because he was gay and in denial. It took me meeting his boyfriend, Cashus, to finally come out the closet, well come out within himself, but he still hasn’t told many people. I guess the fear of what people will say and how they will react is what's holding him back.

"They need to bring Milan fine ass back," he said lustfully. It was an adjustment getting used to him talking sexually about guys the same way I did with Desiree and Krystal, but I never judged him.

"I thought his boyfriend on the show was cute," I said.

"With his confused ass," he said, laughing.

KNOCK! KNOCK! KNOCK!

"I'll get it," he said, placing my feet on the bed and getting up, walking out the room.

"Who was it?" I asked, yelling towards the front with my eyes closed. The one thing I was already hating about being pregnant was that I never had energy, got tired quick, and fell asleep at the drop

of a dime. Feeling him pick my feet back up stirred me from my sleep.
"That feels in better than the first time when you was massaging them," I moaned. "Shit feels so good; if you wasn't gay, I would have raped you," I said, laughing.

"Oh yeah? So you was gone give my pussy away?" I heard Midos say as my eyes popped up to see him massaging my feet, sitting on my bed. Sitting up, I nervously looked at him trying to read the expression on his face. Glancing towards the door, I was trying to see where Tyron was and had he did anything to him.
"Where Tyron?" I asked.
"He had somewhere to go, said to tell you he would call you. Got a phone call as soon as he opened the door," he said to me as he continued to massage my feet. It was feeling so good, but I wouldn't let a massage blind side me from the real issue at hand.

"Midos, don't hurt him; he didn't do anything. He's gay; we were not having sex," I said.
"Damn, didn't I just say the nigga got a phone call and left? Shit, call the nigga if you don't believe me," he said. Picking up my phone, I dialed Tyron's number as he sat looked at me smirking.
"Yo," Tyron said when he answered the phone.
"What's up Tyron. Are you ok? Where did you go?"
"My boyfriend called me, he drove down from school and is at my house. Girl, I wanted to go see my man, and figured you needed alone to talk to yours."
"Damn, dissed me for some dick, just like a bitch," I said, laughing.
"And you better know it, baby. Now, this the part where I'm supposed to say be good and don't do anything I wouldn't do but fuck that bii; you better do anything I would do to that fine ass nigga," he said.

“Hell naw, get the fuck off the phone,” I heard a guy in the background say.

“See, you done got in trouble,” I said laughing as I hung up.

“Happy now?” Midos said as he still sat calmly rubbing my feet.

“Yes.”

“Do I scare you that much that you think I’m capable of killing someone in your parents’ home for no reason just because he opened the door? No lie, I had rehearsed what I was going to say to you in my head over and over again on the way over here, and when he opened the door and not you, I was a little mad. But not at him, at myself because I thought I was too late. I kept telling myself I’ll go tomorrow, until tomorrow didn’t seem like it would ever come unless I actually got up and put forth the effort.”

“Listen, Midos-” I started, but he put his finger to my lips for me to be quiet.

"Let me get this out. I was an idiot. My biggest problem is I react before I think and that caused me to lose the best thing that's ever happened to me. Before you came along, I was lonely, but in denial. A nigga had everything in the world but no one to share it with, that's why I switched girls daily. I was trying to feel a void in my heart. When I met you, that void felt filled; I felt whole. I couldn't exactly explain it at the time, I just knew having you around made me feel good, so I selfishly kept you there for my own selfish gain until feelings developed, and I kept you there because I didn't ever want to have to let you go. I love you, Yemani Jacobs, and shit that scares me. I've never told another woman that other than my mom. Hell, I've never even had a serious girlfriend so yeah; I fucked up royally, but I can admit that. And if you give me another chance, I'll spend the rest of my life trying to get it right," he said, dropping to my feet, pulling out a box and placing it on my leg.

Reaching down and picking it up, my breath caught in my throat as I stared in awe at the most beautiful ring I've ever laid eyes on. The ring was so big and sparkly that it took the saying 'diamonds dancing' to a whole new level.

"Nigga, if you think for one fucking minute you can come into my life and turn it upside down, make me fall in love with you, accuse me of being a hoe, put your hands on me and deny my child. Then have the audacity to come back, admit your wrongs, and give me that weak ass proposal and expect my ass to just give in and say yes," I said, pausing as I glared at him.

Putting his head down, he got up without saying a word, then paused and said, "I'm sorry to bother you. I would like to see my child though and attend appointments."

"Ask me," I said to him as he was halfway out the room.

"Huh?" he said, pausing and turning around.

"Nigga, fuck you mean, huh? If you can huh, you can hear. You want something, you gotta ask for it," I said, throwing his words back at him.

Smiling, he walked back over to me and did the unthinkable, he dropped to one knee, grabbed my hand, and said, "Yemani Jacobs, you gone marry a nigga or naw?"

"Close enough," I said, laughing. "But of course I am," I said, smiling as he picked me up and spun me around excitedly before he leaned down and kissed me.

Pulling away, he said, "Bae, when you came out to the H, did you ever think you would be falling in love with the king of Houston?" he asked, giving me another peck on the lips.

"Nope, but I'm happy that I did. I actually fell in love with two," I said.

"Two?" he asked with his eyebrow raised.

"Yes, baby. I fell in love with you and my son," I told him placing his hands over my stomach.

"You giving a nigga, a junior?" he asked excitedly. I just nodded my head.
"Oh shit now, Houston ain't gone be ready the both of us."
I just shook my head at him as he picked me up effortlessly, even though I was big as hell, and laid on the bed with me, catching me up with everything that had been going on. He was truly my best friend, and we talked like homeboys sometimes, it was just that crazy. He seemed content and at ease as he replayed his accounts of events and telling me about the happenings. I couldn't help but admire him as I closed my eyes to say my daily prayer on what I was thankful for.
Today I was thankful for love and it coming back to me. They say if you love someone, let them go, if they come back, then it's meant to be, so I guess fate once again, stepped in to help us along the way. It's funny how life works. Who would have thought a small-town girl from Sicily Island

would fall madly in love with the king of Houston?

THE END............. or is it?

Hold up, wait a minute, y'all thought I was finished, huh? No. Once again, thank you for taking time out of your day to read another one of my books. I hope you guys enjoyed this stand-alone book and all its characters. I'm far from done with them because we need all the hot tea on Debo and Krystal. Did she keep the baby?

Did he break up wit her? What's really going on? And what about Zac and Desiree? Yeah, I'm not leaving you guys hanging like that, that's why I'm doing a spin-off series with these characters. Please be on the lookout for that, so all of your questions can and will be answered. You know how I do so strap in, and hold on tight because this ride is far from over. As always, peace, love and blessings.

Interested in becoming a part of the Treasured Publications family?

Submit manuscripts to

Info@Treasuredpub.com

Like us on Facebook:

Treasured Publications

Be sure to text **Treasured** to **444999**

To subscribe to our Mailing List.

Never miss a release or contest again!

CPSIA information can be obtained
at www.ICGtesting.com
Printed in the USA
LVHW081331280319
612176LV00032B/626/P

9 781977 54367